The Alzheimer's Association notes that 5.5 Million Americans suffer from the disease. This does not account for other forms of dementia that plague our older citizens. And, of course, that number only represents the victims living inside the United States.

The World Health Organization puts the worldwide number of dementia cases at 47.5 Million.

47.5 *Million.*

It's not the kind of condition that draws headlines. There are no star-studded Hollywood telethons to raise money.

And yet, odds are you know, or have known, a victim.

A horror novel may seem like an odd—or even inappropriate—place to stare down the issue. I don't think so; I think the whole issue, and our society's complacency around it, is exactly the stuff of nightmares.

The monster is real.

BLEAK
DECEMBER

"Come closer, night
Come here and cover me in darkness
I'm gonna wear you like
a big black coat."

—Casey Scott
Rattle My Bones

INVOCATION

Birkenau: a place of mud and brick and the lingering scent of sweet spun-sugar and incinerated flesh; a railway destination for boxcars filled with short lives and endless misery; the hub of an unthinkable new industry. This is how it was remembered by those who chose to hold on to the memories, the stubborn few not lost to alcoholic amnesia or suicide, or ultimately both. But that was later.

Now, with the black smoke still pluming from four crematorium stacks, his young mind recorded everything—the labor, the incoming crowds from Hungary, rumors and speculation, the unspoken but well-known reality, the bright colors of the encroaching swamp, the buzzing flies circling the horse stables and barracks alike.

"Nineteen," he'd told them, "an understudy to an engineer."

All new arrivals were asked. Had he answered honestly, "Sixteen, assistant to a book-keep," he'd have been herded to the showers by the SS and told to remember the number of the hook where he'd hung his clothes. No one ever needed to remember it, but the deception remained, reinforced right up until the moment they released the gas. Like his captors, he'd lied; he'd lived. Sometimes a few of the others would playfully chide him in a whisper, calling him Safran the Librarian.

A lie, a forgotten past: a history of little acts of treason.

One of the others, a friend, another man with a string of numbers tattooed onto his arm, ran to him as he finished mopping the selection platform. New arrivals sometimes vomited when they first stepped down from the boxcars. Influenza, and worse, bred on the trains. He thought at first his friend had come to his side to share good news; perhaps they'd managed to poach some vegetables from the stables, or better yet, that one of the guard dogs had killed a rabbit and left it behind. Food was a common topic.

But his friend said, "They've caught a demon."

"A demon?" Safran said, squinting. The sunset behind his friend's head blurred his vision into blotches of gold and gray.

1

His friend nodded. "Come back, now, and you'll see."

Stepping down from the ramp, they bowed their heads and walked back to the barracks. Anything more than a shuffle might draw the attention of the soldiers, or worse, the kapos, and the distance between suspicion and punishment was never very far. The Germans were shepherds watching over their herd. Kapos, prisoners given the functionary role of labor enforcers, earned a better lifestyle through cruelty to their fellow Jews. They were the sheep dogs.

Together they weaved through the camp, passing by a group of prisoners digging a new irrigation trench, their skins glistening with sweat. Two soldiers sat on a nearby stoop, watching with large, passive eyes. He was careful not to stare. Entering the grid of alleyways between the barracks, his friend took the lead and they continued on single file. Blank faces stared back from each open doorway. In one, an old man, naked and gasping, rested on the floor, hands groping the air, a kitten playing with dangling string. His ribcage seemed ready to burst from his emaciated body. The other residents of the barrack, recognizing the man's end was near, had stolen away his clothes.

Dignity, always the first victim of desperation.

Safran's barrack was indistinguishable from the next. The older brick buildings on the other end of the camp were more distinct from one another, but the newer, cheaper wooden structures hadn't stood long enough to develop character of their own. Like the men that resided inside, they were differentiated only by the numbers stenciled on them. Removing their hats, they entered the place where they lived but would never be home.

The barrack could house more than four hundred men, and at times it did. As they walked the hall, Safran saw many empty bunks. Another culling, perhaps as early as this morning while he'd been out working. His friend said nothing; the disappearance of dozens of men did not merit comment. But Safran noticed, filed it away in his mind. In earlier days at the camp, he'd tried to remember each face that went missing, but now there were too many. Many too many.

At the end of the barrack, a group of men stood around the last column of bunks. Grim frowns, gargoyle faces. Every day he saw misery on their faces, but this was something else entirely. His friend whispered, "They're deciding what to do with him."

The men broke from the huddle to allow Safran and his friend to pass through. Their pale, long faces regarded the new arrivals without any change in countenance. Black marble eyes shifted in their sockets, following Safran. The weight of so much attention made his stomach tighten. Why was his opinion so valuable? Why had they sent for him?

The last thin man stepped out of his path and he understood, at least in part. The man sitting on the last bunk stared back at him with a broken, wild expression. His cheeks and temples were bruised. A trickle of blood ran down from his right eye. The man was his half-brother.

Safran blinked, hard, as confusion set into his thoughts. No, this sallow, starving man was *not* his half-brother. He didn't even have one. Why had he thought it was so? And why with such pressing certitude? He was tired, surely, and overworked. And hungry. And heartsick. And–

His friend leaned in close and whispered, *"Be careful."*

Safran bent his knees and crouched down beside the man his friend had called a demon. Their noses only inches apart, he gazed into deep brown eyes and saw the same loss and sadness as he found in every prisoner here. Safran did not see a demon. "What is your name?"

"I don't remember," the man mumbled.

They'd beaten him senseless, he thought. "What do I call you?"

"Kloum," he said. *Nothing.*

Safran asked, "Are you a demon, as they say?"

Kloum shrugged. Bones cracked. "Don't you know me?"

"No," he said, "I do not."

The battered man smiled, not much, but a little. It was not the sort of smile that celebrated a great moment in life. It was subtle and sad. And infectious. "You sleep three beds down from me each night. Have for the last two months. We've shared our mother's recipes for shlishkes."

Safran shook his head. "I've never seen you before."

"Of course you have."

"Why would you say I have?" Safran asked.

The smile grew larger, but no happier. "When did I say that?"

"Just now."

3

Kloum's face went slack. "Are you sure?"

Safran stood up and waved a hand. "He's stupid from your fists."

The men murmured. One of the elders, sitting on a nearby bunk, raised his crooked walking stick and pointed it at Kloum's head. "Two years ago, I witnessed this man take a child into the woods behind the temple. That child was never seen again."

One of the younger men, arms folded, added, "I know him as well. He went to the Germans, believing they would spare him. A family of nine, safe in hiding, rounded up and sent to a camp like this one."

"He's escaped the noose in my town," another yelled.

And then they were all speaking, many boisterous voices competing for his ears, all condemning Kloum with accusations. Vandalism; rape; adultery; theft; murder. The uproar went on, each testimonial more passionate than the last. Some of the stories were personal; others detailed offenses against entire cities.

When the voices finally died down, Safran turned to them and asked, "But how can all this be true? You're all from different villages. Could one man be in all these places at once?"

"No," his friend said. "A *man* could not."

Demon. They believed his half-brother was a demon.

Safran had no half-brother.

"There's something wrong with all of you."

Their voices roared, repeating their charges, a new urgency rising. Their faces reddened. Spittle sprayed from their lips as they yelled out each slurred syllable. Their dead eyes came alive with a dangerous, fiery passion. They stepped forward; Safran stepped back.

Somehow amidst the ruckus, he heard a gentle laugh, not much more audible than a giggle, as if the sound had been projected directly to his ear. Stumbling over his own feet, he twisted at the waist and stared back at Kloum.

Except that a different man sat there.

But for the bruises, there was nothing about the new man that matched the old. This new face had eyes farther apart and a wide, sloping nose. Whereas Kloum's cheekbones protruded, this man's profile was a simple curved slope. Yet when he quit laughing and spoke, Kloum's voice said, "For your sake, don't forget me."

Feeling lightheaded and uneasy on his feet, Safran lowered himself to the floor. The men stepped over him, kicking his legs aside as they went. Fingers gripped Kloum's collar. Knuckles tightened. They took turns striking him, until their patience wore too thin and their bloodlust was too raised, and then they all attacked him at once, fists and feet pounding his flesh. The prisoners grunted and yelped as they beat him, one voice yowling like a wolf, another singing a child's rhyme.

Panic rising in his chest, Safran scooted away from the blur of motion, but not quickly enough to avoid the spray of blood when a punch crushed Kloum's nose flat between his eyes. He screamed and spasmed, his body rocking back and forth, painting his closest attackers red. Their assault continued, now with calloused fingers raking down his face and clawing at his throat. His arms were pinned back. Chunks of hair and scalp uprooted. One man stomped on his ankle until his foot spun backward, not merely broken but distended.

Watching them torture Kloum, Safran retreated across the floor, crawling and kicking away from the madness. More men ran down the barracks hall towards the assault. For a moment he thought they came to stop it. Instead, they joined in. Kloum continued to scream until, with a pop, a thumb plunged through his neck and blocked his windpipe. Another finger sank into his eye socket to the knuckle.

A moment later, Kloum stopped screaming. And moving.

Still pulling himself across the floor, Safran vomited.

The men continued to defile the dead body, reducing what remained to unrecognizable handfuls of strewn meat, wads of bloody cloth, and lengths of broken bone. One of the attackers held a severed arm up over his head like a tribal bludgeon.

And what was that sound? Were some of them... *chewing?*

Bringing himself to his feet, Safran ran, wobbling and unsure, but moving fast. At the doorway, he lost his footing and tumbled outside, landing in a heap at the doorstep. And a shoe.

The kapo spit. A wad of saliva and mucus landed an inch from his face. "What's going on in there? What is all that noise?"

He rolled over and clutched his chest. "They've gone mad."

"Who?" the kapo asked.

"All," he answered.

*   *   *

When Safran was allowed to return to the barracks, he did so with the same mop he used to clean the selection platform. It was empty, except for the blood. The bodies were gone, already turning to ash in the crematoriums. The soldiers had killed them all, those who attacked Kloum and those who had not. Bullet holes peppered the walls. There would be a draft this winter. He knew the camp administrators wouldn't fix it. Nothing, he realized, could fix it. Nothing. *Kloum.*

Had they killed the demon as well? He doubted they could.

"Who?" the kapo had asked him, and he'd answered, "All."

They died because of his answer.

Then the same man had asked him his name, and, unlike the time when he'd been asked his age and occupation, he told the truth. "I don't remember."

December 1st

"-Okay, Dad?"

Maddox Boxwood studied the mirror for an answer to his son's question. He could see no answers, no cryptic Sanskrit symbols hidden inside the heavy folds of his leathery skin, no Morse code spelled out in the random sprinkling of liver spots across his cheeks and forehead, no cave glyph carved into the tight knots of crow's feet at the edge of his eyes. He looked into the eyes of a tired and weathered old man and saw *nothing*. He should have felt *something*-sadness, loss, fear of his own mortality-but didn't. Emptiness swirled inside him, the sensation in a starving man's gut when mercy sends the hunger away and a horrible, droning peace takes over.

"I'm fine."

Steven stood in the washroom doorway, face long and pale, with a look of rapacious concern. Ever since Maddox had moved into his forty-two-year-old son's house, the younger Boxwood had been searching desperately for a father-son bonding moment, some kind of late-in-the-day coming-to-Jesus experience that doubtlessly involved tears and hugging. Maddox would need to get a whole hell of a lot more senile before any of *that shit* would happen.

Cocking his head to one side, Steven asked, "You're sure, 'cause y'know, it's okay if y-"

Shaking his head, Maddox said, "Getthehell outta here."

Defeated, Steven retreated. The door closed between the men. Steven had *always* been needy. Always. Steven hadn't needed training wheels on his first bike, he needed a surrogate driver. Maddox remembered walking beside his son, one hand steadying the handlebar as Steven pedaled too slowly to even keep the bike upright, a look of absolute terror burning on his face.

Maddox had seen plenty of terrified faces over the course of his thirty-six-year career in law enforcement. Shell-shocked, slack-jawed victims and numb and dumb witnesses were one thing, but the ones that really stuck with him were the criminals. Almost without fail their expressions would change the moment they realized they were caught. Those were the ones that haunted him: greedy, selfish fear writ large across faces unaccustomed to humility and surrender.

A scared kid on a wobbling bike. A hysterical mother crying for her murdered son. A gang banger, face unnaturally pale, lips quivering as he raised his hands over his head. Maddox could close his eyes and see them all, every detail vivid, but when he opened his eyes he still saw nothing. His own face was the real mystery.

Stan Mancuso, his closest friend for five decades, dead, his face added to the memorial wall inside his head. *You don't belong there, Stanny, you belong here.*

"Fuck it," Maddox muttered, wiping a hand towel across his face. Soft cotton ran over rough skin and tough stubble with a sound like sandpaper and dry wood. Turning to the toilet, he unzipped, pissed, and flushed. No need for his enlarged prostate to interrupt a perfectly good funeral with the need to empty his bladder.

Steven drove to the First Assembly church, no better with an automobile than he had been with a bicycle as a kid, both hands rigid on the steering wheel, eyes never glancing away from the road. The drive would have taken twenty minutes tops for Maddox, even if he followed the posted speed limits, which he didn't, but with his son's light foot on the accelerator it took a half hour.

They didn't speak. For once, Steven didn't even try.

Thank God for that.

The church, a modern stucco and brick affair, bristled with badges. A retired cop's funeral meant time on the clock but off the beat, so every twenty-five-year-old buzz cut in the city lined the pews. Maddox recognized a few—a very few—but doubted that more than one or two had even met Stan Mancuso while he was alive. They'd go home today with a memory of a body in a box. That would be all he'd be to them, a room-temperature caricature of a man. They came for the hour of pay and the food at the reception. Parasites of the highest order.

"Y'call around to see what you should wear?" Maddox grumbled as he passed the last row of pews. He wore a suit; they wore their uniforms. Was there really anything more to say?

The first two rows, empty except for two of Stan's cousins, were roped off and signed *For Family*. Maddox ripped the sheet of paper off the backrest and dropped it into the literature slot behind a well-worn copy of *Devotionals and Responses*. Dropping down, he motioned to Steven to take the seat beside him. He could tell from the anxiety spelled out on his son's face that he didn't feel right about taking the reserved spots. Maddox reached up, took his arm, and pulled him down beside him. "Stan's wife's dead six years. Never had kids. Those two over there? They're only here 'cause they're hoping something's written into the will for them. Leaving these seats empty, now that would be offensive."

"Okay, Dad," Steven said. His expression didn't change.

Maddox sighed. "How do you even walk?"

"Huh?"

"With your panties so far up your ass. How do you walk?"

The service began. The pastor was a balding, effeminate man with John Lennon eyewear and the posture of a method actor auditioning for the role of Quasimodo. His voice reminded Maddox of Robert Mitchum, withdrawn and full of awkward pauses.

Maddox pondered the kind of man who could memorize hundreds of pages of Biblical verses but didn't use that particular skill to count cards at casinos. A higher calling, they might say. Bullshit–he'd seen the plates of tax-exempt donations flow down the church aisles. They just played a different game.

"This seat taken?" Darcy MacAteer whispered, kneeing his way past Steven and Maddox. Still heavy even into his seventies, Darcy made the pew creak when he sat.

Maddox frowned in an impatient way that only old friends would interpret as affectionate. Not taking his eyes off the pastor, he mumbled, "Late again. At least you're consistent."

"Blair was late getting back with the car," he said.

His frown changed into a devious smile, though the expression on Maddox's face didn't change all that much. Thirty-odd years before, Darcy's wife earned a reputation on the force as a flirt–possibly more. "I'm sure that's true."

"Shuddup," Darcy said.

Thirty minutes later, the service ended as it had begun, with the recitation of a prayer and a moment of silence. Maddox had a clear opinion which of

9

the two had more value. The congregation's heads finally raised, and the pastor invited them all to form a single line to pay their final respects. A glum altar boy, no doubt having pulled the short straw backstage, opened the casket's hood and stepped to the side.

As Maddox stood up, Steven took hold of his arm. "If you need—"

"What I need is for you to let me go," he said. Steven obliged. Maddox reminded himself that his son meant only to comfort him. "I've seen bodies before."

Steven waited in the aisle as Maddox and Darcy ignored the building line and approached the casket. This wasn't the box they'd bury Stan inside, he knew. The Department wouldn't pay for something this nice. He ran a hand down its sleek, glossy side, as sexy as a sports car. They stopped at the head of the coffin.

"Horrible job," Darcy said. "He looks like shit."

Maddox shook his head and pointed to a collage of photos propped up next to the casket. "What you talking about? He's looked this bad for years. Long time since those were taken."

In the photos: smiling Stan, bright pearlies and winking eyes, early hints of crow's feet at his temples, flowing black hair; handsome as a gray fox. Nothing like the walking corpse he'd been since the chemotherapy and pharmaceuticals took their toll. Black and white photographs: the only evidence left of the good years. Maddox wondered what would become of them. Would the cousins take them? And do what? File them away in a shoe box somewhere until they, too, died? If not, Maddox couldn't imagine the church holding on to them. Once in the trash, young Stan would be gone forever.

Gone. The word consumed his thoughts for a moment. A horrible word, maybe the worst. How many people had died without as much as a footnote in their family trees? And what of the people who didn't find a place in history's narrow breadth? How long before no trace of Stan remained? *Or anyone else.*

"You okay?" Darcy asked.

Maddox waved a finger at his friend. "Don't you start, too."

"It's just... ya looked pale just now," he said.

Steven had taken a few steps towards them. He must have seen it, too. Damn. "What the hell's wrong with you two? It's just the lighting in this place.

All the stained glass and florescent lights. Bad mix."

"Yeah," Darcy said, faking agreement. "That's probably right."

Maddox curled back his finger and rapped his fist lightly on Darcy's shoulder. Sometimes the best thing a real friend could do was lie. "What you say we get out of here. You've had enough of this?"

"Hell, yeah, I have," Darcy said.

One last look at Stan's sunken, pale face. So very tired, even in death. "Guess Persephone Alford's gonna have to do without you, old buddy. You rest up."

A look of confusion and concern passed over Steven's face.

Maddox stepped back into the aisle. The swarm of cops were heading out to the reception at the funeral home next door. Maddox and Darcy headed in the opposite direction.

"Where we going?" Steven asked.

Maddox continued on to Darcy's beaten-up station wagon. The car should have been retired back when they did. "Why don't you just head on home and I'll catch up with you later, son."

"I'm not going home, Dad. Wherever you're–"

Maddox swung open the passenger side door. "Hop's."

"*What? Now?*"

The car's shocks protested as Darcy dropped down behind the wheel. One hand on the open door, Maddox spoke to his son in as patient and caring a voice as he could muster. Which wasn't much on either count. "It's Sunday; it's what we do. You think I want to go home and mope around the rest of today? Maybe watch some black-and-white cowboys and Indians show on cable? Stan's dead. I only got two friends left in this world. *I'd* like to spend some of the time *I* have left with them."

"At Hop's," Steven said, disbelief bulging at the seams.

Maddox nodded. "It's what we do."

Darcy called over from his side of the car, "Why don't you come along, Steven? Your dad doesn't want you to, but I'm game for anything that pisses him off a little."

"Fuck you," Maddox said.

"We're both too old and y'know it," Darcy responded.

11

Maddox cocked a thumb towards the back seat. "Get in, kid."

*　　*　　*

The bell dangling over the door rang out as they entered, a familiar and comfortable jangle of copper, indistinguishable from any of its previous rings. Janey, the fifty-something redheaded waitress with hair dyed twenty years younger, glanced up from the dry erase board as she scribbled out the lunch specials. "Your regular booth's empty, guys."

Maddox led them to the corner booth. The table, as always, was accented by a neat stack of paper napkins, a set of half-filled salt and pepper shakers, a small wire cage filled with sweetener packets, and a beehive-style syrup dispenser. If they'd come in a half hour later, as sometimes they did, the pancake topping would have been replaced by a standing dessert menu. Two decades earlier, there'd been an ashtray and only a single choice of sugar alternative. It all depended on *when*.

Sliding into the booth beside his father, Steven groaned and reached for a napkin. Wiping away a smudge of butter and some toast crumbs, he asked, "Table's filthy, why don't we move over to—"

Maddox groaned.

Steven sighed. "What makes *this place* so special?"

"Nothing," Darcy said. He pointed to the pie case by the cash register. "They've been making the same blackberry pie for forty years. Never was much good, and it won't be today, either. But we're both gonna order a slice. And it'll taste right. Not good, but right. Does that make sense to you?"

"No," Steven said.

Maddox groaned, louder this time.

"It's like this: How long have you owned your car?"

Steven shook his head. "I lease. Fourteen months, about."

"There you go." Darcy reached for a napkin of his own, but instead of cleaning, he placed it on his lap. Maddox followed suit. "You reach an age, the car you drive becomes part of you. Or the restaurant where you eat breakfast on Sundays. Or the bland pie. There's cars that get better fuel economy, and there's better pie, but none of that's me. That's someone else."

A confused look crossed Steven's face. "Really? Why not enjoy the best that life has to offer before—"

12

"Before I'm *dead*?" Maddox grumbled.

"I didn't mean it like that," Steven said.

"You can't understand this right now, but someday you will. Sometimes *better* isn't *better*. Sometimes *okay* is the best, because it's your *okay*." Darcy bowed his head, moved his lips, and signed a cross across his heart.

Steven bowed his head, a clear gesture of respect towards Darcy's silent prayer. Maddox did not. Rolling his eyes, he caught sight of a young woman across the diner. An attractive brunette in her early thirties sat, alone, at a tiny, two-chair table. She wore a zebra print blouse with a black scarf. Returning his stare, his eyes locked with hers. A rush of déjà vu clouded his thoughts. "Hey, Darce, do we know that girl?"

Darcy opened his eyes and craned his neck to see. "Which one?"

"Dark hair."

Darcy shifted in his seat. "Some kind of joke?"

"The girl right there. We know her, or not?" Maddox said, his voice loud and impatient. "It's not a tough question. I feel like I know her, but can't make out where—"

Janey stepped into his view, order pad and pen in hand. Her smile always seemed so genuine and sweet, yet her eyes were always filled with distance and sadness. "Two slices of pie, I take it, and coffee. Anything else today?"

Maddox and Darcy shook their heads.

"Anything for you, sweetie?" she asked Steven.

Steven's smile wasn't as genuine. "Herbal tea?"

"Hibiscus, ginger, or oolong."

"Ginger, please."

Janey thanked them and took off back to the counter.

The two-seat table was empty. The brunette must have finished and left. Distracted by the waitress, Maddox hadn't heard the doorbell ring.

"You just order hot tea? Y'think we're in England?" Maddox said with a snicker. He held a straight face for a moment, then let out a grin to let his son know he was joking. "Just tell me this, please, for the love of Christ, you're not gonna use the little pink sugar, are you?"

Steven laughed a little, playing along. "Dad—"

The doorbell chimed and Mia Cresswater stormed in, open jacket and purse swinging, her heels tapping the vinyl floor tiles like a metronome. Plopping the heavy bag on the table, she collapsed into the chair beside Darcy, groaned, and began rummaging through her pockets. Finally coming up with a tube of lip gloss, she stroked it across her lips with an artist's precision. Then she made eye contact with Maddox and said, "All you white people, you're fucking insane, y'know that?"

"Know it? I endorse it," Maddox said.

Darcy put a hand over hers. "What happened?"

"Got a damned parking ticket over on Fremont."

The old men burst out laughing. Mia was five years younger than Maddox; he'd met her in the late sixties when he'd answered a call about an altercation between a rookie meter maid and the mayor's son. The kid had parked in a loading zone, clearly marked, and assumed his father's name would exonerate him on the spot. Mia, headstrong and full of righteous indignation, insisted the ticket stand. Maddox could picture her still, plucky black girl, pretty in a modest way, hands on her hips, leaning into the face of a twenty-two-year-old white boy who had no reason to fear anyone. In the end, he backed down. His father got the ticket pulled; she never cared. The moment mattered, not the outcome, she'd told Maddox. He never forgot. "That's karma."

"Karma's never met me. I'm the bigger bitch," Mia said, then shot her gaze over to Steven and smiled. Wide. "You must be pretty hard up, hanging around with two old shits like these guys."

Steven smiled back. They'd always gotten on. "Hey, Mia."

She nodded, motherly, and then turned her attention back to Maddox and Darcy. "I missed the whole service trying to straighten this man out. He thinks that uniform makes him something special? I was writing out fines before his ass was even born."

"Were you parked–" Darcy started.

"Don't start with me, Officer MacAteer." She rapped on the table twice. "You know I know the parking restrictions better than anyone. That whole block never had meters before at all. How was I supposed to know?"

"Would you have accepted that excuse?" Maddox asked.

"Hell no," she said, "'cause you crazy white people lie about all that. You'd say anything to get yourself out of trouble. Guy once told me his wife'd gotten bitten by a rabid squirrel, and he'd just stopped the car to go chasing after it to get it tested. Insanity. No wife in the car, bitten or otherwise, and there weren't no fuckin' squirrel, either."

"You're right," Maddox conceded. "No squirrel."

The three old friends laughed. Maddox knew the sound well, their laughter mixing, crossing over one another. Today it sounded a little less full. Stan's laugh was missing. He quit before the others. As they quieted, he bit down on his bottom lip.

Steven broke the newfound silence. "Who's Persephone Alford?"

"Pardon?" Darcy asked.

Turning to face his father straight-on, Steven said, "Persephone Alford–I think that's the name you said back at the viewing. Something about her having to do without Stan?"

Maddox stammered. "Oh, not this *shit*."

Darcy rolled his eyes. "For once, gotta agree with your old man. It's nothing. You don't wanna know."

Steven's brow crinkled. "No, really, what's the deal?"

"Just leave it be," Maddox said, waving a hand.

"Just leave it be." Mia mimicked his voice and hand, a perfect echo fine-tuned by years of experience. "No, I don't think I will. Stevie wants to know, so he asked a question. He deserves an answer. And you two both know Stan would have answered, if he were here."

Maddox bowed his head in retreat. "Whatever."

Mia smiled wide, victory writ large. "Okay, okay. So, there's this old cold case, an old murder from the '50s–"

"She fucked it up already," Maddox said.

Mia's eyebrows dropped. "What?"

"Didn't she fuck it up?" Maddox asked Darcy.

"Yeah," he said, shrugging towards Mia. "You kinda did."

Mia reached across the table and slapped Maddox across the face. Not an unusual occurrence. "Shut your flabby face. Not gonna tell you again, old man, no interrupting me, understand?"

Steven chuckled.

Mia turned back to him. "Your daddy's squawking because it ain't really a cold case. It ain't even *that*. More like a rumor of crime. What happened was this: a little boy walks into a police station and tells the desk clerk that his friend, a little girl that lived across the street from him, Persephone, she died. Said she told him that she was gonna get murdered right before she disappeared. Clerk took down the story, called his parents. Parents come in and say the whole story is nonsense, there is no little girl across the street. Never was."

"Okay?" Steven said, his voice full of curiosity.

"But back then, everything got investigated. So, a beat cop goes to the house across the street. A couple live there, but they assure him they never had any children. They invite him in, get him a cup of tea. Nice people. He's ready to go and he notices something weird. Half a crayon on the floor under the table. Now why would these people have a kid's crayon?"

"Dun-dun-dun," Darcy said, imitating an old movie's score.

Mia's voice deepened. "So, now the cop's thinking that maybe there's something to the kid's story. So, he goes to the records building. He finds all the paperwork for the couple, everything's in order, nothing suspicious. But nothing on any daughter. No birth certificate. No school registration. Nothing. He even asks the other neighbors on the block. They never saw any little girl. None of them can think of a bad thing to say about the couple. But he doesn't give up on it. Ever. Never gets any closer to figuring out whether the little boy made the whole thing up, or why there was a crayon, or nothing."

Attention rapt, Steven said, "But that couldn't have been Stan. He wouldn't have even been on the force in the '50s."

"You're right," Mia said. "Cops are worse than a laundromat full of house-wives. They gossip incessantly. The story passed down, year after year. A cop here or there would investigate it, as much as they could, with what little there is to go on. And each of them added a little bit more to the story."

Maddox slid his chair back, out of Mia's slapping range, before he opened his mouth. "It's nothing more than a schoolyard game of telephone. One kid says *elephant* and the last kid says *meal I ate*."

"Probably so," Mia said with a smile. "But Stan believed it. Spent his entire retirement working on *The Case*. Used to come in here and try to tell us all these little things that he'd discovered, or suspected, or hoped to suspect to discover."

Steven nodded, understanding. "Like a hobby."

"Like a moron," Maddox said.

Darcy's eyes glazed over. "I'm gonna miss that moron."

"Already do," Maddox whispered.

They ate, not much, as always. Maddox was aware of his son's gaze as Steven watched the conversation in silence. Steven seemed peaceful as an observer, not at all the impatient child he remembered. *He's an adult, goddammit. When did all that happen?*

Taking a last bite of his pie, Maddox's eyes drifted across the diner. The attractive brunette was gone, her table already clean. He felt a sudden stab of regret that he'd forgotten about her. She'd seemed so familiar, even if Darcy couldn't remember her. He sighed. Pretty girls, always a distraction... even now, with no real chance of ever launching another romance.

Janey entered his view, leading a new customer to the table, her easy smile already plastered across her face, small talk escaping from her lips. Maddox froze as confusion overtook his thoughts. The customer that sat down in one of the table's two chairs was easily in her eighties. Wisps of gray hair dangled out from beneath a head scarf. She shook as she reached for the menu Janey dropped into her hands. Such a fragile, pathetic creature.

She wore a zebra print blouse and a black scarf.

December 2nd

When the previous television set had finally died, Maddox searched stores for a *replacement*. A replacement, not an upgrade. He wanted another piece of furniture— thick, boxy, and heavy. *Familiar.* The newer sets, like the one in the living room, reminded him of a prop from one of the many low-rent science fiction films he'd watched as a kid. He'd wander Schleifer Park until the truant officer started sniffing around, then sneak down Elizabeth Avenue to the Cameo Theater, drop a nickel, and catch a double feature of Poverty Row kids' adventure movies. Sometimes he'd have a friend in tow, but not often. His was a childhood spent drifting through the city, exploring, daydreaming. He loved those flicks back then, saw some of them a half dozen times.

The television in the living room belonged in one of those movies. Not in his son's house. Or even in the real world. Fantasy belonged on the big screen and cabinet television sets too heavy for one man to lift belonged in reality. Simple.

Thank Christ for garage sales.

Maddox stared into the antique screen at an image fuzzy enough to make him feel drunk, and smiled. He'd seen this episode of the game show before, several times. He knew which questions the pretty blonde with mile-high hair would flub, the lame jokes the host would make, the winner of the final puzzle. Far from boring him, he found comfort in the lack of suspense. She'd lose. The used car salesman from Minnesota would win. All was right with the world.

He reached for the beer on the end table beside his recliner, lifted it, placed it back down. Empty. He glanced at the doorway, thinking of walking to the kitchen for another, but made no effort to lift himself off the chair. He sighed, closed his eyes, and folded his arms across his chest like a corpse. Like Stan Mancuso.

Maddox napped.

He woke to canned laughter and the swell of a theme song. Opening his eyes, he squinted through the blur until his vision cleared. Credits rolled over a freeze frame: a father and his two sons, head cocked in surprise and good-natured outrage, both kids wearing devious smiles. Black and white.

Then commercials. Maddox thought some were funny, all insipid, a few outright nonsensical. He had no idea what product most of them promoted, except that they all seemed to involve cell phones or the Internet. He reached over to the end table beside his chair for the remote control, but his fingers came up empty. Leaning over the side of the armrest, he caught sight of it, face down, on the floor.

He didn't bother.

Another show started up, another re-run from decades before. A western, shot on the same set each week, always featuring the same story. He'd never liked those types of shows. He'd watch it anyway, he decided.

He reached for his beer. Empty.

Maddox napped.

Startled out of sleep, he tensed and straightened in the recliner, unsure what had shaken him from his rest. The last rays of orange sunlight retreated across the floor. His stomach growled. Disoriented and uneasy, he glanced to each corner of the room, pausing for more than a moment at the dark open doorway. Someone standing there, just beyond the light's reach? *No, of course not.*

The phone rang in the living room, loud and shrill. The modern electronic bleeps and buzzes never sat well with him. A phone should ring, like a bell over a door, not make a sound like a machine beside a hospital bed. He stared into the dark doorway as the sound repeated; he made no move.

The answering machine picked up after the seventh buzz. "You've reached Steven and Maddox Boxwood. We're not available to take your call right now, but please leave a message and we'll return your call."

Not available? Not *interested.*

Another obnoxious bleep. "Hey Dad, just checking in. Wondering how your appointment with Dr. Van Stiehl went. Remember that there's cold cuts in the fridge. We threw them all out last week, so please eat them, okay?"

Appointment with Van Stiehl? *What goddamn appointment?*

"Be home at six... ish. Sixish. Love you."

Bleep.

Maddox grimaced. Not the first doctor's appointment he'd blanked out on, but lately it happened more and more. Not only visits to Van Stiehl's office, either. Last week he'd forgotten to get his prescription filled at the supermarket pharmacy, even though it was the sole reason he'd gone out. He bought bread and ketchup instead, even though they needed neither, simply to avoid the nagging thought of wasted gas and lost time. Birthday cards never went out on time anymore. He'd gone as far as to buy a stack of belated greetings in anticipation of the future.

But just these little things escaped him, he reassured himself. Nothing a second visit to the store couldn't fix. And really, they ate a lot of bread and used a lot of ketchup anyway.

On the television, a huckster in a sleeveless muscle shirt chopped an onion into bits with a hand-held contraption. Because a knife wouldn't do the same job, Maddox supposed. The offer of a second unit for free, with only the additional charge of separate shipping and handling, did nothing to entice him to call in an order. Did people really order these fucking things? Some must, he reasoned, or else they wouldn't be able to afford the airtime.

Things were so different now.

A sensation started in his chest, a slow tightening of muscles and a quickening of his pulse. He reached into his mouth as he felt it intensify and removed his dentures. From experience he knew it was better not to have teeth in his mouth when his jaw clenched. He'd bit into his gums more than once. The first stab of pain struck as he reached to place the dentures on the end table. His hand snapped into a fist, discarding the teeth into the air. They skidded across the tabletop, collided with the beer can, and sent it off the side. It landed atop the remote control. Beer gushed out onto the carpet.

Maddox cramped up, curling his legs to his chest and leaning forward, burying his head between his knees. Spasms of sharp pain radiated out from beneath his breastbone. He yelped as the spasms hit, rocking him back and forth in the chair. He growled, twitched, sputtered, and cursed. Tears streamed down his overheated face.

Not a heart attack. Not a stroke. Not a heart attack.

The phone rang again.

The onion came apart.

The beer hissed and foamed.

Not a stroke. Not a heart attack. Not a stroke.

His hands and feet shook. Pins and needles.

Good, almost over. The next part is–

Darkness spread across his vision. He welcomed it.

Just before consciousness left him a name flashed through his thoughts, clear and unclouded by fright or pain or anger:

Melissa Shelton.

Then, blackness.

Maddox was never out for long after an attack, ten or fifteen minutes at most. Stretching out, he worked his fingers and toes. Whenever he came to from an episode, he woke with surplus energy and without any pain, all the rank-and-file daily aches missing in action. He felt thirty years younger. It wouldn't last, he knew. Endorphins and adrenaline.

He stood, steady on his feet.

The local news team bantered on television. Maddox hated their waxy faces, every expression so practiced and false. Neither the business of delivering the news of a house fire leaving four dead nor announcing the names of lucky lottery winners ever produced a genuine emotion from any of them. He reached down, swept up the remote control, and turned them the fuck off.

The remote control was wet.

He ran a fingertip over its surface, brought it to his lips. Beer. Brow lowering in confusion, he dropped to his knees and felt the carpet. Wet as well. He lifted the can and shook it. Maybe a tenth left.

He didn't remember getting up for a replacement, or throwing out the empty for that matter. Getting to his feet, he walked into the dark hallway, feeling his way with his free hand against the wall, until he found the light switch at the far end. He cut through the living room on his way to the kitchen, pressing the *play* button on the telephone answering machine as he passed.

"You have– ONE– new message," the feminine electronic voice told him. "And– NO– saved messages. First new message..."

Dropping the empty can into the recycling bucket under the sink, Maddox rummaged until he found a roll of paper towels and a plastic bag. As he stood, he listened to his son's voice in the next room. "Hey Dad, just checking in.

Wondering how your appointment with Dr. Van Stiehl went. Remember that there's cold cuts in the fridge. We threw them all out last week, so please eat them, okay? Be home at six... ish. Sixish. Love you."

He remembered the second time the phone rang, just as the attack hit. The second caller must not have left a message. Strange, though. Steven's number was unlisted, a practice strongly recommended when housing a retired cop, and blocked from telemarketers. No one called unless they meant to call. But no message. And no *Missed Call* icon lit on the machine. Odd.

He cleaned up the spilled beer, threw away the mess, and made himself a roast beef sandwich. With ketchup. He ate, watching the digital clock count up to Six o'clock, and tried not to think of Melissa Shelton, or her husband, or the golf club. He'd not thought about any of it in years, maybe even a decade, but now he found himself unable to push it out of his mind. He sighed.

Fuck it. *He'd have to do something about it.*

December 3rd

Maddox pressed the doorbell with his thumb and left it there, chiming, until Darcy answered. His friend appeared in the doorway wrapped in a fluffy cream bathrobe. "Did I wake you, princess?" he asked. Darcy tightened the terrycloth belt. "It's comfortable."

"Bet it is," Maddox said, shouldering past him. As he entered, he pinched the crease of his suede trilby hat, lifted it off his head, and dropped it onto a branch of the foyer coat rack. His tweed overcoat and knit scarf stayed on. "I assume you had enough time to remove the mud mask from your face and the cucumbers from your eyes?"

Darcy shut the door behind him and sighed. "It's five-thirty... a.m."

"We used to be up by four."

"*Used to,*" Darcy said. "'Cause we had to be, not by choice."

Maddox shook his head. "What's that mean? We had plenty of choices. We were young and healthy, maybe not all that smart every second of the day, but we could've done anything we wanted. No, you and me, we chose to get up every morning at four, get to the station by quarter of five, check the roster—"

"Yeah, I remember the routine." Darcy headed into the kitchen and made a bee-line for the coffee maker. "Too well, sometimes. Couple of mornings back, I jumped out of bed in a panic. Alarm clock read six-thirty. It felt like I was late for the bullpen. Thought Lieutenant Caulzcalski was gonna have my ass for breakfast."

Maddox smiled. "Happens all the time to me."

"Programmed, like robots." Darcy loaded a new filter and filled the pot with tap water. "Doesn't make me nostalgic for it. I like sleeping in, waking up with birds chirping and cars honking down the street. When we used to get rolling it was silent. Y'remember that? Just, *nothing* out there. In *this* city? Not normal, not good."

"Did I wake Blair?" Maddox asked.

"No," Darcy said, "but *I* was pleasantly at rest."

Maddox waved a hand in dismissal. "No harm then."

Blair MacAteer, six years older than her husband but aging with considerably more grace, rounded the corner out of the kitchen with a coffee mug in hand. They always made individual cups. Blair liked her coffee stronger than her husband did. A lot stronger. Like Darcy, she wore a cream robe, but Maddox could not object to the way it hugged tight to her lithe, still athletic frame. In her sweet, birdsong voice, she said, "Morning, Maddy. You're up and prancing early today. Need coffee?"

"Please," he said, smiling.

She took a sip out of her mug, handed it to him, turned, and headed down the hallway. "You boys play nice. I've got to slip into the shower. Meeting Jan and Louise for English tea."

Darcy snatched the cup out of Maddox's hands.

"Y'know she only flirts with me to upset you," Maddox said.

Darcy sighed. "I've been married to her for forty-two years. If I ever thought she was the kind of girl who'd find your hound-dog gob attractive, I'd have divorced or murdered her a long time ago."

Maddox laughed. "As if. *You'd* be the one buried out back."

"Probably true." Moving to the kitchen, Darcy set down the coffee mug. "So, what can I do for my oldest friend at 5:33 in the morning? I trust you weren't just lonely."

"No, no," he muttered, sliding into a chair at the kitchen table. He reached out and fumbled with the pepper shaker for a moment, collecting his thoughts before speaking. "We've been friends for a long time. You know that I'm not one to... What I'm saying is that I don't talk bullshit, right? You know that. I mean what I say and I wouldn't come to you with—"

Darcy dropped into the chair across from him. The chair creaked. "You don't talk bullshit. But sometimes you ramble. Like right now. Did you come here to tell me something or do you have some ulterior motive? Should I count the silverware?"

"Okay," Maddox said, tapping the shaker on the tabletop. "This just isn't easy for me. I can tell a parent that their drunk-driving son ain't coming home, that was never a problem, but this? I don't even know where to begin."

Darcy took the shaker out of his hand. "Just say it."

"I want us to go back to work."

26

Darcy smiled. "You're outta your fuckin' mind."

"No, *listen*," Maddox said. "A year before you and me became partners the first time, we get a call. I dunno if you remember hearing about this one. Tenants of the Prince Street Projects complaining about men coming to and from one of the units at all hours."

Darcy nodded. "Remember lots of calls like that."

"Not like *this*," Maddox said. "I respond with this rookie kid, green as a dollar bill but worth less on the street. No answer to the door. Record player blaring. Then, ten, fifteen minutes later a young black guy comes out and we go in. Dude takes off running, rookie goes after him. I go in. There's probably fifteen more guys inside, milling about, smoking. They see me in my blue and they skirt right out of there. I let them go. Can't chase them all."

The shower went on in the bathroom down the hall. Old pipes groaned. It was a relief. He didn't want Blair to overhear the rest of the story if she were listening. "The place was a disaster. Cigarettes and beer cans on the floor. Smelled like shit and piss and rotten food. Something off, y'know, something bad. Pulled out my service piece and kept it down at my hip, cocked, ready. Started down this hall. Wallpaper peeling back from the walls. Ugly, early '70s stuff out of a catalog. Noises coming from a door at the end. Wet, slapping sounds. Coughing. Groaning."

"You better have a good god-damned reason for telling me this," Darcy said. "I have enough trouble sleeping with all of my own memories."

"I do. I get to the door and push it open. Thick smoke in the air, everything hazy. Not just regular cigs, either. A bedroom. Five more guys. Three at a small end table playing cards. Two on the bed. And between them..." Maddox coughed, squinted. "This young woman, nineteen or twenty. Skinniest woman I'd ever seen. Could've counted her ribs. Naked and unconscious. They were *fucking* her, Darce, in the worst ways. Bruises all over her. Track lines on her arms."

Darcy turned his head and closed his eyes. "What'd you do?"

"I yelled, screamed, I don't even know what. But the two on the bed sprinted out of there. Didn't even gather up their clothes, just bolted. I raised my revolver and asked them which one of them lived there. They ratted him out fast and I told them to get lost. They did. Then it was just me and him, and her, I guess. He'd gotten his wife hooked on junk, kept her just this side of breathing so he could whore her out to every scumbag and lowlife that could come up with a ten-dollar bill."

Darcy shook his head. "How much time he do?"

"None."

Maddox's heartbeat quickened. "Had a little shiv knife on him, the kind we used to find on teenager gang bangers. The kind we used to confiscate. The kind that never got bagged or tagged or filed into evidence. The kind that sometimes turned up at crime scenes when justice needed a lifeline."

"Fuck, Maddox. I don't even want to know."

"Found a stubby little golf putter, the kind you'd use for mini-golf. Played a few rounds until he didn't have any teeth left in his mouth. Meant to stop then. But that wasn't happening. One look at the girl on the bed and I was back swinging hard. His face... wasn't a face by the time I was done. Big, red, bulging eyes. Cheekbones out of line with each other. Jaw unattached. And I meant to stop *then*, too. But the girl on the bed woke up, somewhat, and saw what I was doing to her husband."

Darcy opened his eyes and stared at him. "She scream?"

"No," Maddox said. "She said *please don't stop*. So, I didn't."

Darcy made a knocking sound with his tongue. "A lot of things happened back then, horrible things, on the street and in the back of squad cars. Don't take this the wrong way, but why the hell are you holding on to a memory like that? Nothing good's there. Let it go."

"I did," Maddox said. "Haven't thought about it in years. At all. But then, I had one of my... moments, and there her name was, Melissa Shelton. And then it all came back to me, just like that, everything, even the tiny details."

"Just like that?" Darcy asked.

"Like that." Maddox snapped his fingers. "But maybe not. Remember at Hop's after Stan's funeral, I tried to point out a woman to you?"

"No," Darcy said.

"I wanted to know if you recognized her?"

"Still no. I really don't always pay attention to you."

"After I was done with Gerald Shelton, the husband, I went out to the cruiser, called it in. Said one of the johns must have done a number on him.

28

Then I went back inside. Melissa was still on the bed, breathing shallow, pulse near nothing. I don't know why now, maybe it was just who we were back then, but I didn't want the medics to see her that way. So, I searched for clothes. Strange thing is that I couldn't find any in the dresser drawers. Just men's clothes. So, I searched the rest of the apartment. On a hook on the back of the bathroom door I found a shirt. A zebra print blouse with a black scarf attached around the neck. Maybe you remember the style. I dressed her and waited at the foot of her bed until help arrived. I remember trembling, for a whole lot of reasons. Afraid she'd die. Worried that my story about a john wouldn't hold. Real fear. And then, when it all went smooth and she was in the hospital safe and he was in the morgue and I was in my own bed, peace. I'd done the right thing, no matter what anyone might think."

"We all had nights like that," Darcy said.

"Yeah." Maddox nodded. "But normally we don't see that same woman, thirty-some years later, not aged a day, sitting in a diner waiting for a club sandwich."

"That's true, we don't." Darcy smacked his lips together, set down the pepper shaker, and spread out his hands. "At least *I* don't. Whatever. I still don't get why I'm hearing about this at the crack of dawn. This is my kitchen. I eat packaged donuts in here; it's not a confession booth."

"I'm not Catholic–anymore–and this isn't a confession."

"So, *what?*" Darcy asked. "You want us to go chase ghosts?"

Maddox snatched up the shaker and resumed playing with it. "Not at all. Melissa Shelton didn't die. Not that night, anyway. Got out of the hospital a few months later. Lost track of her. But I really don't care. Remembering that case, all of it, so clear, every detail still sharp... I want it all back. I want my life back, my real life, before I became this shriveled-up old man without a purpose, or much hair, a dick that won't get hard."

Blair's shower ended. The house fell silent. Maddox hoped she hadn't heard his speech, at least not the last bit of it. He studied his friend's face, looking for clues, the detective still hunting for evidence. Not so easy. Darcy always had a good poker face.

Finally, the old Irish cop smiled. "Just ask it, already."

"One last case," Maddox said. "Nothing dangerous. No badges, no guns, no one to arrest. Just something to get us back into the world for a bit, before... we run out of time. I just want to *feel something* one more time. Let's put our boots back on. Live for a while. Then, I promise, I'll shut up about it and let you schlep back to mall walking and bingo nights."

"Pinochle, not bingo." Darcy grinned. It was a familiar, impish smile that Maddox hadn't seen in a long, long time. "We play for cash. It's not much of a game if there are no stakes."

Maddox didn't return the smile. "I can't do this alone, Darce."

"Just tell me what you have in mind."

"The Persephone Alford case."

"Oh, Christ."

Maddox tapped the shaker into his palm and threw a pinch of salt over his shoulder.

*　　*　　*

Maddox and Darcy spent the day playing poker, drinking, reminiscing, and laughing. They did *not* discuss Persephone Alford, Melissa Shelton, or Stan Mancuso. When Blair returned from her day out with the girls, Maddox noticed the skies were dark. He excused himself. Blair kissed his cheek and told him to get home safe. As always, Darcy walked him to the door and shook his hand.

Maddox said, "After later."

It was an old cop superstition. Never say goodbye.

With a nod, Darcy said, "I'm all in."

*　　*　　*

The first drops of a steady rain splattered against the windshield. Two degrees cooler and it would have been snow. Maddox set the wipers to intermittent. Just as enough raindrops built up on the glass to blur his vision, the wipers chased them away. The sound of the swashing blades soothed his nerves, a mechanical lullaby easing his thoughts out of focus. He yawned, shook his head, and pulled into a convenience store. A candy bar, maybe a soda, something to keep him awake long enough to get home in one piece.

He parked and killed the engine, freezing the windshield wiper blades mid-streak. Tiny raindrops pelted the glass, now safe to gather. The store's neon OPEN sign blurred into a nightmarish splash of red, a fragment of a crime scene or a Rorschach ink blot.

Maddox reached for the door handle. A drop of water dripped off the tip of his finger. He cracked open the car door, triggering the interior lights, and raised his hand in front of his face. Wet. He frowned. He mustn't have noted the rain had begun before he left Darcy's house. A lot on his mind. He glanced up into the visor mirror. His thin gray hair was plastered to his scalp.

He stepped out into the rain, not bothering with the umbrella on the back seat. A little water never hurt anyone. Not as much as a golf club, anyway. Passing through a set of automatic doors, he entered the store. His eyes fought the adjustment from dim moonlight to sickly yellow florescent lights. He wandered the aisles of bright packages, boxes screaming out with bubble-letter logos and photos of smiling children and cartoon animals. Was this a miniature grocery or an amusement park for kids? Hard to tell anymore.

Against the far wall, he found twelve doors of coolers filled with soft drinks. Mostly energy drinks with names evoking violence and crime, but with a little digging, he came up with a plastic bottle of Coca-Cola. *Classic.* Not diet. Or Diet with Lime. Or Zero, whatever that meant. Or Zero Vanilla. Just plain old Coca-Cola. He *hoped.* Turning it over and over in his hand, he grew confident enough that he headed to the checkout counter.

He passed by the three self-checkout stations and approached the kid standing at the far end reading a magazine. He dropped the Coke on the desk. The boy put away the copy of *People* and stared at him with an expression of bemusement. *Got caught in the rain, so what?*

Maddox's eyes darted past the kid to the cigarette case. He hadn't smoked in twelve years, hadn't even had a stray urge in seven, but now the hunger returned. He and Darcy had always shared smokes on the job. It just seemed right. "Box of reds."

The kid smiled, amusement turning to confusion as he turned to fetch the pack. As he rang up the order and bagged it, he mumbled, "That was fast."

"What?" Maddox said, nearly barking at the kid.

The cashier shook his head. "Didn't say nothing."

"Right, y'didn't, how much?"

The kid rang up the soda and the smokes. "Nine-eighty. Again."

What was this punk's problem? Maddox pulled out his wallet, brought out a ten, and handed it over. The kid slid the money into his till and handed him back his change. "Twenty cents. Again."

In a gruff rumble, Maddox said, "Have a good night."

"See you soon," the kid answered, his smile returning.

Maddox ignored him and headed for the doors. They opened with a sound much like his windshield wipers. The rain was letting up. He opened the door to his car and tossed the shopping bag into the passenger seat.

It landed atop another, identical bag. Leaning in, he opened it. A pack of reds and a Coca-Cola. *Classic.*

*   *   *

Steven waited at the kitchen table. Maddox huffed as he entered, tossing his hat and coat onto a free chair and rolling his eyes. He recognized the look on his son's face. He'd liked it more twenty-five years earlier when their roles had been reversed. "Where have you been, Dad?"

"Out." Maddox swung open a cabinet door and pulled down a glass.

"*Out?*" Steven said, anger seasoning the word.

"Yeah, as in, not here." He turned on the faucet, waited a moment for the water to chill, and filled the glass. "I was over Darcy's place. Talking. Then we got pizza delivered."

"It's 11:30 at night. I was worried."

Another cabinet. He brought down the pill box, opened the section marked with a T for Tuesday, and removed all six pills. He hoped Steven didn't notice. Two in the morning, two in the afternoon, every day. Except today– and a few other days recently. He popped them onto his tongue, chased them down with a swig of water, then turned to face his son. "Didn't realize I had a curfew. Gonna give me the speech about living under *your* roof? Take away the Atari until I prove I can be trusted?"

Steven made a gruff, sputtering sound. "Goddamn it, Dad. This isn't some game. Yesterday you brush off your appointment with Dr. Van Stiehl. You're not home to take your prescriptions. You won't get a cell phone, so I don't even have a way to get in touch with you. What am I supposed to do?"

"Guess that depends," Maddox said. He dumped out the remaining water and set the glass down in the sink. "What *is it* that you're trying to do? You think I'm gonna live a minute longer because you know where I am? Maybe you're worried that I'm getting mixed up with the wrong crowd? That I might be out huffing gas fumes and playing sidewalk dice down on Frelinghuysen Ave? Don't worry, I'll call someone else when I need bail."

Steven snorted. "What, I just shouldn't worry?"

"Oh, by all means, worry," Maddox said, leaning his shoulder against the refrigerator. "Call out a Silver Alert so I can see my name on one of those highway signs. Maybe if the National Guard doesn't have any hurricane victims to rescue, they can look for me."

Steven pushed away from the table and stood. When had he gotten taller than Maddox? Up to this point in life, that hadn't been the case, had it? Maddox straightened up his posture. His spine crackled.

"All you needed to do was call, that's it."

Maddox sighed. "I'm home now. Go to bed. You have work."

Steven, voice still riddled with annoyance, said, "Goodnight."

"Goodnight, Good Knight."

As he headed out of the kitchen, Steven stopped, cocked his head towards his father, and smiled. Maddox knew that Goodnight, Good Knight would bring his son good memories. He felt guilty for using it instead of an apology. But not *that* guilty.

"You've got mail," Steven said, and went to bed.

Maddox turned his attention to the kitchen table. A single envelope rested in the exact center. Steven kept an immaculate house, everything in its place– *precisely* in its place. He glanced over at the two-slot bin on the counter. The bottom slot, assigned for Steven's mail, was orderly but full. The top, his, was empty. As he reached for the envelope, he wondered why his son hadn't filed it away. He tried to remember the last time he'd received anything–a letter, a bill, junk mail, anything addressed to him by name. *There*, he reasoned, was the answer.

No return address. Big, bold, blocky letters.

He tore the edge of the envelope, removing a strip, and reached inside. A birthday card. He scowled. Some kind of joke? He was born in March, not December. A banner read ON YOUR BIRTHEDAY, printed in lettering disarmingly like the handwriting on the envelope. Underneath, an illustration that reminded him in style of a religious woodcut, displayed a smiling grim reaper standing over an unmarked tombstone.

BIRTHEDAY.

He studied the misspelled word. It unnerved him even more than the drawing. Tracing a fingertip over the print, he felt the texture of the raised ink. The card hadn't come from a Hallmark production line. This had been handmade. He opened it.

In the same typeface: LEAVE IT ALONE. FORGET HER.

That didn't cause the shudder that ran throughout his body. No, it was the signature at the bottom. Maddox closed the card, slid it back into the envelope, and dropped it into his mail bin. Then he returned to the refrigerator. His hands shook as he reached for the last beer. He waited to open it until he was back in his room, seated in his recliner. He cracked open the tab and took a long swig.

His nerves didn't settle.

He worried another attack might come, but it didn't.

Turning on the television, he found he couldn't focus on the program. Noise and flickering light, nothing more.

The card was signed by Stan Mancuso.

The stamp was canceled with today's postmark.

December 4th

"Outta your mind. More than usual," Darcy said.

Maddox placed the box of cigarettes on the dashboard. Rebuffed, he stared over at Darcy in the passenger seat wearing an expression of venomous disbelief. "You call me insane for trying to give you a gift? Bet Christmas is a real joy in the MacAteer house."

"My doctor made me give that shit up fifteen years ago," Darcy said, pointing to the box of reds. "Smoking is like a disease. I see that now. It's like you're offering me rheumatic fever and then getting sick when I say *no, but thank you for asking, I'd like to continue breathing a little while longer.*"

"Neither of us got so long to live anymore, anyway." Maddox slid the first cigarette from the box, lit it, and put it to his lips. He took a drag. It was awful. It felt right. "All this non-smoking business, the Surgeon General buzz-kill, it's probably right and good and all that, but it ain't who we are."

"Who we *were*," Darcy corrected him.

Maddox asked, "You like today's *you* better? You like having to squint when you take a piss in the middle of the night even though you had to run to the bathroom from the bloat? Or that sound your knees make every time you stand up?"

"I haven't changed. I'm still *me*," Darcy said. "We're older, man, but that's okay. Smoking a red isn't gonna make me any younger. It's just gonna make my breath stink."

Maddox chuckled. "You're just afraid of Blair."

"Damn right, I'm afraid of her."

"Smart man." Maddox pulled out a second cigarette, lit the end, and held it out to Darcy.

His friend's eyes softened. Darcy took the cigarette. "Gotta die from something. Probably won't be from this cancer stick. A frying pan flying at Mach 5, maybe."

They smoked in silence until both cigarettes were burnt down to their filters. Maddox opened the window and flicked his butt outside. Darcy, after searching fruitlessly for a console ashtray, pinched out the glow and pocketed his. Maddox shook his head. "Gonna burn a hole straight through your pants."

Darcy shrugged. "Y'sound jealous."

"Maybe I just have more to protect down there."

Darcy grinned and cocked a thumb across the street at Stan Mancuso's house. "You must have huge pair to have asked Stan's nephew for the keys. Couldn't stand that little prick, not ever."

"Me either. That's why I didn't ask him," Maddox said.

Darcy tilted his head. "What you mean, *didn't ask him?*"

"Darce, you know how this works. We jim a window. Won't even leave a mark if we're careful. We go in, grab his files, and our asses are back in these seats in five minutes. No sweat."

Darcy said, "You're serious?"

"Sure."

"There are, what, sixteen houses on this block?" Darcy asked. "You sure that none of his neighbors are horny pensioners with binoculars slung around their necks? Jesus-Dishwasher-Christ, man, we're not cops anymore. No one's gonna cover for us if we get caught."

Maddox pointed and waited for Darcy's eyes to follow his finger. "That window, there. Take—what?—a minute, minute-and-a-half, tops."

"I'm too cute for prison," Darcy said.

Turning, Maddox snatched the slim jim from the back seat and cracked open the driver's-side door. Stepping out, he leaned back into the car, locked eyes with Darcy, and asked, "*All in* usually means you're willing to do what it takes. Not that you're willing to bitch like a runner-up prom queen scared of giving her first gumdrop humjob."

Darcy sighed and opened the passenger door. Heaving himself out, he reached over his head with both hands and yawned. Maddox extended both hands. *What the fuck are you doing?*

"At our age, it could have serious consequences if we don't stretch before breaking and entering," Darcy said.

Maddox closed his door. "Tell it to the union."

As they crossed the roadway, Maddox studied the block. Darcy was right—this *was* risky. Any of the street's darkened windows could obscure the face of a curious neighbor. Stepping up onto the sidewalk, he glanced north and south, his eyes darting between windows of parked cars. No one.

He led Darcy past the concrete lions on either side of the porch's short set of stairs, his hands dropping down to pet the closest cat's ear. Stepping up onto the porch, he reached for the front door.

Darcy came up behind him. "You should be wearing gloves."

"I'm not that cold," Maddox said, snickering. He wasn't afraid of fingerprints. They'd both visited Stan hundreds of times. Their prints on the doorknob—and inside the house—wouldn't pass muster even as circumstantial evidence. He tried the knob. Locked, as expected; nothing came easy. He moved down to the window. With one final glance back at the street, he ran the jim flat to the window stool and pushed. It slid underneath without resistance. *Thank God Stan's too lazy to winterize.*

Was too lazy, he reminded himself. Dead men don't winterize.

Moving the jim from side to side, he frowned. He expected to run across the lock near the middle. Instead, the jim slid back and forth without coming into contact with anything. Was it unlocked to begin with? Maddox pressed his free palm against the pane and pushed. Nothing. It *was* locked. Somehow.

"Y'doing up there?" a voice asked from behind.

Maddox and Darcy turned. A young black kid stood on the sidewalk holding a dog leash. A brown and white shih tzu squatted on Stan's small rectangle of lawn, relieving itself. Besides the reins to the leash, the boy's hands were empty. No bag.

Darcy blushed. Maddox couldn't tell whether he was embarrassed about the dog taking a shit or being caught breaking into Stan's house. Both, probably. He stammered, "Hey now, look we're not doing..."

The kid smirked. "Y'not what?"

"Nothing," Darcy said, voice soft and reassuring. "We're not doing nothing. Why don't you..."

Maddox slid the jim out of the window and held it up for the boy to see. Darcy's face paled. Ignoring him, he pointed with the tool. "You got a name?"

"Fuck kinda question is that?" the boy asked.

Maddox grinned. "Nice to meet you, Fuck Kinda Question. I'm Jim and this is my friend, we call him Crow. You know Stan Mancuso, the guy who used to live here?"

"He died," Fuck Kinda Question said. "Old cop, or some shit."

"That's right," Maddox said, shaking the jim. "*Or some shit.* You know how friends sometimes borrow stuff and forget to return it? We got a situation like that. We're breaking into his house to get some... some *shit* that belongs to us. If we leave it here, his asshole nephew's gonna keep it."

Fuck Kinda Question nodded. "Sucks."

"Yeah, it does suck."

Darcy, a white man sounding white, said, "*Fucking* sucks."

"You wanna make twenty bucks?" Maddox asked.

Fuck Kinda Question bit his bottom lip and squinted, a dramatic show of *thinking it over.* "Seems, dunno, risky for twenty. Maybe worth it for fifty."

"Fifty? I almost had it. I don't need your help for fifty."

"You almost had it?" Fuck Kinda Question burst out laughing. Tugging the leash, he pulled the dog off the grass mid-shit. He handed the leash to Darcy and joined Maddox on the porch. "Y'haven't done this for a while, right? They stopped making windows like that a long time back. Even old white cops could figure out how to bust in. They knew they had to change it up."

The kid pointed through the window at two small arms on the inside rail. "Now they lock in the middle, so you can't just jimmy it open."

Maddox tapped on the window. "So, we can't get in?"

Fuck Kinda Question snorted. "Didn't say that."

"How do we, then?"

"Need a special tool."

Maddox asked, "A special tool?"

"It's called a fifty-dollar bill."

Maddox grimaced, handed the kid the jim, reached into his back pocket, and pulled out his wallet. Rifling through it, he removed two twenties and held them up. "I'll go forty. But that's it."

Fuck Kinda Question grinned. "S'okay, long as I get to come in."

"Why would you want to?" Maddox grumbled.

The kid shrugged. "Never been in a white person's home."

"Just for a minute, that's it—"

"Hey, Mad, no. It's Stan's house, man..." Darcy said.

"—And you're not gonna touch anything, understand?"

Fuck Kinda Question nodded and plucked the bills out of Maddox's hand. Lowering the jim to the porch, he stomped the heel of his sneaker on its tip and lifted the handle, bending it. Back up on his feet, he worked the tool under the window's center rail, wiggling back and forth, until the bent metal met the lock arm. With a quick twist of his wrist, the window was unlocked. Fuck Kinda Question withdrew the jim, handed it to Maddox, and slid the pane open. The whole operation took less than thirty seconds.

Popping the screen out of place, he asked, "You wanna me to duck inside and let you in, or y'wanna squeeze your old ass through?"

"Be my guest," Maddox said with a sigh.

Darcy chuckled. "I wondered about that part."

The boy crawled through the window. In another moment the front door opened and he gestured Maddox to enter. Darcy hesitated, an expression of apprehension on his face. *He really didn't want to do this.* Maddox waved him off as he stepped over the threshold. "It's fine, stay out here with the dog. Maybe walk the block, let it shit on lawns. Me and the kid-who's-never-broken-into-a-white-person's-house will only be a minute."

"I ain't never broken into a white person's house," Fuck Kinda Question insisted. When Maddox gave him a tough glare, he added, "Black people, Hispanics, Asians..."

Closing the door behind him, Maddox mumbled, "First time for everything, I suppose."

Stan's house was dark. Weak sunlight drifted in through the windows but didn't penetrate far. Maddox waited for his eyes to adjust. They didn't. He patted down his coat pocket for his reading glasses, then stifled a laugh when he found them and realized they'd only exacerbate the problem: dim shapes and shadows, now closer, in sharper detail. Instead, he put a hand against the wall and searched for the light switch.

"Man, I can't see nothing," Fuck Kinda Question said.

"Working on it."

Maddox's hand moved over cheap paneling as if reading Braille, fingertips skimming over tiny bumps and nicks, each one no doubt the only remaining testament to a moment in Stan's family history. Had an old picture frame hung here? A string of Christmas cards? When Stan died, any remaining memory of those events evaporated. All that was left was tiny marks on old wood. Once his nephew sold the place, the new owner would doubtlessly tear down the unfashionable wall and put up fresh, perfectly featureless drywall. No memories, no evidence.

He found the switch.

A single shaded lamp sputtered to life, glowing in the corner of the living room but casting very little light beyond a small halo around Stan's well-worn recliner. Bookshelves, a card table, a television on a cart: all indistinct shapes at the edges of the light's reach.

"Little better," Fuck Kinda Question said, jerking a thumb towards the kitchen doorway. "Y'think there's maybe still some food in the fridge? 'Cause I ain't eaten and..."

Stan wasn't dead a week. It was possible. "Help yourself–to food. Nothing else."

Fuck Kinda Question grunted out an answer and disappeared into the darkness. Young eyes. Maddox envied him. So much new yet to see. He approached Stan's recliner and dropped a hand onto the armrest. New, the upholstery had been soft and luxurious. Now, it was as rough as old canvas. Same could be said of the skin on his hand, he realized.

Tears? No, not yet. But, if he wasn't careful, soon.

He imagined Stan sitting in the chair, one hand full of playing cards, the other wrapped around a beer bottle. Tuesdays were poker nights for years, up until...

It'd been a while.

At the end of the last poker night, after the others had left, Stan pushed back against the headrest until the chair fully reclined, closed his eyes, and asked him, "How bad do I look, Mads?"

Awful. Maddox remembered a young beat cop, curly hair long enough to keep him in hot water with the deputy commissioner, bright winking eyes that won the office girls every time, a lawyer's devious smile, a fit, muscular farm boy's physique. Gone, grape to raisin. "You look like shit, Stan, but that's hardly a new thing."

Stan smiled, weak and gentle. "It's eating me from the inside."

"Y'gonna beat this."

Stan closed his eyes. "This time the charges are gonna stick."

"Talk that way? You can't leave me with Darcy and Mia, can you?"

The recliner was empty. An empty chair in an empty house.

Maddox withdrew his hand from the armrest. Somehow, this moment, standing over Stan's recliner, affected him in the way he supposed he should have felt at the viewing. The dead body had just been flesh. The chair, and the memories it brought, were much more. He whispered, "Dammit, Stan. Already miss you."

Turning away, he ignored the tears building in his eyes and listened. From the sounds coming from the kitchen, Fuck Kinda Question was rummaging through the refrigerator. *Check the expiration dates, kid. Stan loved to shop the 'reduced for quick sale' shelves at the Food Cabinet.*

The staircase leading to the second floor was even darker than the living room. Clutching the handrail, Maddox climbed, each step tentative and uncertain, wary of unseen obstacles. The stairs creaked, a different voice with every step, higher and lower pitches. Walking on a xylophone with its bars out of order. At the landing, Maddox pivoted and reached out for the wall. Another light switch. He flicked it. No change. Flipped it off, then on, and repeated the process. Nothing. He could only see a few feet ahead.

Annoyed, he worked his way down the hall in the same halting manner as he'd handled the stairs, one hand on the wall, each step labored and slow. An old man's walk. His hand free hand twitched as he approached the door to Stan's study. It wanted him to reach into his side holster and draw his sidearm. Old habits. No holster, no sidearm. And no threat, either. Sure, he could create nightmare scenarios in his head—homeless squatters or drug dealers setting up shop—but he was confident that they were the first to break in. The first, in fact, to be inside this house since Stan left for the hospital.

No squatters, no drug dealers.

No holster, no sidearm.

He quickened his pace, eager to throw open the door and put his lingering fears to rest. He shuffled to the end of the hall and reached for the doorknob, then stopped. His hand twitched again, and this time he didn't protest.

Etched into the office door was a rough illustration of a grim reaper standing over a tombstone. Maddox's heart raced. He moved his hand over it, just as he had done the card, and realized the reaper hadn't been scratched into the wood, it had been engraved there, burnt in. This time, however, the tombstone wasn't blank. It read:

PERSEPHONE ALFORD

? - 1958

Oh, Stan. He'd known his friend made a hobby out of the case—he'd teased him mercilessly for it, they all had—but *this*? It chilled Maddox to think that Stan's final act before leaving his home for the last time might have been to send him a card with this same illustration. *As what?* Some sort of warning? *Of what?*

He opened the door and reached inside for the light switch.

As if.

Maddox recoiled, hands up, fingers outspread. His reaction owed as much to his surprise as it did to an attempt to block the sudden blaze of light. Eyes adjusting to the brightness, he lowered his hands and stepped into the room. Nine lamps. Stan had gathered every mobile light fixture in the house inside his office, removing shadows entirely. The room glowed.

But that wasn't the strangest part.

Maddox stepped inside.

Bright-colored yarn zigzagged from wall to wall like an insane Technicolor spider-web. Many converged in the center of the room, to a central hub on Stan's desk. A large spike protruded from the workstation, with the tail end of the lengths of yarn tied to its shaft. Maddox reached out and touched a pink thread, following it to the wall beside him. It ended at an antique photograph of a man in a wheelchair, pressed to the wall by a T pin. Underneath the image, a five-by-ten index card held the caption *RUDOLPH JACOB THEISS, 1927.*

The walls were littered with photographs and index cards. Sometimes the yarn connected two; others went back to the spike. Maddox followed *THEISS*'s yarn-line to a photograph on the opposite wall, ducking and weaving through the web as he went. *MARY KAITLYN TANNER, 1992.*

An orange line also connected to *TANNER*. He followed that to a campground map pinned to the eastern wall. *MERRYTOWN, VA.* Seven small X's dotted the map in red pen. Six more lines led away from the map. The map was from the '70s. There were hundreds of other photos, maps, index cards—even mortgage receipts, obituaries clipped from newspapers, pages torn from grade-school history books.

Turning away from the walls, Maddox traced a yellow thread to the central spike. Beside the spike sat a thick manila folder bulging with paperwork. Across the cover, in Stan's handwriting, was the name *PERSEPHONE MELISSA ALFORD*.

Maddox lifted the folder off the desk. As he did, the corner caught one of the threads and tugged it away from the spike. It fell to the desktop, then, no longer pulled taut, retreated to the floor. Maddox twisted in place, watching the yarn move across the carpet like a snake, for a moment. Then it came to a rest. Curiosity building, he followed the red line with his eyes to its corresponding photograph. This one was different from the others.

An intense, almost painful tingle ran under Maddox's skin.

He recognized the face. He damn well better have.

The index card underneath read *MADDOX BENJAMIN BOXWOOD*.

Pulling the folder to his chest, he hit the light switch and hurried into the hallway. Plunged into darkness, this time he did not hesitate at all, rushing towards the stairwell without worrying about his step or guiding himself with the wall. He only cared about one thing: getting the hell out of there.

"Kid—"

Halfway down the stairs he felt his balance fail and his bodyweight shift. Stumbling, he scrambled for the handrail, latched on to it, and steadied himself, but never stopped moving. He continued down, swaying and tripping over his own feet, until he reached the ground floor. He yelled, *"KID—"*

He spun into the kitchen. Empty. *Where'd he gone?*

"KID, WE'RE LEAVING. NOW—"

Bolting out of the kitchen, Maddox felt his heartbeat quicken and panic overcame him. Not now. No. Not a heart attack. *Not a stroke. Not a heart attack—*

He opened his mouth to yell again, but a rough, chest-burning string of coughs came out instead. Staggering, he clutched a fist against his breastbone. Losing his grip on the folder, it fell away, spilling its contents. His legs wobbled, but he kept moving, rushing towards the living room. *Not a stroke. Not a heart attack. Not a stroke.*

His balance finally succumbing, he slammed one shoulder into the door frame, hard, and slid down to one knee. *Please, no, not now. Later's fine, not now. Have to go. Have to get out—*

"But where'll you go?"

Maddox's head spun towards the voice. "*KID—*"

It wasn't Fuck Kinda Question.

Stan Mancuso sat in his recliner, half his face lost in darkness, the other half lit by the only lamp he'd not moved to his study. His features were waxy and cold, more mannequin than human. His shriveled, frail body took up very little of the chair. His voice, however, was strong and clear. Only, it wasn't *his* voice. "When you leave here, Maddox. Where will you go?"

"Stan?"

Stan grinned. His devilish old smile. "No."

Confusion. "Wha—"

"Stan's dead," Stan said.

Heart pounding, legs shaking, fingertips bulging with each thump in his chest, Maddox stared at his dead friend and managed to ask, "Then who are you?"

"A friend," the friend said, then clarified, "or not. Yet. You and I, we're going to know each other very well, soon. But don't call me Stan; it dishonors his memory."

The friend, or not, glowered as it spoke the word *memory*.

"What are you?" Maddox croaked. His eyes bulged with each heartbeat, blurring his vision. His stomach muscles constricted. He bent forward but kept his eyes trained on the man in the recliner.

"Kloum. I... am nothing."

"You okay, old man?" Fuck Kinda Question called out from behind. Maddox felt the kid's hands on his shoulder, lifting him from his crouch. He glanced at the boy, eyes wide with distrust. "Y'gotta be careful. It's dark in here, remember?"

"*I'm fine*," Maddox barked, though his voice disagreed.

Fuck Kinda Question eyed him with both distrust and sympathy. The latter must have won out. He pulled Maddox's arm around his head and held him up. "Who was you talking to?"

He doesn't see Stan. *Kloum. It.*

Maddox turned back to the recliner.

Kloum remained there, still smiling. He leaned back in the chair, closed his eyes, and said, "In twenty-two days, choose channel seven."

"Get... the... folder—"

And then, as always at the end of an attack, his vision darkened. The living room sank into blackness. The last image to go was Stan's face, half in and half out of the light, a dead man and nothing at all.

December 5th

White walls, white curtain on a yellow runner. Hospital bed.

Oh, fa'fuck's sake.

Steven sat on the faux-leather guest chair, hunched forward, elbows on knees, reading an electronic device of some sort. Not that Maddox read much, but if he did he'd have a yard-sale paperback in his hands, not a gadget that needed to be plugged in at night. He cleared his voice, pushing gravel in the sand, and asked, "Not *The Long Goodbye*, by chance? Didn't finish it, always wanted to."

Steven didn't move.

"Hey, Stevie–"

Head still down, his son mumbled, "You're still asleep, Dad."

*   *   *

White walls, white curtain on a yellow runner. Hospital bed.

Oh, fa'fuck's sake.

Steven sat on the faux-leather guest chair, hunched forward, elbows on knees, reading an electronic device of some sort. Not that Maddox read much, but if he did he'd have a yard-sale paperback in his hands, not a gadget that needed to be plugged in at night. He cleared his voice, pushing gravel in the sand, and asked, "Not *The Long Goodbye*, by chance? Didn't finish it, always wanted to."

Steven's head shot up, smiling.

"Nah, you know I don't like that stuff." He fiddled with the screen, then flipped the device over: a green and white close-up image of a black man's face and text, *Giovanni's Room, a novel by James Baldwin*. "Not your kind of stuff."

"Probably not," Maddox said.

He reached for the bed's armrest to sit up. A tube followed. An IV in his arm leading up to a clear drip bag handing from a rack. He'd visited plenty of hospitals both on the job and off. He knew the drill. Hydration.

"How y'feeling, Dad?"

"Besides the déjà vu? Fine, I feel fine." Maddox studied the room. It wasn't just the dream—there was something more here tripping his sense of familiarity. He squinted, trying to connect the dots. "Maybe a little foggy."

Steven got up, dragged the chair closer, and sat back down. "Well, it's okay. You had a helluva day yesterday. Just relax and rest."

Across the room, a second bed, unoccupied, drew his attention. Above it, a watercolor painting of a foreign city was mounted to the wall, ever so slightly askew. He knew the painting.

Maddox settled back down into the bed.

Jesus. It was the same room where he'd visited Stan near the end. He turned his head away, staring instead at the empty wall behind Steven. Bad art or nothing, he realized. No place in a hospital room for a mirror.

"Darcy and Blair were here all morning," Steven said. "She has Pilates. He just walked her down to the car. When they came in she was holding—" He pointed to a large potted flower on the bed stand. "—that geranium. He had her purse. Held it like a dead skunk, by the tail, at arm's length."

Maddox smiled. He could picture it.

Steven's voice lowered. "You really scared me, Dad. When I got the call, the caller ID said it was the hospital, and then I pick up and hear Darcy's voice... I thought... *you* really *scared me,* Dad."

Scared? You know nothing of it.

"Look," Maddox said, trying his best to sound gruff and nonchalant, "this is just a little thing, I'm sure. Nothing to get worked up about. I don't want you going all—"

Steven interrupted him with a blunt, "I love you."

I love you, too. The words were close.

"I know that," Maddox said, careful not to make eye contact. "You and me, we've been through a lot, since forever, right? That time when you stepped on that rusted nail on the basketball court? You were, what, nine?"

"I love you, Dad," Steven repeated.

Maddox nodded. "I love you too."

It hurt to say. Not because it wasn't true—it was. But it *felt* like a lie. It *sounded* like a lie. He could have said it a million times to nine-year-old Steven, roofing nail protruding from his heel, to soothe his pain, without any doubt or question. But now... it felt... procedural.

Guilt settled into his gut, bedding down in the nest it had built there long ago. When had it all changed? When had *I love you* lost its resonance? Somewhere between Steven's high school graduation and the day he returned from Princeton? Somewhere in there, yes.

"Was Van Stiehl here?" he asked, voice low and grumbling.

Steven nodded. "Last night and again this morning."

Needle marks on his arms. "Blood tests?"

"Mmmm-huh, and CAT scans and MRIs and everything else you can imagine," Steven said. His lip curled and head tilted, barely perceptible motions, but a familiar tell: the conversation with the doctor had frightened him. "Dr. Van Stiehl said the results'll be back today."

Maddox grinned, for his son's benefit, mostly. "School, I was shit at tests."

"Not just at school," Darcy said as he entered and dropped his coat on a spare chair. "If I hadn't helped you cheat, you'd never have passed the LE exam."

"LE exam?" Steven asked.

"Can't be a cop if you don't know the law," Maddox said.

"You were the exception that proved the rule," Darcy said. He reached out, took hold of Maddox's shoulder, and squeezed. "You scared the shit out of us, y'know?"

"Impossible," Maddox said, grinning. "There's too much shit in all of you. It's too big a job for any one man. Thanks for the vote of confidence, though."

Darcy pointed to his arm. "Damned junkie, always talking outta y'ass."

"You kiss your mother with that tongue?"

Darcy laughed. "Mom's been dead for thirty years."

"Wouldn't stop you," Maddox said.

"Okay," Steven barked. "Enough of that. Making me sick."

Maddox ignored him. "Tell Blair I'm sorry I missed her."

Darcy shook his head. "She didn't want to see you anyway."

"No?"

"No, she just came to point and laugh."

"Really, stop," Steven demanded. "Or you two should get a room."

Maddox rolled his eyes. "That from you?"

The room went silent.

"What's that mean, Dad?" Steven said, rising from his chair with a hurt expression freezing on his face. He shuffled his feet, head down, before mumbling, "Been sitting too long in here. I'm gonna take a walk."

Watching him go, Maddox called, "Hey, Stevie, wait, it ain't—"

Steven disappeared into the hallway.

Darcy shook his head again, this time not in jest. "Smooth."

Maddox exhaled. "Yeah, father of the year."

Darcy squeezed his shoulder again, then stepped back and sat in the chair with his coat. Maddox studied his expression, searching for the familiar pain he'd seen on his friend's face any time the subject of children arose. He and Blair conceived six times during the first half of their marriage. None of the pregnancies ever made it to term. That weight did hang on Darcy's face, but it was all but buried under a more obvious strain: fear. Maddox knew where *that* came from: losing Stan, he feared losing Darcy and Mia next. The thought of being the last man standing out of his old circle of friends... terrifying.

"What happened to the file?" Maddox asked, breaking the silence.

Darcy moaned. "Hoped you'd forgotten about it, or at least that they'd have you drugged up enough that it would take a while before you remembered."

Maddox tapped a finger to his temple. "Steel trap."

"A trap, all right."

"So, you have it?"

"No," Darcy said, fiddling with the drawstring on his coat. "That kid pulled you out of Stan's place, you were white as toothpaste. I really thought your ticker'd gone south and you were taking the expressway to flatlinesville. The kid whips out a phone, dials 911, hands it to me and goes back inside."

Darcy shrugged. "I was just worried about you; I didn't give a shit what the kid was doing. He could've gone in and cleaned out Stan's house, I wouldn't have cared. But then, after I talked to the dispatcher, he comes back out with this file. Papers spilling out of it from all sides. Takes the phone and the dog leash from me and tells me he can't be around when the ambulance shows."

"So, the kid's got the file?" Maddox asked, aggravated.

Darcy held out his hands. "Yeah... Man, that's not important right now."

"It *is* important," Maddox said. "I *need* that file."

"You need to shut up before I have one of these nurses sew it shut. They're good with a needle and thread, and frankly, I'm sure none of them want to hear you mouth." Mia turned the corner, sashaying into the room.

A smile brewing, Maddox growled, "Don't they have security procedures in this place? Or do they just let any homeless schlub wander in off the street?"

"Told them I was your great-granddaughter."

Maddox asked, "Was the receptionist blind?"

"No," she said, "just smart enough not to challenge me."

She stopped at his bedside, leaned over, and kissed his forehead. It felt good. He wiped a hand across his brow anyway in protest. "Hey, you could leave some *black* on me doing that shit."

"At least a little bit of you would be handsome, then."

"That's not very nice," he told her.

"Tell me you love me," she said.

"Hell, no." It felt like a lie.

She reached into her purse and pulled out Stan's file.

"You sure?"

"I love you."

"Yeah, but you can't have me. I'm too good for you." Mia dropped the file onto Maddox's lap and turned to Darcy. "Passed Blair on the road. She was crying. You believe that? Crying over this worn-out old gasbag?"

Darcy winked. "Probably had something in her eye."

"It would take a lot in my eye to get me to cry over him." She cocked a thumb over her shoulder at Maddox. She spun, fixed her long skirt, and sat on the edge of Steven's chair.

Maddox patted the file. "How?"

"I knew you'd be pissed, but I wasn't sure what to do," Darcy said. The corners of his mouth raised in a self-satisfied smirk. He knew he'd done the right thing and Maddox would be happy. "So, I called in the bulldog."

"I may be a bitch, but I ain't a bulldog."

"*May* be a bitch?" Maddox asked with an arched eyebrow.

Leaning forward, Mia reached for the file. "Can take that back, y'know."

"How'd you find the kid?" Maddox snatched up the folder and pressed it to his chest. "You knock on every door in the neighborhood like a Jehovah's Witness on a bender?"

She shook her head. "Wouldn't know the two of you were ever cops. Called Animal Services, talked to a friend of mine, was just outta college when I retired, but he remembered me. Had him search for shih tzu registrations within a few blocks of Stan's. Figured there wouldn't be many."

Darcy nodded. "That's damn good work."

"You two wouldn't have survived a day working meters." Mia settled back into the chair, smug and confident. "So, I knock on one door, just one, and a young boy answers. I tell him I know he has the folder. He looks at me sideways, sizing me up. Doesn't know nothing about no file, but maybe he could help me find it... for a finder's fee."

"Let me guess," Maddox scoffed. "Fifty fucking bucks."

Mia said nothing. Finder's fee confirmed.

"You pay him?" Darcy asked.

Mia's brow dropped. "You outta your mind? I grabbed his wrist, pulled it back and up, slammed him sideways into the doorway and told him he'd be jerking off with his other paw if he didn't hand it over."

"It's a wonder your kids survived adolescence," Maddox said. He imagined Fuck Kinda Question pinned in his doorway, yelping in pain, praying none of his friends were watching him get rolled by a woman old enough to be his grandmother. He almost felt bad for the kid.

"You're welcome, Grumps," Mia said.

Grumps. She hadn't called him that in years. There was no specific memory attached to the pet name, he couldn't say when and where it started, but damned if it wasn't good to hear. "You're welcome, Witchy-poo."

"Christ, look who's coming to dinner," Darcy mumbled.

"He tell you what we're doing?" Maddox asked her.

"Didn't need to. Put it together myself," she said.

Maddox pointed a finger in Mia's direction. "You're good at this. Better than you should be, by any right. We might be able to find a spare seat in the car if you want to tag along."

"I didn't hear a question," Mia said with a theatrical pout.

Darcy patted her hand. "Don't make him beg. He's fragile."

"Fragile?" Maddox waved it off.

Mia leaned forward and grabbed Maddox's foot. He jolted.

"HEY—"

"I know you," Mia said, voice rising. Holding him by the ankle, she wiggled the fingers on her free hand like a dancing spider. "You're ticklish. And I've had my good practice at tickling. You ask nice, like a gentleman, or—"

"—torture isn't legal, miss—"

Darcy's face lit up. He leaned into Mia's ear and said, "Do it."

Her hands went wild, fingers disappearing into a blur of motion. Maddox kicked and wailed, unable to free himself. Laughter filled the room.

"—OKAYOKAYOKAY—"

Dr. Van Stiehl walked into the room, followed by Steven, followed by dead silence. Van Stiehl wore no expression whatsoever, a perfect poker face—straight flush or empty hand, no evidence either way. Steven was not difficult to read. Eyes puffy and red, he'd aged noticeably in the time he'd been out of the room. Lips pressed tight together, Adam's apple bobbling, his face painted the portrait of a grieving orphan.

Well, fuck.

Darcy darkened as he noticed Steven's expression. His head dropped. Mia released Maddox's foot and receded back into the chair. She shook her head slightly.

"I'd ask how you're doing, doc," Maddox said, his voice barely more than a whisper, "but from the looks of it, you're doing a whole lot better than I am."

Van Stiehl's attention darted between Darcy and Mia as he ushered Steven into the room and to his father's bedside. "It would be better if it were only family here."

Silence.

When he was ready, Maddox cleared his throat and said, "That's all that is here."

Van Stiehl nodded. "Very well."

Mia stood, took Steven's hand, and navigated him into the chair.

"Creutzfeldt-Jakob disease," Van Stiehl said, tapping a clipboard against his thigh. "Degenerative brain disorder. Transmissible spongiform encephalopathy."

Maddox asked, "Tell me what it means, not what it is."

"Fatal. In one hundred percent of cases."

Maddox breathed out. "The attacks—"

Van Stiehl's poker face remained. "Not even a direct symptom. The panic attacks were more or less your body telling you that something's wrong. More likely, you've been experiencing problems with memory, mobility, and instances of hallucinations."

Hallucinations. Stan in his chair. I am nothing.

Steven broke down, head in hands, tears and wet hiccups.

Mia squeezed his hand even as her own tear ducts bulged.

"Well, fuck," Maddox said, this time aloud. Numbness spread through his body. A chill set in. His fingers felt rubbery and heavy against the file folder on his chest. When he could speak again, his voice crackled like radio static. "How long?"

"Not long." Van Stiehl brought the clipboard up and reviewed it. Maddox had the impression this was just for show, to assure him the results were accurate and no mistake had been made. "Typically, patients expire less than a year after initial diagnosis... but in your case the disease is already in an advanced stage. It wouldn't have mattered if we had caught it early. The timeline is the timeline. You have less than a month."

Steven wailed.

Maddox held his breath. His heavy fingers itched to reach down to his hip for the security of his sidearm. The security he'd felt with the weapon drawn had gotten him through many tense moments on the job. But now, no handgun. No trigger.

Darcy lost his bid to remain stoic. He cried.

"There's nothing you can do?" Maddox asked. His voice sounded distant and thin, even to his own ears, an old recording, something from the early days of radio.

Van Stiehl hung the clipboard on the wall behind Darcy. "Nothing."

Maddox nodded and sat up. "In that case, get my clothes."

December 6th

The cushioned booth seat let out an audible whoosh as Maddox sat. Dropping his hat, he stared across the table at Darcy and Mia's incredulous faces. They still wore pained, helpless expressions. "Two of you, you look like the intern at the pound in charge of euthanizing the puppies."

Darcy had a pile of napkins ready. "How you doing, Mads?"

"I'm dying, Darce," he said. "Otherwise, I'm good."

Mia's voice took the tone of an infomercial voice actor advising medical malpractice victims to dial a 1-800 number. "You need to get another opinion. May be something that—"

"You getting the short stack?" Maddox said, pulling the breakfast menu out of its holder and opening it. "No strawberries on top this time, though. Remember last month? Black spots all over them. Awful."

"Mads," she tried again.

"Getting extra whipped cream. At this point, why not?"

And that was that. Message sent. Subject changed.

Janey strolled over, smiling, perfect in her ignorance. "I see the ringleader has arrived. That mean I can get an order and put a few bucks towards *my* retirement?"

"You can try. Darcy plans on running out without leaving a tip." Maddox winked. "Might have to run him down and tackle him in the parking lot. Shake the coin out of his pockets."

"Not my sweet Darcy-Darce," Janey said, leaning down and wrapping her arms around Darcy. He blushed. She straightened up, tussled with her hair as if fixing it from a long night of intimacy, and pulled out her order pad. "What can I get you guys?"

"Another ten years," Maddox quipped.

Mia's mouth opened in disbelief.

Maddox waved her off. "Short stack. Whipped cream. Coffee."

"Black?" Janey asked.

"Every bit as much as your strawberries."

Her hands went to her hips. "That was one time, mister."

"Abe Lincoln was only shot *one time*. He didn't enjoy it."

"French toast, wheat toast, milk," Darcy ordered.

Mia finished up. "Just coffee. Strong stuff. Yesterday's pot, if you still have it lying around."

Wagging a finger at Maddox, Janey turned and retreated to the counter to deliver their order. Maddox pulled out Stan's folder and placed it on the table. For a moment, no one spoke.

"If this is what you want, we won't question it," Darcy said.

Maddox turned to Mia. "What about you? Too busy?"

"I got a few lines free on my dance card." The infomercial voice was gone. Her face hadn't regained its rigid countenance, though. He supposed that meant something good.

He knew he should have said *thank you*. "Let's get started."

Out came Stan's file. Maddox opened it and slid out the topmost sheet of paper. It was an old photocopy, yellowing and crumbled around the edges, ink blurred and indistinct. A copy of a copy, generation unknown. It reproduced a smaller sheet of paper, a handwritten note in a jagged, unsteady hand. He spun it around for Darcy and Mia to examine.

"This is the original incident notes from the desk clerk who took the little boy's statement," Maddox said, realizing they might not be able to make heads or tails of it. He'd needed to decipher it letter by letter, then make some healthy guesses based on context. He pulled out a second page, this one clean and crisp. His own handwriting. "Here, I've translated. Gotta realize that, back then, a lot of cops didn't have more than a grade school education. Wasn't the same job as when we started, even."

> 9:05P–Missing girl. Persephone Alford, age ?.
> Reported by Troy Turring, age 12.
> 132 Clinton Ave. Interview to follow.

"You have the interview?" Darcy asked.

Maddox shook his head. "Wasn't in the file."

"The name of the desk clerk?"

"That, either."

"Mads..." Darcy's voice took on a stern, authoritative tone. "We don't have the resources we had back at the job. We can't just call down to Suzy and Mark in Public Records to run tags and last knowns. How do you suppose we can even go about investigating any of this?"

"I don't know, Darce. We start with the library."

"The library? Are you fucking kidding me?"

"Afraid of a little reading?"

"The Dewey Decimal System isn't gonna help us find anyone."

"I think that's actually exactly what it does."

"Book, not people."

"Books about people."

"Those books don't exist."

Mia cleared her throat. "14-C, 180 Piermont Ave, Nyack."

"Excuse me?" Maddox asked. Darcy did too, a second behind.

She held up her cell phone. "Troy Turring. Retired high school science teacher. Formerly of Newark, New Jersey. Enjoys gardening and playing with his great-grandchildren."

Darcy pointed at the phone. "Faster than Suzy and Mark."

"And doesn't require a library card," she said, palming the phone before sliding it into her blouse and between her breasts. "The two of you need to claw your dinosaur asses out of the tar pit and get a damned phone."

Maddox grinned. "Fucking things. Making people retarded."

Her head dropped. Into her cleavage, she said, "Don't you listen to him, baby doll. He's just jealous, 'cause he's never had the honor of being where you are now."

"Besides," Maddox added, "If I had one, why would I need you?"

*   *   *

A blast of early winter wind drifted up from the banks of the Hudson River, ruffling Maddox's coat and thinning hair. He shut the car door and faced the rectangular brick apartment complex across Piermont Avenue. As Darcy and Mia joined him, he muttered, "They look like they came out of the Monopoly box."

"Doesn't look so bad to me," Darcy said.

Maddox started across the street, leading the trio. "We all end up in boxes when we're dead. Wouldn't want to live in one while I'm still breathing."

Coming up alongside him, Mia said, "I'll be in an urn."

"Really?" Darcy asked, huffing to keep pace with them.

"Hell yes," she said with a smirk. "Gold with diamonds."

"Pyrite and cubic zirconia," Maddox said.

She punched his shoulder.

The concrete walk up to the complex ended at a short flight of steps. Reaching for the wrought iron handrail, Maddox was struck with a strong sense of déjà vu. He knew he'd never been here before. Nothing about the town, the street, or the building tickled any memory, but the moment itself resonated: stepping up to a door to ask the first questions on a new assignment, not knowing where the conversation would lead him next, the sense of the unknown. It felt good, like home. It also felt sad; it would be the last time.

He opened the door and stepped onto a threadbare rug. Along the hallway, the faded yellow patterned wallpaper bubbled out from the drywall, cracking in places, water-stained in others. Continuing past scraped and dented doors, he listened for Darcy to enter, then asked, "Still want to move in?"

The numbers on the doors were gone, but their sun-bleached shadows remained behind. As he passed 6-C, the door cracked open, stopping only when the chain caught. A young woman peeked out, face pale and stained by purple bruises, patchy blonde hair, her frayed housecoat transparent enough to reveal the outline of a pair of prematurely shriveled breasts. Her nipples poked at the fabric, round and flat like the heads of roofing nails. "Hey, you Bobby?"

"No," Maddox said, stopping.

"'Cause I was *told* Bobby might come today."

Maddox stared into her eyes. Distant. Cold. "I'm sorry, ma'am."

She sniffled. "Is okay, guess. Bobby never comes, just sometimes the man tells me he will, but he *never* does. Maybe he left a package for me on the steps?"

Mia rushed to his side and eyed the woman skeptically.

"I didn't see any package," Maddox said.

The girl nodded and giggled with nervous energy. "He doesn't leave packages anymore, *either*. Guess. Sometimes he says he'll do that, too, but he doesn't.

He doesn't do shit."

Mia prodded. Maddox took a step. "Have a nice day, ma'am."

"You wanna come in for a while?" she called after him.

Mia grabbed his hand and kept him moving. "Keep walking. You're old enough to know not to talk to strangers. Least of all *that* stranger."

As Darcy passed, Maddox heard her ask, "Hey, you Bobby?"

Darcy didn't say a word, didn't stop.

They stopped at 14-C and waited for Darcy to catch up. Out of breath, he bent over, hands on knees, and coughed twice. A far cry from the rookie who'd once chased a purse snatcher nine blocks down Bloomfield Avenue and looked none the worse for wear.

"You're panting. And *I'm* the one dying," Maddox said with a frown. "Gonna make it?"

Darcy straightened up, gulped, and nodded. "Fine. Big breakfast."

Mia rolled her eyes. "Gonna have to tell Blair to get you some more exercise at night."

Darcy blushed.

Maddox knocked.

The door to 6-C shut, the sound echoing down the hall. Quiet. They waited. Overhead, a creaking floorboard, then nothing–no televisions, no radios, no drifting conversations. He envisioned an apartment complex full of coma patients, eyes open in their beds, the world passing them by. *How many of the apartments were even occupied?*

"Maybe he's not home," Mia suggested.

Maddox knocked again, harder. "Could be hard of hearing."

Mia drew her coat's collar tight to her neck. "No heat?"

"It's cold." Maddox bent down to the vent on the baseboard beside the door. Fingers of lint waved like flags from each of the metal slats. Extending his palm, he felt a gentle cool breeze. "Either the furnace's busted or someone needs to drop a check in the mail."

He thought of the girl in 6-C in her thin housecoat. She must have been freezing. If he were still in uniform, he'd have to call in the housing authority to investigate, fulfilling the first half of his oath to serve and protect. He straightened up, balled up his fist, and rapped on the door again.

The door opened wide. A fiftyish man stood in the doorway wearing a white T-shirt, blue jeans, and a Mets cap. His deeply pocked, bulbous nose monopolized his otherwise bland face. When his mouth opened, Maddox expected him to ask, '*You Bobby?*' Instead, he said, "VA or Alford?"

"Excuse me?" Maddox asked.

His unfocused eyes narrowed. "You're either from Veterans Affairs or you've come to ask my father about Persephone Alford. Which is it?"

"Is your father home?" Maddox smiled, not attempting to hide his bubbling excitement. They'd come to the right place. "May we speak with him?"

"That depends," Troy Turring's son said.

"On what?"

"On whether you're from the VA or not?"

Maddox's mind raced, testing out how to reply. He imagined the door slamming shut if he gave the wrong answer. He studied the man's face for a tell but came up empty. He flipped a mental coin. "We're not."

For a moment, the man didn't respond, not so much as a blink. Then, a slow change; his expression melted, changing from hardened indifference to inviting. An unnerving, artificial smile emerged, the Cheshire cat grin of a used car salesman or an unlicensed dentist. He stepped aside and waved them inside. "In that case, make yourself at home."

Maddox crossed the threshold. The apartment was sparsely furnished but tidy and clean. Off to the right, a compact kitchen drew his attention. Polished chrome faucet. Sensible, simple cabinets. Individual trash cans for every conceivable type of recyclable. Modern chic, on a budget. "You've got a nice home."

The man held out his hand. "The building's falling apart, I'm sure you noticed, but we try to keep up our corner of things. I'm Vance Turring."

They shook as Mia and Darcy joined them inside.

"Your neighbor down the hall—"

Vance shook his head. "I don't know any of our neighbors."

"Don't care to?" Maddox asked.

"Would you?" Vance pointed to a closed door at the end of a short hall. "My father's watching *Wheel*. He never misses it. I'm sure he'll talk to you, but have patience with him. He's ninety-two and he likes what he likes. And he

60

loves *Wheel.*"

Maddox started towards the door.

Vance darted into his path. "There is one thing. Well, two."

"Yeah?" Maddox said.

Vance's expression turned bashful. "My dad, he worked hard for many, many years. Served the country, risked his life. First in the army, then at the station. His career ended... messier than it should have. A mistake, a *thing*, whatever. Anyway, he doesn't get much in the way of a pension. And the VA won't provide what they should."

Maddox nodded. "How much you looking for?"

"No, it's not like that. Just maybe, a donation, to help out?"

Mia's lips pressed together. Tight.

Maddox shot her a glance. "Yeah, that's fine. I think I've got a few tens in my pocket that I'm not doing anything with."

Vance bit his bottom lip, released it. "It's been... tight."

Maddox fished two twenties out of his wallet and handed them over. As he did, Vance's face took on the same expression as he'd seen on Fuck Kinda Question. "What's the second thing?"

"Oh," Vance said, stepping back as he pocketed the bills. His face changed again, this time back to the blank slate he'd originally worn. "It's just... not that there's any reason you would... but please don't mention anything about this apartment. He likes to pretend we're still in the old house in Newark. Moving upset him."

"I promise," Maddox said as he broke away. Mia and Darcy followed him down the hall, a few steps behind, as he opened the door. Once inside, his skin tightened and the hair on his arms raised to attention. Confusion. *Is this real?*

Troy Turring sat, sunken in a plush, threadbare recliner in the center of the room, a half dozen feet from a television set. A small love seat rested against the far wall. Six framed photographs hung from the powder blue walls. Floor-length white curtains bookended cheap plastic blinds, the fabric too thin by itself to block out the light from the only window.

The love seat, he knew, had a handle under its skirt, a little too hidden to be easily reached. The sleeper bed rolled out like an inchworm, arching up until its support legs folded underneath and then touching down with the sound of cheap rubber grips hitting hardwood. The photographs ran across the molding on the ceiling because they were easier to line up that way. Steven hated the blinds, called them *trashy*.

The room was identical to his own.

Turring stared–eyes wide, lips not quite meeting–at the television with an expression approaching religious fervor. On screen, Pat Sajak chatted with a ditzy blonde contestant. From the shoulder pads on her blouse, Maddox pegged the show as recorded around '87. "Mr. Turring?"

Turring didn't flinch. Didn't move. Didn't even blink.

Vance slid past Darcy in the doorway, gestured to the love seat, and put a finger against his lips. It'd been a long while since Maddox had been hushed. Vance whispered, "Wait for a commercial."

A fictional place: _ N _ _ _ N _ _ D   _ _ R _ _ _

Mia and Darcy complied, moving to the love seat and sitting. Mia patted the seat beside her, a span of cushion half the necessary size to comfortably accommodate Maddox's ass. He stood.

The contestant spun the wheel. Asked for a T. Two Ts.

Vance raised an imaginary coffee cup to his lips, then pointed to each of his guests. Maddox ignored him. Gentle and polite, Mia shook her head. Darcy nodded with enthusiasm. Vance mouthed *cream and sugar?* Darcy confirmed both. Vance turned and left.

The answer to the puzzle was *ENCHANTED FOREST*. Maddox read the contestant's faces. None had any clue. He sighed. *Sorry, there are no Ps.* The blonde's face transformed from hopeful to crestfallen. A balding businessman spun next. Asked for an *H*. Vanna gave it to him.

Fucking insufferable.

Troy Turring continued to watch, unmoving, attention rapt. Maddox wondered if he'd worked the puzzle out, or if he were even trying. Were it not for the rise and fall of the man's chest with every breath, he might as well have been frozen in place.

The wheel landed on *BANKRUPT*; the studio audience moaned.

Mia caught his attention, her eyes studying him, the corners of her mouth pulled tight, lips curling. Her enjoyment of Maddox's impatience was palpable. Her eyes met his. Against his will, he found himself smiling, too. He motioned for her to scoot over, then sat next to her.

The third contestant asked for a C. Spun. F. His face changed, relief and pride swelling. He announced that he'd like to solve the puzzle, then did. The audience applauded. Pat read off the scores. *"Don't go away, we'll be right back."*

Turring blinked, wiped his lips with the hem of his sleeve, and turned towards the love seat. His eyes scanned each of them, from face to feet, lingering an extra second at Mia's breasts. "You three, you're all from Ironbound, can smell it on you. Rotten eggs and rubber. Maybe a little gunpowder."

Mia wrinkled up her nose. "I live in Harrison, thank you much."

"Sorry to interrupt your show," Maddox said, intentionally letting his impatience leak through. *Hiding how you feel is no different than lying.* Sometimes Catholic schoolteachers got things right. Not often. "We've come to ask you about Persephone Alford."

"You cops?" Turring asked.

"We're not from the VA." Not as honest, but still not *quite* a lie. "We're just looking to close the books on a few old cases. And your name came up in relation to this one."

Turring nodded. "That seems to happen from time to time. A lot."

"You mind answering a few questions?" Maddox asked.

A shrug. "I guess so. Done it before, I can do it again."

"We appreciate it," Mia said.

Turring grinned, exposing empty gums. "Is no problem at all."

"When you were a kid, you reported Persephone missing," Maddox said, watching for a reaction. A facial tic or involuntary flutter in Turring's eye might say more than his lips ever would. But no, nothing.

"That's what you do when someone goes missing, isn't it?" Turring's grin slid off his face. "Didn't matter anyway. Nothing came of it, and she never got found."

Maddox leaned forward. "There's no records of her at all, actually, except for the missing persons report you filed. And even that's not much more than a note on front desk stationary."

"Ah-yah," Turring said. "Things, they were different back then. Lots of folks born in their homes. No hospitals. Maybe a local doctor, maybe not. Paperwork? Might happen. I dunno, might have been like that with

Persephone."

Mia said, "Tell us about her."

Finally, Troy Turring's expression softened. His bottom lip quivered as if searching for a way to begin. "Y'know a thing? Been asked about her more than a little over the years. Did I see anyone hanging around? Did I ever see her folks being mean to her? But, no one ever asked me that. Don't think anyone ever cared who she was, only what happened to her."

"So, tell us," Maddox said.

Turring turned his attention back to the television. Pat Sajak returned, reading off a random factoid about one of the contestants before announcing that the next puzzle category was *PROFITABLE HOBBIES*.

Maddox counted the tiles; the answer was *METAL DETECTING*.

Turring watched in silence.

The wheel spun, colors blurred.

Vance returned with Darcy's coffee.

"Is it every show, or just this one?" Maddox asked the son.

"Just *Wheel*," Vance said in a hushed tone as he handed over the coffee. "Be careful, it's hot. It's out of a real percolator, not a microwave. Stays warm longer. And got taste."

Darcy thanked him.

Buy an A? Yes, one A. Vanna earned her pay.

Maddox asked, "Is he ignoring us, or—"

"He has no idea you're speaking. When *Wheel*'s on, he's out." Vance said. He pointed at the television. "Once, back around Easter, I got fed up and turned the set off right in the middle of the show. He just kept staring. At a blank screen. I thought it was an act, something he was doing to annoy me. But he stayed like that all night. I turned it back on after midnight. A different show was on, people arguing politics or something, thought it'd bring him back around. Didn't. No talking, no moving. Dad just sat there, breathing and staring. Until the next day, actually. *Wheel* came back on, and first commercial break, he turned to me and asked if I'd make him a sandwich. I don't interrupt *Wheel* anymore."

The balding businessman took a deep breath. *"Metal Detecting?"*

"That's the one—"

Mia whispered, "Some kind of dementia?"

Maddox cringed.

"Dunno," Vance said. "VA won't pay for him to get diagnosed."

Mia whispered, "So sorry."

Vance nodded. "They'll pay for the funeral, they say. There's that."

Wheel went to commercial.

"I was curious as a boy," Troy Turring said, facing them. "Used to peek into any window I could. I know how that sounds, but it was innocent. I just was looking, y'know, not for something in particular, but for anything I hadn't seen before. The house across the street was empty for years before the Alfords moved in. There was this little hedgerow that circled round the house. And in the back, hidden, was a little rectangular window, no bigger than a shoe box.

"One day I took a gander through, and I saw her. Beautiful little girl, light ginger hair and a mess of freckles. And she saw me, too. Didn't scream. She laughed. We couldn't hear through the glass, so we would read each other's lips. Make gestures with our hands. We talked every day like that for months. Then one day, no more Persephone. Her room was gone, too. No bed, no lamp. Just empty."

Maddox leaned forward. "So, you went to the precinct?"

"Yeah, I did," Turring said. "Not at first, only after a week or so. I thought she would come back, but she didn't. I missed her terrible. Y'see, the boys and girls my age... they'd be your friend for a game of stickball or whatnot, but when I listened to the way they talked... they weren't genuine, not at all. Selfish little bastards, every last one. But not her. She was different. Maybe because we had to work so much harder to communicate, hell, I dunno. But I always felt..."

"Less alone," Maddox said.

Turring nodded. "The last day I saw her, I could tell she was upset. I couldn't understand what she was saying, couldn't read her lips the way I usually could. Like she was suddenly speaking another language or something. But then, at the very end, when my mom called out from our front door my name and dinner was ready, I was able to make out one thing. Just one little thing and we were both crying. Didn't even know why at the time."

Mia asked, "What'd she say, Troy?"

Maddox swallowed hard. *Wheel of Fortune* returned. *We're back–*
But Turring didn't turn back to the screen.
"She said this–"
He mouthed the word *Goodbye*.

December 7th

Maddox woke, 3:39 by the alarm clock, and reached for the glass of water on his nightstand. Another nightmare, he thought, then changed his mind: *No, not another at all, the same one. Again.*

He never could remember the dream, not tonight and not thirty years ago, but the sense of it lingered inside him, not quite an emotion or a sensation, but something akin to the feeling of being watched. The nightmare resonated inside him, surging like a low-level electricity, not only in his head but throughout his body.

He drank the water, coughed, and reached for the television remote control. Attempts to return to sleep would be futile. Propping himself up, pillow against headboard, he settled in for an early morning of black-and-white Christmas movies. He'd seen them all dozens of times.

*   *   *

"Fucking cold," Darcy said, hands dipping into his coat pockets. "They're gonna have to chip frozen winos off the steel bridge supports with ice picks."

Mia grinned, her face surrounded by a halo of faux-fur trim. "Whas'ammatter, did Blair forget your mittens when she packed you lunch?"

Darcy glared at her. And hid the paper bag behind his back.

"You two playing nice?" Maddox said, walking back from the corner pastry shop balancing three large coffees. His nose felt as brittle as an icicle. He handed out the joe.

"Thank Christ," Darcy said before taking a healthy swig. Two sugars and three creamers—barely coffee, really. A little color settled back into his face.

"Too kind," Mia said, wrapping her hands around the foam cup. Pink artificial sweetener and a splash of 2 percent milk. Closer to the real thing, anyway.

Maddox drank. Black, pure, bitter—like rolling his tongue through the grinds on the bottom of the can. He closed his eyes and waited for the caffeine to start playing jazz. *Nothing.* Maybe a cigarette. *No, fuck it, could fall asleep standing here.*

Darcy's voice stirred him. "This neighborhood's a disgrace."

Clinton Avenue stretched on, a crooked jack-o'-lantern smile of a street extending from the Garden State Parkway to Lincoln Park, all of Newark in one roadway, from the elegant Temple B'nai Abraham to the dilapidated townhouses on the east side. Peeling paint. Abandoned cars. Beads of broken glass embedded in the cracked sidewalks. Maddox had answered hundreds of calls to CA. Not many pleasant ones.

"Didn't your sister live down here somewhere?" Maddox asked.

"Hell, no," Darcy said, not getting the joke. "Tammy lived over in Maplewood."

Mia winked. "He knows, Darce. He knows."

"What's that mean?" he asked her.

Maddox glanced down at the back of his hand. He'd written 132 lengthwise, starting at the middle knuckle, ending at the wrist. He motioned for Darcy and Mia to follow, then crossed Murray Street. A mid-'90s Toyota honked, veering out of lane as it ran the hexagon.

Darcy and Mia bustled behind him. Maddox counted off the lots. 132 Clinton Avenue was a barren, empty space bookended by a shuttered brick building and an enormous white supermarket. The house where Troy Turring had lived was gone. Turning, Maddox stared across the street. A strip mall. Laundromat. Convenience store. Dollar store. No remnant of the Alford house. He let out an exasperated sigh.

"What now?" Darcy asked, pointing. "We could get some scratch-off lottery tickets and a slushy, but I don't think there's any answers over there."

Mia wrinkled her nose. "Lots of answers in the lottery."

Maddox headed across the street.

Darcy called, "Mads—"

He listened for the sound of their feet on the asphalt. He knew they'd follow and they didn't disappoint. He reached the other side, strode across the small parking lot, and continued around the building's corner. Passing a set of fenced-off dumpsters, he made his way to the back of the building.

Running, Mia caught up to him and tugged at his sleeve. "What're you doing? There's nothing here. What can you possibly hope to discover back here? Y'think ol' Persephone is hiding out next to the loading bay selling loosies?"

"No," he said. He turned in a full circle, surveying. Darcy, a large blur in his moving vision, was just stepping off Clinton Ave. City trees. Patches of sickly grass. Bent beer cans. A discarded, stained wifebeater T-shirt. Then–

Yellow. Maddox walked to the edge of the property and bent down.

"Tell me you ain't gonna pick nothing up," Mia scolded.

He lifted half a yellow crayon off the ground and held it up.

Darcy, in Maddox's peripheral vision, passed the dumpsters.

"Oh, shit," Mia said. "That's got creepy all over it."

Maddox ran a finger over the tip. Waxy. New.

Darcy stopped at his side, huffing. "You do realize... that's just a coincidence... doesn't mean anything. Right? You can't believe that–"

Maddox pocketed the crayon, turned, and headed up the grassy embankment leading to Martin Luther King Boulevard. Mia followed close behind.

"Could we please try *not walking* for a moment?" Darcy pleaded.

Maddox crested the top of the knoll. Hopewell Baptist Church loomed overhead, green dome glistening in the sunlight, massive brick arches revealing three gigantic wooden doors. A young black woman sat on the church's white steps breastfeeding a newborn.

Maddox gestured back towards the strip mall. "None of that was there, but she–" He pointed to the church. "–most certainly was. Come on."

They crossed MLK Boulevard, dodging a speeding taxi, and climbed the steps. Reaching for the center door's handle, Maddox prepared to struggle, but it slid open with ease. And without a sound. Stepping inside, the sounds of Newark's busy streets hushed away completely, leaving a silence so absolute his ears rang. Even on a Saturday, several of the pews were fully occupied by older black parishioners. Some read from Bibles, while others prayed in silence with heads bowed, backs bowed, shoulders jutting forward.

Mia crossed her heart.

"What's that for?" Maddox asked her in a whisper.

"Feel guilty being here," she said, cringing, "'cause all these folks look so sincere. This is their place. I don't belong here, 'cause I don't believe in any of this."

"So, this?" Maddox said, imitating her gesture.

69

"I dunno, just feels like I should. When in Rome—"

He whispered, "The Romans are responsible for this whole *cross* business to begin with. Might as well roll down the aisle with lions on leashes. Probably not be in the best of taste."

Stepping into the main aisle, Maddox ran his hand over the nearest pew, marveling at the slick, oily texture of the hardwood. Craning his head upward, he studied the ornate domed ceiling and stained-glass windows. Like Mia, he'd never found a use for religion in his life, but he understood the awe such buildings birthed. Add a little incense and music, and he had no doubt he'd feel moved as well. *A place where even the most flatulent hold back out of respect.*

He pointed to a middle-aged black man on his knees, not in prayer but housekeeping. The gray-haired custodian was polishing the lectern. As Maddox approached, he turned his head. "H'can I help you folks?"

"Looking for someone," Maddox said.

The custodian stood, knees cracking as he straightened. "Name?"

"It's not that simple."

"Never seems to be, these days."

Maddox nodded. "How long you've worked here?"

"Nine years, as a volunteer, 'course. Can't charge the Lord."

"Who's been here the longest?" Maddox asked.

"Oh, I dunno," the custodian said, biting his lip and squinting with one eye. "People come and go, y'know. Pastor Knox been here for a right stay, came up from Orleans after Katrina. But I think maybe D'ester must have the best run."

"How long?"

The custodian shrugged. "F'decades. He's *old*, man."

"Can I find him somewhere?" Maddox swung his head from side to side, scanning the church. "Is he here?"

"Always here," The custodian pointed over Maddox's shoulder.

Mia frowned. "I hate heights."

"That makes all of us," Maddox said. He thanked the custodian.

Angry and hoarse, Darcy stumbled up beside Mia and Maddox. Red-faced, with his chest heaving, he gave Maddox a cold, wide-eyed stare. "It's not... like you... to look for... answers... in a church... What gives?"

Maddox didn't answer. Instead, he tilted his head upward, eyes following a narrow staircase ascending three stories up to the organ platform. "Ready for a climb, Darce?"

"Don't think... I won't punch you... in a church," Darcy said, wiping his mouth. He glanced up at the stairs, then shook his head in disbelief.

Maddox slapped his back. "You stay down here and unwind. I think they offer free daycare. They might even have a juice box and some graham crackers for you."

Mia smiled. "Does that mean I c'stay down here, too?"

"Absolutely not," Maddox said, taking his first step towards the stairs. Keeping his voice modulated, he told her, "Darce and me, we're the only white people in here. I need you by my side in case the natives get hungry."

Mia spread both hands as she followed. "Y'such an asshole."

With each step, Maddox's shoes squeaked and Mia's heels tapped, a synchronized, percussive pattern. Halfway up to the organist's platform, the tapping fell behind the squeaks. Glancing back, Maddox watched his friend struggle with each step, one hand clutching the handrail. *Heights. Always assumed she was fearless. The Unsinkable Mia Cresswater defeated by a flight of stairs.*

Maddox slowed. The squeaks and taps aligned. Mia took his hand.

At the top of the stairs, Maddox stepped into a small, rounded alcove not much larger than the pipe organ it housed. A small, white-haired man rested on the bench seat, head propped up in his hand, eyes closed behind a thick pair of prescription glasses.

"You D'ester?" Maddox asked.

D'ester grunted in the affirmative.

"You've lived in the neighborhood a long time?"

One eye cracked open. "Long enough."

"You remember when the Alford family lived a block over?"

"Maybe."

"Maybe?" Maddox asked. His hand slipped into his pocket, fingers curling around his leather wallet. *This keeps up, I'll be broke long before the case.*

"Don't want your money," D'ester said with a tired sigh. "You people always think you can buy us off. Come on in here and do what? Put us back on the plantation? Those bills in y'pocket? Poison. You keep them."

Maddox withdrew his hand. "Right... Mia?"

She stepped in front of Maddox and pointed at the organist. "That what you're about? Throw the first stone? What, you sit up here and play the Lord's music but never give a thought what it means? That you?"

D'ester smirked. "You smell like a rich white neighborhood and a pension check. You criticize me? Question my faith? I've devoted my whole *life* to God's work. My fingers on the keys bring folks closer to Jesus. What you spent your time with? Holding hands with old white men?"

Mia leaned in and sniffed. "Guess Jesus got the scent of Sutterhome and no dental plan. This man comes in here, all he wants is an answer or two, but you can't do that 'cause you're brain's pickled and your heart's gone cold. Devoted your life to Jesus?" She snickered. "Sure enough, 'cause no one else ever wanted a share of your sorry ass. Let's go, Mads."

She tugged at Maddox's sleeve as she turned back to the stairs.

"Mads?" D'ester asked, his eyes coming fully awake. He jumped to his feet, stumbling but remaining upright. "Is your name Maddox? It is, isn't it?"

Maddox studied D'ester's eyes. Excitement danced there. "Yeah."

"Another man came by a couple days back," the organist said, reaching down for a duffel bag full of sheet music at his feet and riffling through the papers. "Sat with me and played for a while."

"Played?"

"Yeah, played." D'ester plucked an envelope from the bag and handed it to Maddox. Running his hand over the organ's keys, he played a few quick notes. Obviously written for piano, the song's melody emerged from the pipes off-key and distorted. "Taught me to play this one; hadn't even heard a note of it since all way back when."

Maddox felt an electric chill surge through him, expanding outward from the bridge of his nose to the tips of his fingers. He knew the song. "The man, what did he look like?"

D'ester took his hands off the keys. A blank expression crossed over his features and he shook his head. "A moment ago, had a clear enough picture of him in my head, but now that you ask? Guess it's like I don't remember, not at all."

"Was he white?" Maddox asked in a demanding, booming voice.

D'ester's brow dropped. "Might have been. Having trouble–"

"What's going on?" Mia asked him.

"Dunno, man, all right? I dunno," D'ester said, removing his glasses and setting them down on the organ. He pinched his nose and closed his eyes. "Just remember him coming on up, not like you did; he was... familiar. Like I knew him for a long stretch, but 'course, I didn't. But now he's *not* familiar, not at all. Can't place him, not even sitting right next to me here."

Maddox shook the envelope. "He gave you this, for me?"

D'ester nodded, opening his eyes. "Said you'd come by for it. I can remember that. I remember the song we played. But not him. Not even his voice; just the words he spoke. Said he had something you're looking for, you'd know what to do with that."

"Okay," Maddox said, voice lowered. The electric shocks subsided and he felt calm. Reaching back into his pocket, he removed his wallet, dug out a twenty-dollar bill, and held it out.

D'ester shook his head. "Told you, don't want your money."

"I'm not *giving* it to you," Maddox said, placing it on the organ. "I'm asking you to take it. I don't care if you drop it on the collection plate, buy a bottle, or wipe your ass with it. Delivering this to me, you've performed a service. I pay my way."

D'ester's hand moved over the bill. "Y'know, I *do* remember the Alfords. Not so much them, really. They didn't come out to the church. Of course they didn't; they weren't... colored. That's the word that was used back then. But then one evening they did come. Just sat in the pews and cried. Uncontrollable weeping. Bill Youngs, he was the pastor back then, he went and asked them what was wrong. They told him they didn't know. But they stayed and cried all night, then went away and never came back again."

Maddox patted his shoulder. "Thank you."

"You ain't gonna come back again, neither." D'ester crumbled the twenty into his fist. "The man who played with me couple days ago, that's what he said. You wouldn't come back 'cause you didn't got long to live."

Wide-eyed, Mia tugged on Maddox's sleeve again, this time with more urgency and force. Maddox turned and followed her down the stairs. Mia hurried, heels clapping. Once they reached the bottom, She spun around and locked her eyes on his. "What was all that?"

"'You'll Never Know,'" Maddox said. "By Dick Haymes. It was Stan's favorite song. He used to sing it out on the beat. Whistled it, too, under his breath, just for himself."

Mia's eyes filled with tears. Not the sorrowful kind. The frightened ones. "But he said the man visited him a few days ago. Stan's been dead—"

"Yes, he has." Maddox tore open the envelope.

Darcy joined them. "What's wrong with you two? You look—"

Maddox pulled a sheet of old paper from the envelope. After a cursory glance, he held it out for Mia and Darcy. They both took a step back.

It was a child's crude sketch.

"What-the-*fuck*?" Darcy whispered.

In scraggly bright crayons, red, green and blue, the young artist had drawn two old men-one tall and thin, the other short and fat-and a darker-skinned woman standing inside a church. Behind them, in a round stained-glass window, the shape of a young girl watched from overhead.

Maddox raised his head and stared up at the cathedral ceiling of the Hopewell Baptist Church, settling finally in its north corner. In the same three colors as the illustration, a stained-glass window depicted Abraham at the sacrificial alter, holding his son Isaac at knife point.

You'll never know.

December 8th

Maddox woke with a start, jolting off the car seat until the seat belt caught him. The lingering tingle in his fingertips told the story, but he had no memory of the attack. Or of driving home from the church, for that matter. He stared at his hands for a moment. The sensation waned.

"I used to worry," Steven said from the passenger seat. His hair was as disheveled as the bathrobe he wore. "Now I just wish things were different between us."

Maddox squinted through the foggy windshield. He'd managed to park in the driveway, mostly; that was something, better than careening into a highway guardrail. "How long you've been out here?"

"Since you pulled in at two," he said.

"Steven–"

His son raised his hands. "Not gonna preach at you. How you want to spend your nights, that's up to you. But it scares me, Dad. I hear you pull in. Twenty minutes later, you still haven't come inside. I come out, you're just sitting there, not moving, eyes closed."

"I'm sorry."

"You know what's worse than all of it, though? Worse than not knowing if you were alive or dead until I put my hands up to your mouth and felt you breathe?" Steven paused, his lips quivering. "In a way, I wanted it to be over. 'Cause I don't think I can handle going through this shit over and over."

Maddox gripped the steering wheel. Words? Nothing.

"So, I won't make any demands on you. Wouldn't be right. And I won't ask you to abandon what you're doing. I understand why it's important. But, please–" He wiped his eyes. "–at least let me be part of it, so I know you're safe. I can drive."

Maddox reached down to the ignition.

Tears streamed down Steven's face.

With a heavy sigh, Maddox handed his son the keys.

"Thank you."

Maddox tried his best reassuring smile. Feeble. He sniffed the air. "We both need toothpaste and showers. Let's go inside and get that done. Then you get me to Hop's."

Steven nodded. His face had all the sincerity of a twelve-year-old. In that moment, Maddox saw only the little boy he'd lost so long ago. Christmas train sets. Wooden baseball bats. Science projects built the night before the fair. *What happened?*

He led his son. Steven headed for his bathroom. Maddox went to the kitchen, drew a glass of water, and drank. A short stack of neatly folded clothes in his hands, Steven leaned through the doorway. "You wanna get in first?"

"You need the hot water. I'll jump in when you're done."

Steven smiled. "Just be a minute."

Maddox filled his glass again. "Take your time."

Steven headed to the bathroom.

Maddox drank. He finished the second glass without quenching his thirst. Hand on the faucet handle, he considered a third. Better not, he decided; lots of traveling today. He didn't want to have to stop at every toilet along the way. He lowered the glass into the sink.

The sound of the shower curtain running on its rail was followed by water hitting porcelain.

Maddox waited a moment, anticipating pangs of guilt. None came.

"I *am* sorry," he said. Then he plucked his spare car keys off a hook on the dish cabinet. As he left, he tried to ignore the full glass of water on the countertop.

*   *   *

Darcy's old station wagon pulled up alongside Maddox and parked. Stepping out of the car, Darcy stumbled over his own feet. Bracing himself with the roof of his car, he straightened up and frowned.

"Y'okay?" Maddox asked, flicking away a cigarette.

Darcy raised one eyebrow. "Not Fred Astaire, that's f'sure."

Maddox watched Darcy's feet as his friend came to his side. Still unsteady, each step was accompanied by a shake in his ankles that reverberated up his legs. "You need a cane, old man?"

"As a weapon to use on you, maybe." Darcy reached for the handrail as

76

they climbed the three concrete steps that led up to the front door of Hop's. With a devilish grin, he added, "Blair played a little rough with me last night."

Maddox eyed him with suspicion and worry but chose to play along. "Maybe she just needs a *real* man–one who can take it."

Hop's was busy. As they entered, Janey waved her order pad at them and gestured towards a booth at the back of the restaurant. Maddox took three menus off the hostess station as they passed. "Can't remember the last time we couldn't get our regular table."

Struggling with every breath, Darcy asked, "You kidding?"

"Whaddya mean?" Maddox asked.

"Mads, it's Sunday. It's always banging on Sunday."

"*Banging?*" Maddox dropped into the booth.

"My nephew says it. It means–"

"I know what it means," Maddox said. "Just... don't. Ever."

A stack of three menus already rested on the table. Maddox added the three he'd brought to the pile. Before he could react, Mia came bustling out of the ladies room and slid into the booth beside him.

"You bring menus, too?" he asked her.

She gave him a quizzical look. "'Course. I'm thoughtful like that. Unlike two gentlemen I know, who kept a lady waiting for a half hour."

"Hang up the phone and call 911," Darcy said. "*You* were on time? When's that ever been the case? What happened, your alarm clock work for once?"

Mia blushed. "Not my fault I'm usually busy."

"Whose fault would it be, then?" Maddox asked.

Mia unwrapped her silverware from the napkin and placed it on her lap. "I blame the needs of an adoring public."

Maddox and Darcy opened their napkins, but left them on the placemats. Janey rushed over, blowing hair out of her face, and took their order. Her customary smile was in place, but seemed more like an act than usual. If Darcy and Mia noticed, they didn't let on. Maddox let it go. He leaped right into business.

"Stan tracked Persephone Alford's parents," he said, pulling a sheet of paper out of Stan's folder and pointed out an entry in the handwritten notes. After Newark, they moved to Bartlett, Tennessee. Then, a couple years later, Fort

Lauderdale. Mother dies at a Broward County hospice in '88, complications from diabetes. Father makes it to 2000, dies at home. No cause of death."

"I know old white people like to read obituaries, but how does this help us?" Mia asked. She wasn't just on time, Maddox realized; something else was different, too. Her makeup was heavier–eyeliner darker, blush brighter.

"Ya-huh," Maddox agreed. "Stan must have thought it was a dead end, too, since he never went any further looking into the parents. But I got thinking: they weren't keen on doctors or hospitals. No birth certificate for Persephone. Maybe they handled her delivery like a home improvement project, but back in those days, I'd say it'd be more likely–"

Mia smiled. The lipstick was brighter, too. "A midwife."

Maddox nodded. "Exactly what I thought."

"But," Darcy said, "how do we find the right midwife from half a century ago without so much as a name to go on?"

Mia's phone was already in her hand. "Don't need a name."

"What's she up to?" Darcy asked Maddox.

He grinned. "She's using her Googles. Whatever they are."

"Sounds dirty."

Maddox leaned over to snatch a glimpse of the screen. "I'm sure it usually is."

"Done," she said, setting down the phone. "I belong to one of those family tree sites, let you trace your ancestors back through documents and social media and whatnot. Other people, too; all you need is a name. Or even a place. Or date. I did a custom search for midwives, Newark, 1950s. Bang, got a list of eleven. You give me that pad and a pen, I'll write them down. Then we'll see if any of them are still alive."

Darcy frowned. "Why does it seem like all the hard work we used to do investigating can now be done by typing into a phone?"

"I could have used voice search," Mia told him, "but I knew you'd look at me even funnier."

Maddox handed over the pad and pen. "Do your magic."

"This ain't my magic. My magic, now that *is* dirty." Glancing between the phone and the pad, Mia scribbled out the names. "While I'm doing your legwork, why don't you go over and say hello?"

"To who?" Maddox asked.

Mia sighed. "Men. Oblivious to everything but cleavage and carbohydrates. Your son just got seated over by the window."

"Shit," he muttered.

Maddox closed his eyes. Why? Why couldn't Steven just leave it alone? He didn't need to be walked like an untrained puppy on a leash. He knew his son meant well, but this case shouldn't involve him. It could even be dangerous.

Darcy turned noisily and asked, "Who's his friend?"

Maddox opened his eyes. Steven stared at him from across the room, eyes furious. Across the table, a man in a stylish gray sweater chatted away, obviously unaware of Steven's divided attention. *Cleavage and carbohydrates*: not likely. *Maybe* the carbohydrates.

"We should go," Maddox said.

Mia stopped writing. "Mads..."

"Don't. Okay? Don't."

Darcy looked confused. "He's your son."

"I'm aware," Maddox said, not really as an answer to his friend.

Mia huffed as she wrote the final name. "You're an idiot."

"Aware of that, too."

*　　*　　*

The first five midwives on Mia's list were dead. The next two couldn't be found. Hadassah Boutros, eighth of the twelve, still lived alone in an apartment on Peddie Street. Maddox parked in the shadow of the Dayton Projects, a decrepit brick skyscraper that lumbered over the city like a giant middle finger. The roar of incoming and outgoing planes from Liberty International Airport seemed constant.

Hadassah didn't answer the front door intercom. They waited.

After ten minutes, an old African-American woman came around the building carrying a trash bag over her shoulder. She eyed Maddox, Darcy, and Mia with apprehension. "What's you all here?"

"Looking for Miss Boutros," Mia said, stepping in front of the two white men. "Don't worry, she's not in any trouble or nothing. You know where she's at?"

"You say? No trouble?" The old woman stepped up to Mia, jutted her nose up to Mia's collar, and sniffed. "Y'smells like hotel soap and hand cream. Round here, that's trouble."

A Boeing 78 passed overhead on descent, drowning out all other sounds. Once it'd passed, Mia leaned down to the old woman's neck and breathed in deeply. "All I'm getting off you is body odor and cheap powder laundry detergent. All that wash in the bag yours?"

"Hell no," the old woman said. "Do for all my neighbors."

Mia pointed to a second-story window. "Mrs. Boutros?"

"Yeah, sure. She delivered my great-grandbabies. I do her wash; that's how things get paid out here." She spoke with a sense of working-class pride. "Gather it all up on Mondays and Thursdays, take it on over to the laundry. Get it back to them fresh and folded, yes ma'am."

Mia leaned in even farther, down to the old woman's ear. "And I bet you keep any spare change you find in the pockets, right?"

She laughed. "Suppose I do."

Mia straightened up. "Mrs. Boutros was my mama's midwife back in the day. Helped with my birth. Wasn't sure if she were still alive, but wanted to check in with her. If that's possible."

"Haddie's still living," the old woman said. "God blessed her with a long life, probably f'helping so many of his little angels get to being born safe. Don't do too much midwifin' anymore, not too much call. Honey, you can find her over at the park. She plays checkers there with the boys. Beats 'em all every time, too."

Mia thanked her and turned to Maddox and Darcy.

Across the street, a line of trees and a grassy incline separated the neighborhood from Weequahic Park. "Had an informant used to play cards in the park, between the fieldhouse and the baseball fields. It's not far."

"Not far?" Darcy said with a moan. "I'll wait in the car. Today's not the day for me to tramp a couple-mile hike. I'll take a nap. You two let me know how it goes."

Hands on hips, Maddox said, "Okay."

"Lock the doors," Mia told him.

Maddox led Mia across the street, up the incline, and between trees. They were met with a chilling, fragrant breeze drifting off Weequanic Lake. In summer, the air would have smelled like pine needles and freshly cut grass; the scent now was pure ozone. They walked the park, eyes watering as the temperature dropped. Mia rubbed her hands together furiously. "Should have known to bring gloves."

Without a word, Maddox reached for her hand.

They walked.

Their silence lasted until they reached the first ball field. At the far end, a young Hispanic man played catch with his black lab while his girlfriend chatted on her phone. Mia sighed. "Never did enough of this kind of thing."

"Walks in the park?" Maddox asked.

She nodded. "Or that," pointing at the man and his dog.

"But too much of that." Mia pointed to the young woman on her phone. "Even back when we were young, I was always talking to people about what they did, what they saw, who they knew. Didn't do enough myself. Now I look back and I wonder how much of my history is other people's memories. Sad."

A sly grin grew on Maddox's face. He pointed to the park fieldhouse they approached. A number of senior citizens sat at folding tables, playing card and chess, and chatting. "To piggyback on the sentiment, let's go talk to an old midwife about something we never did."

"Let's," Mia said, squeezing his hand.

Picking Hadassah Boutros out of the pack was easily. Sitting behind a checkerboard, she'd amassed two towers of quarters. Maddox sat opposite her. "Can I have this game?"

Haddie puckered her lips. "If you brought your coins, you sure can. I don't play for bragging rights."

Maddox patted his pants. "I guess I don't have quarters."

"Could sell you some, I guess," Haddie said, tilting her head towards her winnings. "It's three dollars to play. You use the quarters as playing pieces. I jump it, I keep it. Understand?"

"I think I do," Maddox said. "But I'm out of practice. Think I'd lose to you pretty fast. So maybe I can just hand you over the three dollars and you could answer a few questions for me?"

She squinted. "Questions ain't checkers. Answers cost more."

Maddox huffed. "How much more?"

"Depends on the question," Haddie said.

"Persephone Alford."

"Oh," Haddie said in a lower tone. "I'm not so sure I can put a price tag on a question like that. Already cost too much to so many folks."

Mia chimed in. "Excuse me?"

Haddie's gaze shifted from Maddox to Mia and back. "You two don't know, do you? Thought maybe you might, given that you came and asked. Most folks don't... believe in things."

"What *things*?" Maddox asked, his voice growing insistent.

Haddie took a handful of quarters and, as she spoke, arranged them on the board in the shape of a smiley face. "When a baby's born, you hold it in your hands. It's got nothing before your hands, no time in the light. Before that, it's just darkness and grumbling noises. But then suddenly there's bright light and loud, clear sounds, and colors and shapes. Have you ever considered that the first sound a baby hears is that suffering of its mother? That's why a baby cries when it comes into our world. Everything's new, and she learns right off about pain."

She slid a few coins down the board. The smile turned into a long frown.

"So you remember Persephone?" Maddox asked.

Haddie let out a surprised, hoarse chuckle. "Of course. I remember all my babies. The itty-bitty premature ones, the big guys, the twins: I don't forget none of them. After I'd hand the babies off to their mommies, I'd ask the daddies–*if they was there*–what the name was they picked out. I had these big paper ribbons. And I'd write their names on 'em and tie it around their wrist, real loose, but not so much that they'd fall off. I sure do remember little Persephone. Had to have Mr. Alford spell it out for me." A se nior citizen seated behind Haddie, playing cards in hand, announced, "P-E-R-S-E-"

"You two just ignore Mr. Lonaghan," Haddie said. "His brain's gone a few years past its sell-by date."

"–P-H-O-N-E."

Haddie rolled her eyes. "I remember asking Mrs. Alford–she was just a tiny little thing, and Persephone wasn't a small baby–so I asked her what her favorite color was; I could barely make out what she was saying, she cried so hard. Remember, no drugs, just a woman and her willpower. I brought a new box of crayons, like I always did, and picked out the yellow one. Wrote PERSEPHONE on that ribbon, tied it to her wrist. Then I handed Mr. Alford the box and winked. Always gave my babies their first crayons. Deal was, once they was old enough to write, they'd send me a letter using 'em.'"

Maddox's hand dropped down to his pants pocket and felt the shape of the broken crayon inside. He thought better than to present it to Haddie. "Did you ever get that letter from the Alfords?"

"Matter of fact, I did not," she said.

"Any reason?"

"Because the *nothing* took her."

"The *nothing*?" Maddox asked. "What's that?"

"N-O-T-H-I-N-G," Mr. Lonaghan called out.

Haddie laughed. "Now, sir, *nothing* ain't a thing—that much anyone should be able to figure. If you could describe it, it'd be something, even if only an idea. Nothing's nothing. And sometimes it comes in and swallows a person up. Don't know why; no one does. And afterward, no one remembers. Little Persephone isn't even a memory anymore. Even her parents forgot."

"How do *you* know?" Maddox asked.

Mia added, "And why do *you* remember?"

Haddie lifted up her hands. "I help bring new lives into this world, but each one gives me something in return. A better view of things, or maybe something more. I never forget any of my babies, no matter what nothing might try."

"Did you ever see the Alfords after Persephone went missing?"

"Plenty of times. In the market. Community events." Haddie retrieved her quarters off the checkerboard and stacked them up. "They always remembered *me*. With a look on their faces like they got sucker-punched. Could make out who I was and what I did for a living, but had no idea *why* they knew."

Haddie folded up the checkerboard and stood up. "I best be getting home. Think it might storm tonight. Temperature's dropping."

"Miss Boutros, just one more question," Maddox said, following her to her feet. His knees cracked. "You said that sometimes nothing comes and takes people. You've seen this happen with more than just with Persephone?"

"Oh, yes."

"How many times?"

Haddie grinned. "Good day, sir. Ma'am."

She pocketed her winnings, slid the board under her arm, and headed back towards Peddie Street. In her nineties, the midwife still moved with easy grace, legs crisscrossing as she walked.

The wind picked up, colder now. Mia tugged the collar of her parka tight around her neck. Caught in the airflow, a deck of cards blew off one of the folding tables and tumbled through the air like autumn leaves before settling on the grass. A frail woman in her seventies rushed over, dropped to her knees, and scurried after them.

Mia bent down to help.

The woman's head snapped towards her. "Get back."

Mia raised both hands, straightened up, and backed away. "I was just trying to help."

"No one comes round here to help." The woman spit on Mia's shoes.

"N-O-O-N-E," Mr. Lonaghan said. "K-L-O-U-M."

Maddox spun and ran to the old man's table. "What did you say?"

Mr. Lonaghan stared back at him with vacant eyes.

The old Irish man sitting next to him said, "Leave him alone; he didn't say nothing."

"He spelled a word," Maddox said.

The Irish man shook his head. "My hearing's gone to shit, but I don't remember him sayin' nothing."

Nothing. *Exactly.*

Mia joined Maddox at the table and pulled at his sleeve. "Let's go."

They did. Walking across the baseball fields, Maddox's eyes returned to the young man and his wife. His dog was nowhere in sight. The couple seemed to be arguing, though their voices were drowned out by the ascent of a Boeing 787 overhead.

Mia didn't reach for his hand.

They didn't speak.

Haddie disappeared from view.

Passing between the tree line, they stepped down onto the street.

A plastic bag, torn and flapping in the wind like a flag, rested in the street.

Dirty laundry was spread out over the asphalt. Like a deck of windswept cards. Maddox turned his head, up and down the street. He called out to Haddie as she climbed her front steps, "MISS BOUTROS–"

Haddie turned.

Maddox pointed to the laundry. "Your friend who does the laundry–"

A look of confusion washed over her face. "Who?"

"Old black woman. Does your laundry. She was here–"

Haddie shrugged. "I have no idea who you're talking about."

"Let's go," Mia said for a second time.

Maddox assumed it was the second time, anyway.

December 9th

The whisper in his ear came quick and sharp, like the whistle of a paper cut. *"Not a heart attack. Not a stroke."*

Maddox bolted upright in his recliner. Stan's folder, open on his chest, dropped into his lap and spilled its contents down his legs and onto the floor. Loose paper and photographs settled across the room in an array that reminded him of the laundry spread out over Peddie Street. His head snapped from side to side, from one corner of his room to the next, until he was satisfied he was alone.

He checked his watch. Three-fifty a.m. When had he fallen asleep? He didn't know.

On hands and knees, he gathered up the photocopies, clippings, and prints. He rose to his feet, set the folder down on the bedside table, and stared at his fingertips. Ink from the newspaper clippings stained his skin. Touched enough, he wondered if any of the print would remain at all. Maybe not. And then what? A blank page? Just black smudges on the hands of anyone who'd touched it? In time, not even that. Words fading into haze into nothing at all.

A dry snap drew his attention to the door. A creaking floorboard under the pressure of a shoe? The settling of an old house? He considered calling out but thought better of it. Steven had work in the morning; he'd need his rest. Maddox slid on his slippers.

Always drafty, the house caught a breeze off the interstate that seemed to creep in from every pore in the old house's siding. As Maddox entered the hall, a rush of cold air tickled his skin, teasing out goosebumps. He stopped at thermostat on the hallway wall and nudged the needle up the dial. Continuing on, he listened to his footsteps. This creak of old wooden floorboards was different than the one he'd heard. With a smile, he considered the idea that he probably could recognize the sound of his own movements through the house, the same way he'd been able to track Steven through their old home when his son was a teenager; so different from his wife's gentle shuffle, or his own heavy stomp. *The sounds we make*, he thought. *Our aural fingerprints. What's that make the echo of our voices?*

The door to Steven's bedroom was open. Awake or asleep, his son kept it closed. Maddox had only been inside a handful of times, never without Steven or for more than a moment. He peeked in. Steven's bed, unmade, was empty.

Maddox let out a deep breath and headed to the kitchen. Surely, he'd find his son there, maybe searching the cabinets for an antacid tablet, or a sleep aid. Steven never kept medicine in the bathroom vanity, as Maddox had. Something about fecal contamination from an article he'd read on the Internet. Didn't even allow toothbrushes or toothpaste to be stored there. Absurd.

The kitchen was empty.

Peering out through the window over the sink, he searched the driveway for Steven's car. Gone. Suddenly, the empty house around him seemed larger and darker than usual.

Where are you?

Maddox took a step back towards the hall but stopped when his foot skidded. He leaned down and pulled the greeting card out from under the toe of his slipper. He stared at the grim reaper drawn on the front. A grinning skull with wide black eye sockets. A long scythe held in skeletal hands.

ON YOUR BIRTHEDAY.

Standing, he placed the card on the table. It opened like a flower responding to daylight, exposing the inside text. It wasn't the same card he'd received earlier in the week. *Couldn't be.* Where there had been the warning to *leave it alone*, the card now read:

STILL LOOKING FOR ME?

And below it, in smaller print:

I FOUND YOU FIRST.

Maddox closed the card and buried it under a heavy pan from the stove. He hurried away from the kitchen and checked the front door. Finding it locked, he retreated down the hall to his room and slammed the door behind him.

A petite figure sat on the edge of his bed, facing the window, lit only by moonlight. Naked, she turned her head and slowly revealed herself in profile—button nose, full lips, a sharp and delicate chin. Then she twisted at the waist, bringing her body into view. His gazed dropped from her prominent collarbones to the swell of her breasts and prominent upturned nipples, and from there to her narrow waist.

"Blair?" Maddox said.

Her mouth fell open, but her lips remained motionless, as if painted on. As smoky and ariose as a torch singer, her voice was not spoken, but instead seemed to emanate from her presence. "If you like."

Maddox backed himself against the door.

"*Do you, Mads?*" she asked. She cupped her breasts in her hands and squeezed. Her eyes glimmered in the moonlight, silver electricity over hazel irises. "*Like me? Still?*"

"You can't be here," he whispered. He felt lightheaded. His hands went cold. *No, not now, not again.* His chest tightened and his throat constricted.

Blair stood up, shaved legs crossing as she turned to face him full on. Releasing her breasts, she let her hands fall to her sides. Her fingertips swung far below her knees–too, *too* low. Her thin arms were impossibly long. "*Not a heart attack. Not a stroke. I need you conscious, Mads. I need you with me, in the now.*"

Fighting his closing windpipe, he croaked, "The fuck are you?"

She stepped closer. Mouth still gaping, her breath carried the strong scent of black licorice. It burned Maddox's nostrils as he breathed it in. Although her legs moved with an uncanny feline sensuality, her torso and shoulders jerked and buckled with each step, head bobbing like a puppet. "*A warm spot in a cold life.*"

Maddox reached for the doorknob. Numb and tingling, his fingers wouldn't close around the chrome ball. He shrank back as Blair raised one long arm out to him, pale fingers moving through the air with an unnaturally quick tremble. Her fingertips landed on his face, forefinger under his right eye.

Hot.

Her hands slid down his cheeks, leaving a trail of warmth behind. The sensation burrowed into his flesh, relaxing his muscles. As her fingers glided over his chin, his jaw unclenched. His throat opened as her touch reached his Adam's apple. His chest muscles loosened. He felt a pleasant stirring as she reached under his waistband. As she took hold of him, her lax expression changed, the corners of her lips curling as a satisfied smile painted itself across her face.

Maddox whispered, "Darcy–"

"*Always a wet noodle,*" she hissed, tightening her hold on his manhood. A surge of energy and power exploded within him. His hips jutted forward, working her hands around him, building friction. "Unworthy."

Maddox groaned. The first of its kind in decades.

Blair moved closer still, until her face was flat to his, eyelashes tickling his cheek. Her tongue darted out and teased his. As she continued to massage him with her hand, she nipped at his nose with her teeth. The scent of licorice intensified in the heat of her breath, now as intoxicating as a shot of absinthe. "*He knows, you know, deep down. He knows what you and I did. That you and I did.*"

The warmth inside became an inferno. The intensity rising to an unbearable level, Maddox took ahold of Blair by the shoulders and pushed her away. She stumbled, falling to the floor on her back. Propping herself up on her bent elbows, she pushed her chest upward and moaned. Her knees rose. And parted.

Maddox dropped onto his hands and knees and crawled on top of her. He buried his face between her breasts. Her legs locked around his and pulled him forward. He slid himself out of his sweatpants and into her. She rested back onto the floor.

She felt familiar. Even after thirty-four years, he knew the feel of her.

He pumped. She moved to his rhythm underneath him.

The blistering heat under his skin continued to rise.

As his climax neared, he dropped his head against her chest.

Blair had no heartbeat.

The heat turned to ice. Pain.

Maddox tried to withdraw but the strength of her legs held him in place and forced his hips to continue to grind. The passion turned to panic. He scrambled to free himself, frantically twisting and jerking, but without success. Balling his hands into fists, he struck out, striking her in the face. Her skull slammed down against the hardwood floor with each blow.

She laughed.

Summoning all his strength, he drew back his fist and brought it down. Her skull cracked. Blood flowered in her hair. Her legs buckled. She moaned in ecstasy before her body went totally limp.

Maddox pushed away, tumbling across the floor before balling himself up against the bedroom door. Drawing his knees to his chest, he rocked in place, eyes fixed on the unmoving body.

It wasn't Blair. The woman spread out on his bedroom floor was young. She lay on the remains of a torn zebra-print blouse. A long black scarf led from her neck to an inch from his foot. Her name was Melissa Shelton.

The laughter still echoed in the room.

*   *   *

The morning came.

There was no body on the floor.

No Blair MacAteer.

No Melissa Shelton.

No sleep.

Maddox sat, hunched over a cup of black coffee, at the kitchen table. Bleary eyed and clutching his robe tight around him, he rocked back and forth as he tried to read the previous day's newspaper. Although a beam of cheery morning sunlight lit the page, he was unable to constrict his eyesight enough for the ink blots on the newsprint to narrow into letters. Removing the magnifying eyeglasses he called cheaters, he sniffed at the air and frowned. Did he still detect the faintest whiff of licorice? *No, probably not*, he decided, but he *felt* like he could still smell it, the same way an amputee could sometimes still feel a lost limb tingle.

Creutzfeldt-Jakob disease.

Degenerative brain disorder.

Transmissible spongiform encephalopathy.

He folded the eyeglasses and rested them on the napkin beside the newspaper, where it shared space with an oatmeal raisin muffin with a single bite missing. *No ghosts. No appetite. Makes sense.*

The front door opened and Steven slid through, a bundle of loose clothes under one arm. He glanced at Maddox, brow low and eyes squinting, and said nothing. He headed for his bedroom.

"Steven–"

Without a pause, Steven mumbled, "My house, my rules..."

The bedroom door closed. The lock clanged.

Maddox raised his fist and brought it down on the eyeglasses, knocking one lens out of the frames and snapping the plastic at the bridge of the nose.

He raised his hand, inspected it. No harm that he could see.

But he knew better.

*　　*　　*

Janey's day off at Hop's; the scab waitress, Wendy, was an impatient brunette with bubblegum in her mouth and garish red fingernails. They clicked together as she wrote out Maddox's order on her pad, reminding him of a grasshopper using its hind legs as percussive instruments. "You sure you're good without having nothing, honey?"

Mia smiled from across the table, amused by the woman's grammar.

"Yeah, I've had plenty of *nothing* for today," Maddox said.

"Okay," Wendy said with a dismissive shrug. The effect was roughly the opposite of Maddox's understanding of good customer service. She turned to Mia and said, "I'll have you your chamomile tea over to you real shortly."

Once the waitress disappeared from earshot, Mia let out a guilty laugh and dropped her head down onto the table.

"Public school," Maddox grumbled.

Mia snatched a paper napkin out of the dispenser and dabbed at her eyes. Dropping it, she wondered aloud, "You ever wonder about waitresses and napkins? I mean, we think nothing of blowing our noses in them, then leaving 'em on our dirty plates. Don't give it a second thought. Probably don't even remember doing it by the time we're out the door."

"It's a shit job. They know it when they take the gig," Maddox said. He glanced down at his wristwatch. "It's almost nine."

"Is it?" Mia checked her own. "I guess it is. So?"

Maddox tapped the table with impatience. "Darcy."

"He'll be along," Mia assured him. "Probably overslept."

Maddox shook his head. "He's not here in five minutes, we're going over to his place to herd his counted sheep to market."

Mia's expression darkened. "Someone piss on your toothbrush?"

"I'm dying," he said. "Every moment matters."

"Mads, you know I didn't mean—"

Maddox reached over the table and tapped her hand. "I know."

"I just ordered tea."

"Get it to go."

"And they say you can't take it with you," she said.

"Chamomile," he said, sliding out of the booth. "Why would you want to?"

*   *   *

"Knock again," Mia told Maddox, gesturing with a fist.

He frowned. It'd been a full five minutes since he'd rapped on the door. His mind reeled–had he forgotten something Darcy might have said in passing? Some appointment? He didn't trust his memory as far as he could throw his voice. And he was no ventriloquist. He glanced over his shoulder at Darcy's car parked at the curb. No sign of Blair's boxy little hybrid.

Maddox's watch read 10:12.

"He say anything to you about going outta town or anything?"

Mia's face scrunched up into a questioning expression. "If he had, you think I'd have the two of us out here freezing our asses off? Of course not."

He smacked his lips. "Didn't say nothing to me, either."

Knuckles met door. They waited in silence.

Maddox's watch read 10:16.

A bird song called Maddox's attention to the peak of a telephone pole across the street. A brown and yellow cedar waxwing perched there, wings pulled tight to its body. Its flute-like chatter sounded sad. *You should already be down south, bird*, Maddox thought. *Won't make it through the winter. But you already know it, don't you, old bird? Not gonna bother flapping your wings all the way down to Florida just to go beak-up once you arrive.*

Mia paced the porch. "It's too cold for this. He ain't home."

Maddox's watch read 10:18.

Maddox moved to a flower pot near the railing. The plant inside was a mass of withered limbs. A chrysanthemum? Maybe months ago. Lifting it, he lifted Darcy's spare key off the concrete. He held it up for Mia.

"Is that cool? To just go in?" she asked.

Maddox shrugged. "Or you can stay out here with the bird."

"Bird?"

Maddox unlocked the door and dropped the key into his pants pocket. The rush of heat that met him as he crossed the threshold forced him to blink back tears. As Mia followed him inside, she brought a hand over her nose. "Jesus.

Gotta be eighty degrees in here."

A warm spot in a cold life.

Maddox pointed his lips towards the stairs and yelled, "DARCE–"

Moving to the wall thermostat, Mia tapped it with her index finger. "It's set to sixty-eight. Must be busted. Darcy's living on a fixed. Why wouldn't he get someone over here to fix it?"

"DARCE–"

He peeked into the kitchen. Three empty cereal boxes sat on the counter. Dirty dishes filled the sink. An empty ravioli can rested on the table, spoon handle rising from it like the flag raised at Iwo Jima. The microwave oven's door was wide open, the digital display's countdown frozen with five seconds left to go.

"Place is filthy," Maddox grumbled.

Mia gave him an annoyed glare. "What you expect?"

"Wasn't like this a few days ago," he said as he headed upstairs. As he climbed, the temperature rose. He unbuttoned his coat. At least heat still rises. *Can't rely on much else anymore.*

At the landing, Maddox faced a framed black-and-white portrait of Darcy and Blair on their wedding day. The new husband wore his Navy service dress blues. The bride's dress was a quarter of a year's salary's worth of satin and lace. Big, genuine smiles and glistening eyes.

Blair's arms were of normal length.

Maddox continued down a hallway and stopped short outside the bedroom. Darcy lay on the bed wrapped inside a cocoon of sheets and comforters, with only his face peeking out from a tiny cave entrance. "Darce?"

Darcy did not move.

Mia strode into the doorway behind Maddox. Eyes wide, she gasped and reached for Maddox's hand.

"DARCE!"

No movement.

"Oh, Jesus." Mia's voice trembled.

Maddox stepped up to the bed and dropped a hand down over Darcy's shoulder and shook. Even through layers of sheets, he felt skin and bones instead of muscle. An old man's body.

Body.

"Oh, Darcy," Maddox whispered.

Mia sobbed.

Maddox sat on the edge of the bed. *Not right. Not supposed to be you, Darce. Sure, Stan went first, but it was supposed to be my turn next. Even Dr. Van Stiehl agrees with that. You have to be difficult once last time and cut in line?*

"No... no... no," Mia stammered.

Maddox tugged at the top comforter, pulled back a section, and straightened it out to cover his friend's face. A curious custom, one he didn't understand, but given the moment, it was the only thing he knew to do.

Darcy opened his eyes.

Maddox dropped the comforter.

"Mads?" Darcy said, stretching. "Mia? What are you two doing here?"

For a moment, Maddox couldn't answer. *What* was *he doing there?*

"Checking on your sorry ass," he said finally.

Darcy pushed himself out of the sheets and sat up. "Why?"

"You didn't show at the diner," Maddox replied.

Darcy raised an eyebrow. "And you got yourself worried?"

Maddox stood up. His expression hardened. "I don't worry."

Mia rushed to the bedside and wrapped her arms around Darcy. He didn't return her embrace. Instead, his face rearranged into a look of exasperation and annoyance. "I have a cold. Maybe flu, but I don't even think so. You two think I can't take care of myself anymore? Gonna try to put me in a home?"

Mia pulled back. "Not like that. We just—"

"Well, don't *just.* Okay? I've been telling you for months, I'm fine. Really." Darcy's eyes didn't look fine; a deep sadness had set in, something like homesickness. His voice took on an accusatory tone. "I don't appreciate you breaking into my house just because I overslept a little."

Mia took a step back. "Sorry."

"I'm not," Maddox said. "Thought you were dead."

Disbelief on his face, Darcy shook his head. "Sorry to disappoint."

Darcy stood. He wore a T-shirt and boxers. Neither appeared to have been washed in weeks. He pointed to the robe hanging from a hook on the back of the door. Mia retrieved it. "How'd you get in? Hire a local kid to bust in through a window like at Stan's house?"

"Used your spare," Maddox said.

Darcy snatched the robe out of Mia's hand and climbed into it. With a huff, he said, "Well, you can be damned sure that next time you want to traipse in here without permission, there won't be any key under any flower pot."

Mia said, "Darce, we were only–"

"What's gotten into you?" Maddox asked, stretching out his hands in a questioning gesture. "You act like we came in here to steal your pension check and raid the fridge."

"Do I know you didn't?"

Maddox sighed. "I think you're sicker than you realize. Maybe you should see a doctor. At the least, I don't think you should be alone. Where's Blair?"

Silence.

Mia's hand covered her mouth.

Anger blossomed on Darcy's face. "Fuck you."

"What?" Maddox said. "I'm lost here."

"Get out," Darcy said.

Maddox took a step towards his friend.

Darcy retreated. "GET OUT."

"Maybe we *should* go," Mia called over.

"I–"

"GET THE FUCK OUT OF MY HOUSE!"

"Darce..."

Mia pleaded, "Maddox, let's go."

"GET OUT–"

"–we just–"

"–MADDOX–"

Darcy rushed towards Maddox, palms out, and pushed. Maddox stumbled back, not from the force but the surprise. In all the years they'd been friends, he'd never seen Darcy raise a hostile hand. Not even to perps. He did what he had to do on the job, but never did it out of anger. But now, there was no mistaking it.

"FUCK OUT OF HERE."

Mia tugged at Maddox's sleeve.

"YOU THINK It's EASY BEING YOUR FRIEND?" Darcy screamed. "YOU KNOW HOW MUCH I've HAD TO OVERLOOK? HOW MUCH I've HAD TO FORGIVE?"

'He knows, you know, deep down.'

Maddox turned away.

Darcy's voice lowered in volume, but not in tone. "I'm *done* forgiving. I'd rather just forget you."

Maddox and Mia left.

*   *   *

Settling into his car, he asked Mia, "What was all that?"

Mia shook her head. "He's sick. And tired. And still dealing."

"Doesn't answer it." Maddox started the car.

"Maddox," Mia said. It was clear she meant to sound compassionate, but it came off as professorial. "You have to be careful. We all know how bad things are for you right now. I can't even imagine what's going through your head. But you know that Darcy never got over it. You can't go off and–"

"You talking about?" he asked. "What'd I do?"

Mia cocked her head to one side. "Blair, Maddox, you mentioned Blair."

He drummed his thumbs on the steering wheel. "And...?"

"Mads," Mia said slowly. "Honey. You've got this thing eating away at your brain, I get it. Darcy gets it too, even, but that doesn't mean that sometimes things you say aren't gonna hurt feelings."

"What did I say? Honestly, I don't know."

Mia didn't answer at first. Her face contorted. Maddox watched her choose her words. Finally, she said, "You don't remember, do you? Blair passed away four years ago. You were a pallbearer."

Maddox turned off the ignition. His hand dropped to his leg. He felt the impression of Darcy's spare key still in his pocket. He breathed out. His heart raced.

A bird sang.

December 10th

Maddox tugged at the hospital gown to cover more of his legs.

"You haven't heard a word I've said." The expression on Dr. Van Stiehl's face resembled the disappointment of a parent with his child. "Have you?"

Clutching the edge of the examination table, Maddox rocked forward and back. He needed coffee. "At this point, what's it matter, anyway?"

Dr. Van Stiehl dropped the clipboard of Maddox's charts onto the table. He reached up and pinched the bridge of his nose and exhaled. "You're here. You came in. For what? To argue? Mr. Boxwood, I've got better things to do. People to see who actually want help. I know you're confused and angry and depressed. But so are all my patients. If you're not here to participate, go bitch to a bartender instead."

"What am I supposed to do?" Maddox asked.

"Whatever you'd like," Dr. Van Stiehl said. "Anything you've always wanted to but never had the chance. Go skydiving. Climb a mountain. Chew peyote out in a desert. Whatever it is. And then, when it's time, die with dignity. Not sniveling and full of regrets."

Maddox said, "That what passes for your bedside manner?"

"You'd prefer I refer you to the hospital chaplain?"

Maddox plucked the prescription bottle beside him and shook it like a maraca. The label read SODIUM VALPROAT, 500mg. Little purple pills rattled inside the translucent orange tube. "I'll stick to the drugs."

Dr. Van Stiehl nodded. "Only when you feel the disorientation begin. Stops the seizures most times. But they'll make you sick to your stomach. Might be difficult to sleep."

Maddox put down the bottle. "There's another thing."

"There always is," Dr. Van Stiehl said.

"I've been... seeing things."

Dr. Van Stiehl blinked. "I would imagine so. Blindness is not a symptom of Creutzfeldt-Jakob."

Was that a joke? From *this* man? Maybe he was hallucinating right now.

99

"You know what I mean. Things that can't be real, but they're *there*. Solid."

The doctor pulled a stool over and sat. "Tell me."

"People who shouldn't still be around," Maddox said.

"Ghosts?"

"No," he said. "Not like that. I don't know how to—"

"It's the disease."

Maddox shook his head. "That's what I was thinking, but these aren't memories. These are things happening *now*. Right before my eyes."

Dr. Van Stiehl took a moment to reply. "Did you know that it takes an eighth of a second for the brain to interpret the information it gets from the eye? It has to decode what it sees, and put it in context. Nothing you see is happening exactly at the moment you think. We're all a fraction of a second behind. Some people a little more or less, but none of us is really sentient in real time."

Maddox leaned forward.

"We store memories all around our brains. Smells over here, tastes there, a little color over in the corner. We all manage a card catalog, like the libraries used to have. When we remember, we pull out a card and it tells us where to find the elements of the memory. Then we grab them, put them together into a whole. Thing is, we do this same thing with our eyes and ears and nose every other minute too. You're doing it right now. Instead of stored information in the brain, it's the sensory organs, the live feed. But the process is the same."

Dr. Van Stiehl leaned in, too, bringing them face-to-face. Was there a cloudiness in the man's eyes, or was Maddox's own vision failing? The onset of cataracts? Not a reassuring trait in a physician. *What are you not seeing, doc?*

"The disease is shuffling your card catalog. But it won't stop there. It'll burn all the books in time. And then it'll go after the ones still being written," Dr. Van Stiehl said.

"So how do I know what's really real?" Maddox asked.

"Mankind has been asking that question for a very long time," the doctor replied.

Both men reclined back. A long silence followed.

Maddox pushed off the examination table and reached for his clothes. He gestured to the bare wall behind Dr. Van Stiehl. "Shouldn't you have an eye chart or something? This room is so sterile. Maybe a poster with a cat clinging to a tree branch."

Van Stiehl glanced over his shoulder. "I dislike clutter."

"We're different. I've nothing against it," Maddox said.

*　　*　　*

The most direct route home from Dr. Van Stiehl's East Orange office was to take Cedar Avenue down to Route 510, a quick eight-minute journey, give or take a jaywalker or two. And that was the path Maddox meant to take. But instead of a right turn at the end of Cedar, he took a left and passed under the Garden State Parkway. He cursed under his breath. Too many years of the same commute; his muscle memory was too strong.

He decelerated the car as Holy Sepulchre and Fairmount cemeteries passed on his left, two huge tracts of parkland jam-packed with tombstones and monuments. *But fear not, always room for one more*, he thought as he turned his attention to the other side of the road. The streets counted down from South 19th to South 6th over the course of thirteen blocks, alternating between empty lots and row homes. One lot always caught his attention. Behind a low chain-link fence, the property was bordered by a brick wall painted white. A graffiti artist had painted an old man sleeping on his side, covered by a blue blanket decorated with white stars. Big, uneven block letters spelled out NEWARK DREAMS.

What dreams are left? Maddox thought as he took the right onto South 12th. Brick homes lined the street, separated by tiny rectangular lawns and wrought iron fences. Maple trees rose up from islands of soil between slabs of sidewalk at regular intervals, the product of the city planner's Renaissance Trees program a decade and a half earlier. Maddox pulled to the side of the road and parked.

He lit a cigarette and smoked.

Why'd I come here?

So how do I know what's really real?

What dreams are left?

In the time it took to smoke down the cigarette, the street darkened as the sun slid behind the rooftops. Maddox glanced at his watch. Four-eighteen, only a few moments before the sun would set. He rolled down the window and flicked out the butt. The wind took the litter and sent it down the curb. Maddox followed its progression towards the corner of 14th Ave until it changed course and tumbled to a rest at the foot of a doorstep. Glancing up, he stared at a lighted second-story window.

No. Don't even think about it. Just go home.

He couldn't. He wished he could have placed the blame with his years of police work, but that wouldn't have been anything more than an excuse. Maddox couldn't turn away for a reason much closer to his heart: his friends were his brothers, and he'd never turn his back on family. He killed the engine and stepped out onto the street.

Then he made his way down the street to Stan's house.

The door was unlocked. Stepping inside, Maddox counted to ten before turning and entering the living room. Uneven light drifted down from the stairs in the hall, illuminating half the room. The dying sunlight did little to help the remainder. Stan's recliner, half lit, sat empty in its place. Maddox spun, crossed the hall, and found the kitchen unoccupied as well. The refrigerator door hung open a crack. He closed it.

Moving upstairs, he followed the light to the end of the hall. To Stan's office. He placed a hand against the door, as if testing for a fire, felt only cool wood, and pushed.

A figure sat at the desk, shorter than Stan and slumped over in defiance of healthy posture. The young man stared back at him with a look of fear and anticipation. But not surprise.

"What're you doing here?" Maddox asked.

Fuck Kinda Question's eyes filled with tears. "You remember me."

"Of course I remember you. Only been a few days," Maddox said.

"No," Fuck Kinda Question said, blubbering as he spoke. Tears filled his large brown eyes. The fear and anticipation was replaced with relief. "You remember me."

It took Maddox a moment to understand the kid. The first time he'd spoken hadn't been a question—it had been a declaration. He stepped up to the desk even as the kid pushed out of the chair and stood. "Why wouldn't I?"

Fuck Kinda Question laughed. Not pleasantly. "No one else does. Why should you? Other day, after we broke in here? Went home, my moms, she acted all funny, like she was scared of me. Told me to get out of her house.

Man, she didn't recognize me. Didn't know me. Her son. And she wasn't playing, I saw her eyes. You don't know the look maybe, the way a stranger looks at you with suspicion, but I do. That's how she was looking at me. My mom."

"Jesus," Maddox murmured.

The tears didn't stop as Fuck Kinda Question continued. "Went to my boy's house, my friend. Thought maybe I could crash there until I figured shit out. Same thing, except he hit me." The kid pointed to a dark purple blotch under his right eye. "Kicked my ass. I didn't fight back, couldn't, 'cause I was in shock. Walked the neighborhood for a long time, making eye contact with people I know. They didn't know me. Nobody knows me anymore. Nobody but you."

"Why'd you come back here?"

Fuck Kinda Question pulled a small handgun out of his waistband. Maddox recognized it instantly. Accu-tek AT-380, a two-hundred-dollar waste of money that could nevertheless put a .380 diameter hole in any fleshy thing in its aim. "Cause I figured you'd come on back here."

Maddox raised both hands and stepped back. "Whoa, kid."

"I don't wanna hurt you," the kid said. "I just want things back how they was. I want my Mom to know me again. And my boys, too. Whatever you did here, whatever you involved me in, you take it back. Hear me? You make it right."

"I'm not doing it," Maddox said, taking another backward step.

"*GOTTA BE YOU*," Fuck Kind Question yelled. "It started here. You still know me. That ain't some kind of coincidence. You're the reason for this. So, you do what you gotta do, make this go away."

Maddox kept eye contact with the kid. "I wish I could."

Fuck Kinda Question aimed the gun at Maddox's chest. Tears fell from his face, creating translucent splotches on the chest of his white tank top. "That ain't all, though. *THAT AIn'T MOST FUCKED PART–*"

"Kid, don't–"

"*I DOn't EVEN REMEMBER MY NAME–*"

The gun in his hand wavered.

"*I DOn't KNOW WHO I AM NO MORE–*"

"–just put the–"

"*YOU SAY IT. YOU SAY MY NAME–*"

"–gun down–"

Fuck Kinda Question's knuckles tightened on the Accu-tek's grip. His eyes squinted down to slits. "*DOn't WANNA HURT YOU. BUT I GOT NOTHING LEFT.*"

Maddox motioned for the kid to lower the weapon. "We'll get some help, I promise we will, and we'll find a way to make it all okay again, all right?"

The kid's voice softened. "Just tell me my name."

Maddox opened his mouth, but the words came slowly, lingering in his throat for an eternity before he finally said, "I'm sorry, I don't know your name."

Fuck Kinda Question's expression collapsed into despair. He lowered the gun and pressed it flat against his chest. His head dropped. He wept.

Maddox took two steps forward and reached out for the kid.

"Then there's no point," he whispered. He slid the muzzle of the gun under his chin and pulled the trigger.

A sharp crack, like a leather belt being snapped, assaulted Maddox's ears. He turned away and closed his eyes. With his face stretched in a tight grimace, he felt every wrinkle and every old scar. Suddenly, every moment of his life had added weight to his soul and it was very, very heavy. Gravity brought his knees to the hardwood floor. Maddox screamed.

He stayed in darkness, eyes locked closed, for a long time. He'd seen violence and death many times before, but always with a context he could understand. Even the most brutal crimes could be rationalized in some way, even if only by appeals to mental illness or chemical imbalance. Not this.

A snippet of whistling drifted in from the hallway, muffled and distant, like an old transistor radio from another house. He recognized the melody. "You'll Never Know."

"Goddammit, Stan," Maddox whispered.

He opened his eyes and stood up. No one in the hall. He turned. No one in the office. Fuck Kinda Question's body was not sprawled out on the floor in a pool of blood. He was gone.

The Accu-tek rested on the floor. Maddox picked it up and weighed it in his hand. It felt real, for whatever that was worth. He dropped the magazine into his palm. Three rounds. Accounting for the one in the chamber, four. It held five at maximum capacity.

He knew where the fifth had gone... but where had it *gone?*

He slid the gun into his pocket.

December 11th

Maddox woke, stumbled out of bed, and shambled down the hall to the bathroom. Steven's door? Untouched. He still hadn't come home. As he relieved himself, Maddox rehearsed a speech in his thoughts, a fifty-yard narrative that stopped two inches short of an apology. He promised himself he'd speak those words when his son finally came home. He was a good liar. Not good enough to fool himself, though.

*   *   *

He opened the lid marked Monday and emptied the caplets into his palm. He studied them for a moment. The idea that a few grams of one compound or another could make a dent in a body his size caused him to smirk. He popped them into his mouth and washed them down with a glass of water.

It was Wednesday.

*   *   *

Hadassah Boutros wasn't home; he could tell this the moment he pulled up alongside the curb on Peddie Street. The windows were dark, though that had nothing to do with his conclusion. Shifting the automatic transmission into park, Maddox stared at the ruins of a long-burned-out apartment building. The slanted, collapsing roof gripped four charred brick walls. The front door rested against the front porch rail and displayed a frayed CONDEMNED – NO TRESPASSING – OCCUPANCY PROHBITED sign.

I led it to her, he thought. *She'd managed to fly under the thing's radar for decades. I walk up to her and ask her questions about Persephone Alford. And this.*

The windshield wipers streaked across his view, displaced rainwater distorting the ruined apartment building on the upswing. Maddox killed the engine, freezing the wiper blades at eleven o'clock. Reaching over, he plucked the cigarette box off the passenger seat, slid it into his coat pocket, and stepped out onto Peddie Street. A gust of cold wind punched him in the chest, drawing a hiccup of steam from his mouth and nostrils.

A young dark-skinned kid, no more than ten, darted across the road. He dragged an aluminum baseball bat behind him. The sound of the metal tapping and grinding against the asphalt threatened to dredge up the fine details of a golf club meeting Gerald Shelton's skull. Maddox turned his attention back to the apartment building. As he approached, another blast of wind streaked down Peddie Street. Pebbles of freezing rain danced on the asphalt.

"Need an umbrella out here ta-day," an orotund voice called.

Maddox pitched his head towards the caller. A young Dominican stood on the curb, the stem of a large black umbrella in one hand and a steaming Styrofoam cup in the other. Well-groomed and dressed for business, Maddox would have bet a pension check the man was a government employee. He called back, "Don't own one."

"Never seen rain before?" The Dominican hustled over, joining beside Maddox and lifting the umbrella over both their heads. "Or winter, from the looks of you. This coat you wear? Better for early spring."

Maddox inspected himself. Wrong coat. He shrugged. "Maybe I'm a slave to fashion."

The Dominican smiled. "I'll walk you. Where you going?"

"You a Boy Scout?" Maddox ran his eyes over the man. The rain intensified, vacillating between liquid and solid. He slowed his pace. "You new?"

"New?"

Maddox added, "To here. Newark. America."

The Dominican shook his head. "No, well, yes. I've lived here all my life, North Ward, Roseville. Came up with some boys that ran through Branch Brook Park, got into some trouble. More than some. But not now, not anymore, I'm changed, *new*. Redemptoris Mater."

"Seminary." Maddox stopped at the apartment's porch step. He faced the Dominican, stared into his eyes. There was something earnest there, maybe a little misguided, but the man wasn't lying. "Gonna be a priest?"

His smile withered. "If God will have me. I've not always..."

"Who has?" Maddox cast a thumb towards the apartment building. "I'm here to visit a woman who clearly doesn't live here anymore. Why're you slinking around this part of town?"

The Dominican pointed to a dented and rusted panel van parked at the end of the block. "I deliver food to the needy. Three days a week. Could do it every day and it wouldn't be enough. There's lots of needys."

"You know the neighborhood?"

The Dominican nodded.

"You remember the midwife that lived here? Hadassah Boutros?"

"No," he said, shaking his head. "Do not."

Maddox sucked in his bottom lip, bit it lightly, and then released it to the cold. "She's the only one that can answer some questions I have. Maybe answer, I dunno. She's the best chance I've got."

"A wrong address?" he said.

"I don't think so." Maddox's foot slipped on the first step. The Dominican grabbed his arm and steadied him. The man's grip was firm. Maddox took hold of the cast iron handrail. "Just... tell me about this building. You know anything about it?"

The Dominican released Maddox's arm. "Not much. Been like this for ten years at least. I remember seeing it like this back as a kid, riding my bike to the park to play ball."

"Baseball," Maddox said.

The Dominican's smile returned. "Of course, baseball."

Kloum's just fucking with me now.

"But, you know, I don't think it's really empty. I've seen homeless people on the steps, seemed pretty comfortable." He gestured to the CONDEMNED sign. "Piece of paper on a door doesn't mean much to them. If they can find a dry corner to curl up in, then this is home."

Maddox stepped up onto the porch and peeked through the doorway. Too dark to see very far. He lowered his voice. "You think they're dangerous? Safe to take a look around?"

"Depends," the Dominican said.

"On what?"

"Not *what*. On *who*," he said. "Some of these people, they're not thinking the same as you and I... not anymore. They don't see things in our way. This old building, there's no telling what it is to them. Home. Prison. Something else." He pointed to Maddox's chest. "Or what *you* are. Maybe they see you as someone evil. They'll protect themselves. Or, if you're lucky, they don't see you at all. If you're nothing to them, that's safer."

Maddox mumbled, "I'm safe if I'm nothing."

The Dominican turned back to the street. "What do I know? I've got to go. I've kept my needys hungry long enough. You be careful, old man, whether or not you go in there. God bless."

Maddox stepped through the door. The stench of mold and rot struck his nostrils before his eyes could adjust, a scent like stewing mushrooms mingling with wet dog. Covering his nose, he stepped further inside, his foot brushing aside debris. Shapes took form in the darkness, hazy at first until his eyes focused in the dim light. The apartment building lobby was a small square of bunched-up carpet, collapsed furniture, and a wall of metal post office boxes. Against the far wall, a framed portrait hung–still perfectly level–against cracked and faded wallpaper. Maddox brought his face close to the glass. It was a black-and-white photograph of the building in its prime, proud Georgian revival white ashlar stone and tall rectangular windows against a clear sky. The handwriting at the bottom of the photo read BUILDING 6 – 1929.

But whose 1929? he wondered. *Hadassah's?*

The stairs had collapsed into a haphazard tower wall of broken lumber that left no access to the upper floors. Navigating over some of the planks spilling out into the lobby, Maddox headed down a short hallway lined with apartment doors. Overhead, the ceiling became a quilt of dislocated sections with gaps between them. Subdued sunlight trickled down through the ruined floors above, better illuminating his path and aiding his steps. He avoided the most bloated and rotten floorboards, but even those not exposed directly to the elements creaked as he put his weight down.

Maddox passed apartment number 6A on the left, then 6B on the right. Both doors bowed outward as if struggling to hold back intense pressure. Sidestepping a pile of fractured ceramic floor tiles, he tilted close to 6C, then stopped. The door was partially open, the top hinge no longer connected to the doorframe, and a flicker of light came from within the apartment.

"Hello?" he called. "Miss Boutros?"

Maddox side-stepped into the room. The light from the hallway penetrated only a few feet. A few shafts of errant sunbeams filtered down from overhead. Clouds of dust danced in the spotlights. The room was small, square, and furnished with a decaying couch, an overturned ottoman, and an ancient cathode-ray television set on a cart.

A naked, feminine figure was perched on the television, toes curled over its edge like a bird's talons, feet arched. Leaning forward, her emaciated body shook as she brought a lit cigarette to her lips, sucked at it, and exhaled the smoke through her nostrils. Her eyes were glassy and unfocused. Tears streamed down her face. "Hey... you? You Bobby?"

Maddox stepped closer. No doubt, it was the same woman he's seen down the hall from Vance Turring's apartment. Unclothed, her small body seemed even more withered, the contour of each rib visible beneath her stretched skin, her hips protruding like fins.

He didn't want to get any closer. "Yeah, I'm Bobby."

"You are?" she said, her voice squeaking. The tears intensified, drenching her face. "He said you'd come, I heard him say it, but I didn't think..."

Maddox slid a hand into his pocket and around the grip of the Accu-tek. She looked real enough. But so had Blair MacAteer. He wasn't up for another round of *that*. "*Who* said I'd come?"

"The guy," she said, jumping down from the television. She landed with her knees bent at odd angles, as if her legs could no longer support normal posture. "The one with the dead baby face."

Maddox stepped back. "Dead... baby face?"

She snorted–possibly a laugh–and wiped her nose with the back of her hand when a mucus bubble inflated from her right nostril. "He's got regular faces, a lot of 'em, but only when he thinks you're looking." Her voice turned into a whisper. "He doesn't know I peek sometimes. I see him. You ever see a fetus in a jar at the circus? That pale, unfinished face? Like clay? That's him."

The gun felt small and ineffectual in Maddox's hand.

"But if he knows I'm looking, sometimes he's got my daddy's face," she said as an expression of shame and guilt washed over her. "Other people, too. First-grade teacher. The woman that delivers milk to the store on the corner. Once he looked just like Jesus on the television."

The television behind her was dark. Off. Empty.

"Why are you here?" he asked. "Don't you live in Nyack?"

She shook her head. "You're silly. A silly man."

Maddox asked, "Why'm I silly?"

She spread her hands out wide. "Where do you think we are, Bobby Silly

Man?" She stepped up to him, her body pushing up against him as she stared up into his eyes. The smell of body odor and halitosis drifted up to his nose. "Shit, you don't know, do you? We're *in* Nyack. This is my place."

Whose 1929? he reminded himself.

"Doesn't matter," she said, stepping back and away. "You're here now. I can give you what he wants you to have. Then maybe he'll leave me alone. I'm so tired."

He tightened his grip on the Accu-tek. "He gave you something for me?"

"Yeah," she said, walking to the far side of the room. Her curved backbone crackled as she walked, vertebrae shifting, aligning and dislodging. "I keep it hidden in my safe place."

Maddox followed her into a second room, keeping a careful distance between them. His eyes focused on her feet. Should she suddenly turn and lunge at him, he'd have warning. Hand on the gun, he hoped it'd be enough.

Moving past a tower constructed of dresser drawers, the thin woman pointed to the corner of the room. The ceiling had collapsed. Wooden beams, drywall, and firewall brick cascaded down in a chaotic mound. Without hesitating, she scurried up through the debris, climbing even as the structure shifted beneath her feet, until she disappeared into the room above.

Dust sprinkled down. Maddox covered his mouth and nose. He might not have much life expectancy left, but he saw nothing to be gained by breathing asbestos and mold. He waited, listening to the sounds of the woman moving overhead, like hearing a mouse move inside the walls.

Hadassah Boutros was gone. Fuck Kinda Question, erased. Persephone Alford. He thought of the hundreds of photo portraits he'd recovered from Stan's house. If Kloum could make all the people in those pictures disappear, why had it spared him?

Not now. Think later.

The woman reappeared, climbing down the scrap heap with one hand. She cradled a shoebox in the other. As she reached the floor, she turned and handed it to Maddox. He paused, not wanting to release the gun, before taking the box from her. He moved into a shaft of sunlight. A stray pellet of rain struck his face.

"He told me to make sure you got it, but that I couldn't open it up, not even a quick peek-a-boo." She giggled. "Said he'd do me right wicked if I did, something worse than he done to the others. Don't know what, but I believe him."

Maddox took he lid off the box.

It was full of ribbons, each inscribed with a name.

The one on top read PERSEPHONE.

There were dozens of ribbons, dozens of names.

Maddox closed the box. "Did he say why he wanted me to have this? Is it some kind of threat?"

She jutted her chin out and smiled. "He never tells me much. If you really wanted to know, you should have asked him yourself when you had the chance."

Maddox studied her face. Insane, yes, but there was no deceit in her eyes. If anything, she looked relieved, as if finally reaching the end of a long journey. "When would I have asked him?"

"Oh, right," she said with a shrug. "That hasn't happened yet."

December 12th

The shock of reheated instant coffee jousted with the artificial mint of tooth-paste. Maddox swallowed the mouthful of joe and grimaced. He stared down at the paper plate on the breakfast table. He'd buried three quarters of a slice of toast under a napkin. *Why did I even bother? Wasn't hungry. Just part of the routine.*

He lit a cigarette instead and dragged.

Still no sign of Steven. Best not to think about *that.*

But how not to think of it? Get to work.

Maddox stood, walked to the wall, and plucked the telephone handset off its cradle. Pulling a creased note out of his pocket, he dialed the first number. It rang once, connected, and a computerized female voice stated, "The number you are attempting to reach is not in service at this time. Please check the number and try again."

Maddox dropped the cradle with two fingers, cutting off the call. He dialed the second number. It rang. Again. Again. Again. Then a man answered in a thick Russian accent. "Hah–llo."

"Is this Vance Turring's number?" he asked.

"Hoo?"

"Vance. Turring."

"No, no Turring," the Russian said, then hung up.

The third number on the paper was Steven's cell phone.

A dial tone filled his ear.

Find out. Just dial.

Maddox closed his eyes, breathed out, and hung up the handset. His heart quickened and goosebumps raced down the length of his arms. Doctor Van Stiehl's voice echoed in his ears, reminding him to distract himself and curtail the escalation of anxiety.

In his early police days, he memorized a massive list of radio close-out codes, used to signal the resolution of a call. While he waited for his breathing and heartbeat to return to normal, he recounted as many as he could remember:

644 shots fired, 633 kidnapping, 438 disorderly persons, 539 domestic violence—

Melissa Shelton, a memory in a zebra-print shirt, emerged.

His heartbeat did *not* stabilize.

404 graffiti, 601 bomb threat, 710 fire report—

Hadassah Boutros's apartment building. Beating faster.

737 shooting, 543 drug activity, 711—

Maddox's knees bent. He scrambled to steady himself, but his hands slid across the wall. Sparks of pain gathered in his chest, popping like fireworks. He lost balance, twisted, and collapsed to the floor. Bones cracked. He screamed.

711... missing child. Not a heart attack. Not a stroke. Not a heart attack. 641 screams for help. Not a heart attack. Not a stroke. Not a heart attack. 855 officer in need of assistance—

Pins and needles. Fog spreading through his thoughts.

Balling up a fist, Maddox struck the wall. Hard.

—attack. Not a stroke. Not a heart—

He struck the wall again. The drywall dented. Glasses and ceramics rattled across the room.

—a stroke. Not a hea—

Maddox's vision blurred, cleared, blurred.

His knuckles struck out again. The dual-slot mail bin toppled off the counter ledge, spilling its contents across the floor. As Maddox's sight dimmed, he followed a single greeting card-sized envelope drifting to his hand and sliding under his fingertips. For a moment the return addressee was MIA CRESSWATER, then it blurred into a black smudge as his eyesight failed.

Then nothing existed for a while.

*   *   *

Maddox knocked on the door—the latest in a chain of knocks on doors that stretched back fifty years—and waited for a response. Unsteady on his feet, he held tight to the porch rail behind him and concentrated on his breathing. The wind whipped down the street, rustling his hair and coat. On his drive, he'd heard a weather forecast calling for near-blizzard conditions on Sunday. Catching a taste of ice and ozone in the air, he believed it. They'd had three mild winters in a row. He didn't hold out hope for a fourth.

C'mon to the door, dammit. He told himself that his agitation came from being out in the bitter cold, but he knew better. There'd been no answer to his calls, just like the others, but the vanishing of the Turrings and D'ester the organist was one thing. Mia was another entirely.

He knocked again.

C'mon... please.

*   *   *

In 1974, Maddox linked arms with a dozen of his fellow police officers as rioters screamed in the streets. Blocking the entrance to the public library on Washington Street, they spent the day facing down angry Puerto Rican protestors, some bold enough to shout in the cops' faces, others flashing clubs and knives. PD resources stretched thin, he'd spent sixteen hours there, unmoving, without a break. Thirst and hunger and stress became unbearable, until walking off the job seemed less a temptation than an inevitability. But then a single dark face cut through the crowd, fearless and shouting for the mob to make way. Mia stepped up to the police line with her arms full of bagged lunches. It wasn't lost on Maddox that his contained a homemade oatmeal cookie that the others did not.

Come to the door, girl. Be here. Don't be... gone.

He knocked a third time.

Nothing.

Maddox's chest tightened and his throat constricted. Heat rushed over his eyes, followed by hot tears. Wiping them away with his sleeve, he reached for the lid to the aluminum mailbox posted beside the door and flipped it open. He pulled out the single envelope inside.

An electric bill. Addressed to ROBERT MADISON.

Hey... you? You Bobby? echoed through his head.

"Jesus Christ," he muttered. He'd never considered the idea that he might someday be alone. Since childhood, he'd always been surrounded by family and friends. Over the decades, the family tree had performed a steady self-pruning: grandparents, older aunts and uncles, parents. He lost a few friends on the force, as many to addictions as to crime. His wife. Then, after retirement, the floodgates opened. He bought a supply of condolence greeting cards and kept them on his desk. But still, even with all of the absent friends and family, he'd never given serious thought that he might be the last man standing. Now that it'd started, the idea wouldn't shake free. He stood on Mia's porch and ruminated on those who'd gone, tried to remember as much as he could about each one. It was depressing how little he came up with for most of them.

A large crash from across the street shocked him out of his woolgathering. He spun on his heel in time to watch the last sheet of frozen snow fall from a second-story rooftop. It demolished the snowman on the small patch of grass beyond the sidewalk. In the aftermath, the street fell into a droning, empty silence.

The door opened.

Mia stood in the doorway in a long purple housecoat, hands on her hips. She wore no makeup and her hair was an untamed mess of tight spirals. "What you doing here, Mads?"

He exhaled, then blushed. "Needed to see you."

"You could've called," she said.

He shook his head. "That hasn't worked out all morning."

"I can't leave you out here freezing," she said as she rolled her eyes. Stepping aside, she guided him inside with one arm. "All the time we've been friends, you never once even asked to come over. And now here you are."

Maddox slid past her. "*You're* here. That's what's important."

She closed the door behind them. She squinted her eyes in a dramatic show of skepticism. "What's up with you? That sounded sweet, and you *never* sound sweet."

He handed her the envelope addressed to ROBERT MADISON.

"Another one? Get them all the time," she said. "Somebody needs to update their mailing list."

The brownstone façade gave way to the telltale signs of converted project housing: a breezeway built over the remains of a common lobby, a narrow hallway leading to a cinderblock staircase, neutral colors on the walls. Living under the ceiling of Mia's meter-maid pension, Maddox couldn't criticize.

Mia pushed ahead of him and led him into the living room. She motioned for him to take a seat on the well-worm chesterfield sofa in the center of the room. A bed pillow and comforter were piled at one end. As he sat, Maddox took a quick inventory of the room, an old habit from his investigative days. A low-end flat-screen television hung on the far wall, obviously not professionally installed. Department-store art decorated the walls. A single houseplant fought for survival under the room's sole window. The hardwood floor under his feet was overdue to be refinished by at least a decade.

What he didn't see was more startling: no personal knick-knacks, no family photos, no vacation souvenirs. Had the room been furnished by a real estate agent on a budget, with no thought to the tastes of the prospective buyer, it would have looked identical.

Maddox crossed his legs. Mia sat next to him. "Coffee?"

"Already made?"

"No," she said, "but'd just take a minute."

Maddox waved it off. "Don't bother. I had a cup at home."

A glimmer of embarrassment lingered in her eyes as she extended both arms and waved them. "This is it, home. Been here since '82; still have boxes in the attic never been unpacked."

"It's nice," he said.

She laughed. "No, but it's the best I can manage, which says something, I suppose. I get this, cable TV, some groceries, a few meals at Hops. I get by."

"You always have bags from the stores on your arm."

"I like to shop," she said with a shrug. "Buy it today, return it tomorrow. Unworn. Tags still attached. I know it sounds pathetic, but it keeps me sane. Makes me feel normal."

"You *are* normal," Maddox said.

She cocked her head to one side and let out a nervous giggle. Large, pearly tears grew in her eyes. "I got no one, Mads. No family. No husband. No boyfriend. No friends beside you and Darcy. I spend my days watching old re-runs, shows that were on the air when you and Darce, and Stan... when I could be around you guys. I know none of you never saw me as anything much, but you included me. Nobody else did, not in my entire life. You can't know how that made me feel."

Maddox let himself join her; they cried together. "Got that wrong. I never deserved a friend as good as you. None of us did. Different times. We used to think with blinders on. Wish I could go back and–"

She leaned forward and kissed him. The heat of her lips against his sent a shiver of excitement through his body. The scent of her so close to him–violet perfume and lavender hair gel—seduced his senses. He snaked a hand around her shoulder and brought her in close.

She softly pulled away. "That didn't happen if you don't want."

"Pretty sure it should have happened a long time ago," he said.

She laughed. "We'd be in a whole heap of trouble if it did."

Maddox pulled her back and held her. She settled in against him and smiled. He tipped his chin to the television's remote control on the sofa's armrest. "What you say we stay here like this for a while and watch some god-awful rerun from forever ago?"

"Uh-uh," she said. "I like right now more. Plenty of time for yesterday tomorrow. But, Mads..."

"Yeah?"

Mia put a hand on his chest. "Tell me why you came."

For a while, Maddox couldn't answer. Sitting here with Mia, in this honest moment, he didn't feel like an old man with a degenerative brain disease eating away his remaining days. He felt young and strong. But he knew the moment he started talking the serenity would fade away. The monster would snatch away that happiness, too.

He wasn't wrong.

"I was worried about you," he said. "This morning I called all of the people we've interviewed about the Alford case. They're all gone, Mia. 'The number you've dialed does not match any known subscriber.' 'Sorry, sir, you must have a wrong number.' 'We've had the same organist for nineteen years and his name isn't D'ester.' Vanished, every trace of them, as if they never existed."

Mia said softly, "Go on."

"There's a thing. It calls itself Kloum, but I don't think it really has a name. It changes things." He snapped his fingers. "Just like that and this guy's gone. His family and friends don't even remember he ever existed. I think that's what happened to Persephone Alford. And when we went looking into the matter, it came for me. It took Blair—"

"Mads..."

"It *took* her, Mia *erased* her. I know you remember things differently. That's because of Kloum. It changed things, messed with reality. I—"

Mia slid out of his arms, but stayed closed. Her eyes met his. "You know what this all really is, don't you?"

"It's not," Maddox said sharply, "the goddamned disease."

He reached into his coat pocket and pulled out a wad of ribbons. He rifled through them until he found the one marked PERSEPHONE ALFORD. "Do you remember the midwife? These were hers. Kloum had them given to me. Why? Maybe a warning, maybe something else. But see?"

Maddox held it out. Mia raised an eyebrow. "Mads."

"Just read it."

She took the ribbon from him, stretched it out, and read, "*Overturned tractor trailer on Route...* the print runs right off the edge."

"What? No." He snatched the ribbon back from her. "It says Persephone Alford. It's in Hadassah Boutros's handwriting. It's clear as—"

He felt very old and very sick. "Oh."

There were no ribbons, only strips of shredded newspaper.

Mia wrapped her hand around his. Crisp newsprint crinkled in their grasp. Her eyes filled with hurt and compassion. "Baby, it's nothing I'd wish on anyone, but to watch you go through this, no, it ain't something I can bear."

He closed his eyes and felt her brow against his.

"Could be you're right, I know that, and it's all my memory going bad," he said between short, sharp breaths. "How would I know? Maybe the disease is something Kloum dreamed into our heads. We wouldn't be able to make heads or tails of that, either. And we—"

She shushed him, then kissed him again.

"You need to rest. Come on," she said, rising from the sofa and helping him to his feet. She led him to her bedroom and pulled the blinds. Lying beside him, he rested her head on his chest. Violet and lavender. An oatmeal cookie in a riot.

As he began to drift into sleep, he whispered into her ear, "I fell in love with you a long time ago."

She pecked his neck. "A whole heap of trouble."

*　　*　　*

He woke. The alarm clock on the bedside table read 11:59 p.m.

He was alone.

December 13th

Mia stared up at him, face yellowed and faded, a solemn blank expression hiding just behind her upturned cheeks and smiling lips. Maddox brought the photograph closer to his straining eyes. In her late twenties, she'd reminded him of Sheila Guyse, the beautiful black actress from *Miracle in Harlem*. Sometimes he'd quote lines from the film and wait for a reaction. Hands on hips, she'd ask him, "What're you all about right now?"

I dunno. I have no idea what I'm about anymore.

A tear fell from his eyelash onto the photograph, magnifying Mia's face for a split second before racing down the surface of the slick paper. The Newark Paramount Theater screened *Miracle in Harlem* in the early '70s as part of a "black cinema" retrospective. He stared at the marquee for a long moment. He wanted to take her to see it. But he was married, and she was black, and the world was much simpler back then, so he never asked.

The image on the photograph: three cops and a meter maid crammed tight on the bronze bench beside the statue of Abe Lincoln; the ever-present paper coffee cup in Stan's hand; Darcy caught mid-laugh, head cocked back. And between them, Mia and Maddox, smiling politely, too politely, as if they had something to hide.

The image faded.

"Goodbye," he whispered for the eleventh time.

The photograph was blank.

Maddox glanced at the ten blank sheets of glossy paper spread out on Mia's couch. They'd been pictures of picnics, social dances, and nights out. Once-treasured moments of a life. Now gone.

A thought cut through the noise of his grief. Mia hadn't vanished from the photo; the entire image–the courtyard, the bench, everything–was gone. His mind raced. He could remember the photograph but not the event it commemorated. Had Stan, Darcy, Mia and he sat together outside the Essex County Courthouse? When?

Nothing. His mind was as blank as the paper in his hand.

It isn't just erasing people; it's taking our memories of them. The idea stole away his breath. How powerful was Kloum? What *couldn't* such a creature control? Then, on top of that thought, a more urgent one: *Don't you forget her.*

He sprang to his feet and rushed to Mia's kitchen. He swiped her grocery list pad off the counter and scrambled for a pen.

Vegetable oil

Bath tissue

Sugar

Window cleaner

Maddox searched the countertop but came up empty. He slid open a utensil drawer, revealing a jumble of cheap silverware, old birthday candles, and a single steak knife–but no pen.

He glanced at the pad.

Vegetable oil

Bath tissue

Sugar

He searched the overhead cabinets. Pots and pans. No pen.

Exasperated, Maddox snatched up the pad and hurried back into the living room. Nothing on the end tables that bookended the couch. The coffee table. The television cart. No pen. No pencil.

Vegetable oil

Bath tissue

Christ. Where'd she drop her purse? Surely he'd find something there. He scanned the room. Nothing. Tossing open the closet door, he patted down the three coats he found inside–palms of his hands, not fingers, like working down a perp. Nothing in the pockets.

Vegetable oil.

Fuck. Abandoning the closet with its door wide open, he hurried into the bedroom. Mia's purse waited on the bedside table. Snatching it up, he emptied its contents onto the bed's rumpled comforter and ran his free hand through the pile. Lipstick. Eyeliner. Nail clippers. Receipts. Bottle opener. A compact.

The grocery list was empty.

A bingo blotter. Debit card. Dental floss. Keys. A folded twenty-dollar bill. Reading glasses. A hair tie. Cell phone. Bundle of coupons bound by a rubber band. Yellow crayon—

Yellow crayon.

His hand shook as he lifted it. Putting it to the paper, he wrote MIA ELIZABETH CRESSWATER. The letters came out crooked and shaky, the barely legible scribblings of a child just learning to scratch out letters.

I won't forget you, he promised.

He stared at her name, reading it over and over as if memorizing a long string of numbers, until the tremors in his hand subsided. Breathing out, Maddox emptied his hands and turned his attention to the bed. He picked up the cell phone and touched its screen.

TO ACTIVATE

DIAL *1010

He dropped the phone.

The receipt slips were empty. The debit card had no embossed numbers, no expiration date, no name. The printing on the receipts faded away.

Heat rushed to his face. Waking in Mia's bed without her beside him, he'd known she'd been taken. That hurt, as bad as anything, but this... *violation*... was worse. *Can't you leave something of her, dammit? Some small thing for me to hold?*

Maddox took a small step towards the bedroom doorway. His knees wobbled. His stomach turned. He bent over and vomited onto the floor. Retching, he lost his balance and dropped down to the floor, one knee and one palm keeping him from falling into the mess. He stayed that way, shaking as if naked in a snowstorm.

When he did rise, the furniture was gone. No coats in the closet. Even the walls had retreated to unpainted drywall. All that remained was Maddox.

And the yellow crayon.

*   *   *

At midday, thickening columns of cumulonimbus clouds towered over the Essex County Courthouse, casting the four-story rotunda into shadow. The normal bustle of a Friday afternoon on High Street was just beginning to die down. The morning riptide of black-tie lawyers and their shuffling clients subsided to a lazy stream's trickle. From his vantage point on the bronze bench, the day looked like Maddox felt: weary to the point of exhaustion.

Abe Lincoln sat next to him and invited any who passed to sit beside him,

125

one hand on the bench as a welcoming gesture. The statue hadn't seemed to age since Stan, Darcy, Mia, and Maddox last took up his invitation. Everything else had changed, Maddox knew, and not for the better.

He closed the zipper of his coat, bringing the neck up to his mouth, and tasted aluminum against his lips. In '79 he'd gotten sucker-punched by a young kid wearing a knockoff Super Bowl ring trying to escape a snatch-and-run robbery. The hit busted his lip and cracked a tooth, but the pain faded from his memory quickly. The taste of metal did not.

Trigger memory. A sensation that evoked a moment.

"Y'okay?"

Maddox cocked his head towards the voice. A young cop, still starching and ironing his uniform daily, stood at Lincoln's eleven. He sized the man up: probably college ball; microbrew beer at a chain restaurant; registered Democrat. He doubted he'd ever taken a punch. "Had better days. Not recently."

"Look... outta it," the cop said. "Sure you're okay?"

Maddox choked back a dark laugh. "Didn't say I was."

The cop's brow lowered. "Something I can do for you?"

"Yeah," Maddox said, rooting through his pocket. He withdrew the shopping list pad and held it out. "Read the name on this."

Confusion spread across the cop's face.

"Just read it, aloud," Maddox said. "I need to know if you can read the handwriting."

"Some kinda joke?" The cop handed the pad back. "I think you need to let me call someone for you. Come out and pick you up. This game you're playing, very dangerous. Some other cop, they might..."

"What's the name on the paper?"

"You know there's no name, you know what it says."

Maddox glanced down. "Mia Elizabeth Cress—"

"*Sir*," the cop said in a sharp, loud bark. "Either you tell me who to call, or you move along, but I'm not going to stand here and—"

Maddox blinked. MIA ELIZABETH CRESSWATER was no longer written on the shopping list pad. Instead, in his own hand, were the words SUICIDE BY COP.

"You win," he muttered as he pocketed the pad.

The young cop took a step back and gave Maddox room to stand. His face took on the glow of an arrogant child who believed he'd won an argument with his parents.

"I wasn't talking to *you*," Maddox clarified.

The cop reversed his step, bringing the two men chest-to-chest. A whiff of department-store cologne and body odor trickled up to Maddox's nostrils. He knew the smell: the cop's shift was a few ticks of the clock over Too Long O'clock. The scent of his breath confirmed it: coffee breath, pastrami, oil and vinegar. Bad diet, worse hours. "I'm trying to give you a break, crazy old man. You don't need to give me attitude."

"You're right," Maddox said. "Long day."

The cop seemed to accept that. "Okay, then."

Maddox waited for the young man to step away again, but when it didn't happen, he turned. As he did, he felt a tug on the waistband of his pants. Before he could react, the gun he'd taken from Fuck Kinda Question dropped from his coat and landed on the concrete.

The cop's eyes went wide. His hand went to his hip.

"Wait," Maddox said, hands up.

With one hand, the cop pushed Maddox's chest. He stumbled back until his legs hit the bench. Knees buckling, he fell back into a seated position, one hand gripping Lincoln's arm. "I didn't–"

The cop drew his Sig P229R, took a firing stance, and centered his aim at Maddox's chest. The gun was dark, stout, and ugly, a far cry from the Smith and Weston Model 10 revolver Maddox had carried for most of his career. But no less intimidating. "*HANDS ON YOUR HEAD–*"

Maddox complied. "Hey, fella, you don't–"

"DOn't TALK."

Hands on his sides, palms not fingers, patting him down.

"You got anything else on you?"

Maddox shook his head.

The cop tilted his head towards the gun on the concrete. "You got a permit to carry? Is it licensed?"

Maddox considered his answers. "Me, yes. The gun, no."

The young cop's eyes glistened with intensity. He nudged the gun with the heel of his shoe, then again retreated a step. "I'm gonna reach down for the piece. You're not gonna move. Understand me?"

"Copy," Maddox said.

The cop knelt, never taking his eyes off of Maddox.

"Newark PD, retired," Maddox said.

"Yeah, and?" The cop pocketed the gun.

He shrugged. "For what it's worth."

The cop toggled his lapel radio mic. It let out a short gasp of static. Some things never changed. "I've gotta 5-4-4 at 4-7-0 High Street."

Suspicious person with weapon.

"Y'should lead with your badge number," Maddox said.

The young cop's eyes softened. A gentle smile followed. He holstered his weapon. His stance softened. His cheeks blushed. He looked baffled and embarrassed. "I'm sorry."

"Sorry?" Maddox said in a soft, careful tone.

"I..." the young cop said, bringing a hand up to the side of his head. "Must be tired. Sorry. I just... don't know what I'm doing right now. I had... my gun..."

Maddox waited a moment before standing up.

Kloum. Messing with me. With him. Sending a message.

"It's fine, it's okay," Maddox said.

"No," the cop said, shaking his head. "It's..."

His radio cackled. A distorted male voice asked, "Backup required?"

"No. Situation... is resolved."

It wanted the gun, Maddox thought. He wondered what the young cop would think when he found it in his pocket later. Then again, Kloum was capable of placing any story it wanted in the cop's head, the same way it filled in the gaps when it made someone disappear.

Maddox pulled out the grocery list pad and held it out for the cop to see. "Can you read this?"

The cop nodded. Even deeper confusion set into his expression.

"What's it say?"

"Strangest damned thing, don't remember what it said before, but I could swear it wasn't *that*," the cop said. "It says, happy birthday, but with an E in the middle of birthday."

Maddox nodded. "Of course it does."

December 14th

A creature of habit, Maddox made a point of parking in the final spot of the first row, under a robust oak tree at the edge of Hop's property. In the thirty-some years he'd breakfasted at the diner, he could count the number of times he'd parked elsewhere on a single hand. Today, however, a pair of orange traffic cones occupied the space instead. A yellow X had been spray painted on the asphalt.

Grumbling, he parked in the next-to-last spot.

Hop's bustled, as always, with a collection of office workers, retirees, and housewives. Two cops sat at the counter, laughing too loud, obviously blowing off steam after an overnight shift. Maddox glanced up at the pie case behind the cash register. Must have been a good night; only lemon meringue and pecan remained.

Two overweight women, both wearing pajama bottoms and T-shirts, attacked a leaning tower of pancakes. They were sitting in his booth. *That kind of day*, he thought as he slid into the booth next to them. *Then again, how long has it been since it hasn't been* that *kind of day?*

"She was like, nuh-huh, not gonna do *that*," one of the women said, causing the other to snort. She followed the reaction up with a trumpet blast of her own, culminating in, "You know, right?"

"Definitely, baby, definitely."

Maddox rolled his eyes.

Was this booth larger than his usual? It felt like it. He stared across the table at the empty bench. With Stan's wide shoulders on the left and Darcy's girth in the middle and on the right, he usually didn't see much of the red vinyl backrest. He felt a tickle in the corner of his eye but couldn't bring himself to peek over to the empty seat beside him.

"Just you this morning, honey?"

"'Fraid so, Janey," he said, and turned to face a twenty-year-old girl with dark eyeliner and a shock of bright blue running through her ruffled black hair. Shirt open to the second button, tattooed letters rose up from her meager cleavage. *COND TO N.*

Maddox thought of Troy Turring and his game show. With a grin, he thought, *SECOND TO NONE.* No need to buy a vowel. He turned his gaze from the waitress to the counter, then to the dining floor. "Janey off today? Don't recall her ever taking off a Saturday morning."

She tapped her name badge with the eraser-end of a pencil. REBECCAH. Smiling, she said, "Sorry, I dunno any Janey. I've only been working here since June, though, so maybe she was before my time?"

"No," Maddox said, aware that his voice took a stern, authoritarian tone. "Janey's been serving joe here since '82 and she was here just the other day."

Rebeccah kept her smile, but her eyes narrowed, a bad poker tell. Had to give her credit where due; she kept her annoyance in check. "Well, I guess I've always just missed her. Probably schedule us opposite. Don't wanna put all your A-list talent on at the same time, I guess."

"Yeah," Maddox said, softening his tone. "I guess so, too."

She winked. "So what can I getcha?"

My parking spot and my booth, for starters, he thought.

"Cup of black, waffle with whipped cream."

"Gotcha," Rebeccah said, scribbling on her pad. As she turned to leave, he caught sight of her wrist. Over a bird's nest of scars, another tattoo read 2ND. The other wrist read *NONE.* "I'll get your order in and be right back with your coffee."

"Thanks."

Troy Turring. Why did he remember the old man and his game shows? Or Hadassah Boutros or Fuck Kinda Question? If Kloum erased them–truly uprooted all evidence they'd ever existed–then why could he still bring up memories of them? Was he the only one? Some kind of aberration? An oversight? Or was there a reason? Did Kloum want him to remember even as everyone else believed that he was losing his memory to the disease?

Too many questions before breakfast.

Except, where was Janey?

"...don't wanna ever get like that..." one of the fat women in Maddox's regular booth said. The other, mouth still full of pancake, mumbled in agreement. One of the garbled words that came out of her mouth sounded like it might have been *senile*.

Rebeccah returned with the promised coffee. Bitter.

She didn't leave. Instead, she put a hand on her hip and stared at Maddox with a baffled expression. She started to speak twice, unsuccessfully, before stammering out, "You said, *Janey*, right? That was the name."

"I did," Maddox said. "But look, it's no big—"

"Crazy," she said. For a moment Maddox thought she meant him, but then she said, "I go back to the kitchen to put your ticket on the spinner, and there's yesterday's mail sitting on the prep table. I'm nosy, so I rifle through it, just, you know, to see."

Maddox nodded.

Rebeccah pulled an envelope out of her apron. "Your name?" "Ma ddox," he told her.

She slid the envelope across the table. "*Crazy.*"

The letter was addressed to him, care of Hop's. The return address was also the diner, headed off with the name JANEY ANN BROSTWILL. He flipped it over. A happy face with XX OO for eyes, the same as she always drew on the back of her checks. Hugs and kisses.

"Your waffle should be right out," Rebeccah said, her expression still locked in disbelief. "Just flag me down if there's anything else you need in the meantime."

"I will," he promised.

She waited a moment longer, eyes flickering down to the envelope, before retreating back to the counter.

Maddox slid a thumbnail under the envelope's lip and slit it open. Emptying its contents onto the table, his eyes widened. The first was an order check. In Janey's flirty script, she'd written *This must have slipped out of your folder. Put it in the mail because things get lost around here. XX OO J.*

The second item was a photograph he'd taken from Stan's home office. As he stared down at the photograph, a knot formed in his gut and twisted tighter. He'd been too disturbed to find a photograph of himself among Stan's inventory of evidence to notice the details. *Impossible*, he thought, and then chided himself. What constituted *impossible* anymore?

The photo featured Maddox from the chest up, standing and scowling. In the background and out of focus, he could make out the unmistakable white peak of the Essex County Courthouse. He recognized the shirt he wore. Just over Maddox's right shoulder, a familiar young police officer approached from behind. The photograph had to have been taken *yesterday*, but he'd pulled it off a wall in his dead partner's house *ten days ago*.

"...see that movie, and I said to her, 'No, I ain't saw it ever...'"

Rebeccah returned with the waffle. Maddox thanked her. Before she could leave again, he held up a finger. "Y'know, you can help me out with something. I can't read the handwriting on this note. Forgot my glasses at home. Could you spare just a moment?"

She nodded. "Of course"

He handed her the note. She frowned.

"What's t'matter?"

"No," she said and waved a hand dismissively even as tears bubbled up in her eyes "It's just... the handwriting, it reminds me of my mom's. The way it looks."

Maddox sensed tragedy and sorrow in Rebeccah's voice. Such a young girl, so much loss hidden just under the surface of her skin. As she read the note silently her composure failed. Tears flowed down without restraint, drawing eyeliner trails down her face. "I'm sorry... it's just... more crazy... it's so much like Mom... God..."

"What's it say?" he asked her.

She reached down for his napkin, wiped her face, and sobbed. "Okay, okay, okay... sorry... it's just a coincidence... has to be... but... holy shit, what a fucking coincidence..."

He waited for her breathing to become more regular.

"It says, *I'm gone but still with you. Always. You'll always be my second to none.*"

*   *   *

The storefronts along Bloomfield Ave beckoned shoppers inside with plastic snowmen and mannequins dressed as Santas and elves. A brisk wind rushed down the avenue, tugging at the hems of heavy coats and fur-lined hats. Maddox walked among the shoppers, paying no attention to the couples holding hands and bundled-up children dancing around their parents' feet. He knew they were there, like every year, celebrants of a holiday that no longer had much to do with virgin births, wise men, or guiding stars. His cynicism began long before his diagnosis. Any cop knew violent crimes increased as the season progressed. He'd spent more than his share of Christmas Eves waiting for the coroner's van to cart away the latest fatalities of the Holy Day.

Without fail, loneliness bred catastrophe.

Maddox couldn't remember most of his family's Christmas trees. Carols and strings of lights on pine branches simply couldn't compete with screaming sirens and the glare of red and blue emergency lights. He wondered if it were different for others, if those moments of getting drunk on eggnog and opening department-store tie boxes still resonated. Maybe it was just him.

The city answered. In the distance, a lonely, shrill police siren sang. He tried to tell himself that someone somewhere would be saved tonight, but he didn't believe it.

He *did* remember shopping with Steven one season. At eight, his son had just discovered shopping. Before that, stores held no interest for him and he'd beg to go back home and play. But that year his mind changed and he became fascinated with the concepts of buying and selling. Steven's mother facilitated the shift in philosophy one afternoon by allowing the boy to pay for groceries at the cash register. Maddox's wife had been a serial enabler.

He'd taken Steven to Bringley's department store on Bloomfield to buy a trinket for his English teacher as a gesture of appreciation. Steven struggled with spelling and grammar more than any kid Maddox had seen, but the teacher stuck it out even when Steven gave up. The C+ on his report card was a kind of miracle.

They settled on a glass ornament, a red ball with a large ornate snowflake painted on its face. Nothing fancy, but a perfectly serviceable thank-you, especially on a cop's salary. When they arrived at the counter, Steven grew uncharacteristically shy and hid behind Maddox's leg.

"What's wrong?" he asked his son.

Steven shook his head.

"C'mon, big man, hand him the money."

The cashier, an older man with a bald head and round ears, blushed slightly and held out his hand. When Steven made no attempt to take the money from his father and hand it over, he cocked his head to one side and said, "No big deal. Sometimes kids get bashful. I was a kid like that."

A kid *like that.* Even in the moment, the way the cashier pronounced those words was unsettling. A week later, two days before the holiday, Maddox knew why. The cashier was one of the men that fled the grimy apartment where Melissa Shelton was victimized, where Maddox had picked up a golf club and–

"'Scuse me, buddy," a homeless man wearing a threadbare flannel said as he approached from an alley between stores. Unshaved and caked with dirt, he wheezed as he spoke, each word trailing off into a short whistle. "Trying to get some coin together, get some coffee in me. Help out?"

Maddox eyed him with suspicion. "No booze?"

"No, man, promise not. Coffee."

"All right," Maddox said with a little huff. He reached into his trouser pocket and pulled out his wallet. "I don't got any change, but I'll give you a buck. Just–"

The homeless man's hand darted out like a snapping turtle's maw and snatched the wallet out of his hand. He took off down the alley.

Maddox didn't think; he ran after the man. Wheezing after the first few strides, he shambled over broken glass and cracked asphalt until the shadow of the store beside him blocked his path. He skidded to a halt. The darkness that extended beyond an overflowing dumpster drowned out all light. Pitch black.

Stupid, Maddox thought. *Seventy-seven years dumb.*

"You coming to get me, old man?" a voice said.

His heart pounded. He expected the familiar pain and panic to rise up inside him–*not a heart attack*, not a stroke–but instead, a strange calm took hold. He balled his hands into fists. "Y'just come out and hand over my wallet."

The reply was a volley of hoarse laughter, as dry as sandpaper. And beneath that, another sound–a rolling, guttural drone in an even lower register. A growl.

Maddox glanced back towards Bloomfield Ave.

A taxi cab passed. Donation bells rang faintly.

The laughter stopped. The growling did not.

A spark flashed in the darkness, transforming into a tiny blue flame, then a floating orange orb. The glow of the cigarette illuminated the faint outline of the homeless man's face. He took a long drag, then exhaled the smoke through his nostrils, evoking the image of a Chinese dragon. "You coming for it, ol' man?"

Maddox took a step towards the shadow.

"Ol' man got big ol' balls," the homeless man said. His face disappeared as he lowered his hand to his hip, revealing the man's tattered trousers. And a quivering shape beside him.

Maddox squinted. "What's that you got?"

The growl intensified.

A pair of eyes reflected the cigarette's glowing tip. At first Maddox thought he saw horns rising from a broad head, but then recognized them as a pair of tall canine ears.

Maddox stepped back, twice.

"You going?" the homeless man asked. "Hot date?"

Maddox's hand dropped to his side. No holster, no gun. He felt heavy and slow and old and defenseless. Thirty years ago he might have had a chance fighting off a dog with his bare hands. Those days were well in the rear-view mirror. *This isn't ending well.*

"Yeah, I'm going," Maddox said, mumbling.

His wallet landed, open, at his feet. He froze. He stared down at his driver's license. The photo showed a man nearly four years younger and still full of life.

The homeless man said, "Let's see what you got. Dog's named Buddy Boy, 'cause he's my buddy. We don't got much but each other. I make sure he eats, even times when I don't got nothing for myself. He knows it, too. Loyal. So, if I tell him to rip your fuckin' faceskin off and shit on your skull, he ain't gonna waste a second doing it. You want your shit? Reach on down for it. And I'll have Buddy Boy sink his teeth gum-deep into your eyes. Or you walk away and the wallet's no longer yours. It's mine. You understand?"

Maddox's fingers twitched. The wallet itself was nothing special, nothing more than a strip of tailored leather bought from a department store. He'd never been one to carry photos. Twenty-seven dollars in the fold. But that photo ID. It tugged at him. The card changed over the years, of course, but he'd never *not* had identification.

Too slow. The dog'll be on me in seconds. Knees won't even straighten up by the time it's got its teeth in me. He'd been bit before, but not in decades. A young man would recover. Not him.

Maddox took a large stride backwards. His heart sank.

"Good choice, ol' man."

Buddy Boy stopped growling.

Maddox turned and hurried out of the alley. Cold wind struck him as he reached Bloomfield Ave, rustling his silver hair and pattering against his coat. His eyes watered, blurring the Christmas lights and bright shop windows into a splash of abstract shapes and watercolor smears. Backing up to a brick wall, he cried.

Maddox's pocket felt unnaturally empty. All of him did.

December 15th

Staring out from the screen door, Maddox watched as his neighbors shoveled out from the overnight snowstorm. Thirteen inches of powder reduced the street to a narrow gulley bordered by waist-high retaining walls. The yellow and orange Essex county plow trucks had buried cars and sidewalks, opening the road while closing off the means to escape. The sound of shovels scraping asphalt mixed with the noise of human labor–grunts, barked swears, and a chorus of panting. Clouds of white vapor rose from mouths and nostrils.

Over the rooftops, black smoke rolled through the sky, moving like a serpent. The local news was reporting a tenement fire in the Ironbound. Maddox thought of the first responders: men in uniforms, some with ventilators, others with caution tape. Accidents were sometimes worse than crime scenes. He'd been able to promise grieving parents that he'd help find a suspect. But what could anyone say once the flames subside and the bodies are counted? The expressions on the survivors' faces were worse, too. The parent of a kid killed by a stray bullet projected overwhelming anguish and anger, but when the child died because of bad wiring their faces went ghostly blank.

Maddox retreated back inside and closed the door behind him. He had a few hours before the neighbors would have the sidewalks clear. After seventy decades of digging out after snowstorms, it was someone else's turn. His stomach growled.

The milk in the refrigerator smelled like cat piss. He emptied it into the sink and then tossed the plastic container into the recycling bin. Back when milk cartons were paper, they used to print black-and-white photos of missing children on one side. He imagined a distraught mother standing over a garbage pail, unable to decide whether to toss away her child's picture. Or... what? Keep it for posterity?

The refrigerator shelves were nearly empty. Normally, Steven kept it well stocked, albeit mostly with health food that Maddox wouldn't touch. What remained teetered on the edge of the expiration dates on their labels: a few slices of yellow American cheese, a couple ounces of orange juice, an upside-down bottle of Russian dressing. The freezer had ice.

Where *was* Steven?

A twinge of guilt tickled Maddox's conscience. *Food.* Was that what it took to trigger some kind of paternal instinct? Maddox closed the freezer door, rapped his fist against the handle, and thought, *Who the fuck are you? This is what you turned out to be?*

Sitting at the kitchen table, he reached for yesterday's mail. No bills anymore; they all came electronically to Steven's phone, to be paid–somehow–by pushing a few buttons.

A credit card offer. Sweepstakes. Coupon mailer. Car refinancing advertisement. Finally, a postcard. The photo on its face was a twelve-year-old black schoolgirl holding up a computer circuit board. The smile on her face suggested a cup of pride with a pinch of well-earned arrogance. Balloon letters over her head read *THE NATIONAL YOUNG INVENTORS SCIENCE FAIR.* In smaller lettering below here it stated *COMES TO THE EXHIBITION CENTER DECEMBER 26th – THOUSANDS OF PROJECT TABLES – $600,000 IN PRIZE SCHOLARSHIPS – JOIN TOMORROW's LEADERS IN ENGINEERING, COMPUTER SCIENCE, AND MEDICINE.*

Medicine, Maddox thought. *Work fast, kids. I'm counting on you.*

The next pang of hunger got him back on his feet. He rummaged through the disorganized cabinets over the sink until he found a stack of canned goods. He settled on a can of tuna fish. Standing at the counter, he microwaved a cup of instant coffee, lifted a spoon out of the sink, and ate from the can. *Breakfast... Christ.*

During his days on the force, meals had always been a fluid concept. If he worked overnight rotation, breakfast meant the meal after he woke, often at two in the afternoon. That was how the Hop's tradition started; diners served pancakes and sausage links around the clock. They could also always be counted on to grill up a cheeseburger at six in the morning. Eating meals at home was a rarity, then and now. He was certain that Janey knew more about his tastes than his son. *Knew*, he reminded himself, in the past tense.

"Hold the mayo," he said to himself before finishing off the last spoonful of tuna. He and Janey had a joke about mayonnaise and the Mayo Clinic. Sometimes he owned the punchline and sometimes it was hers. It was part of a ritual, no different than spitting out *gesundheit* after a sneeze. He doubted he'd ever speak the joke again.

He felt tears tug at his eyes.

Asshole. Can't bring yourself to feel anything for your own son, but you get all weepy about a waitress who probably only cared about you because you left a 20 percent tip? Forget the kids at the expo center—there's no cure for what you've got, old man.

The phone rang. The sudden blast of sound startled Maddox and his hand jerked reflexively. The empty can of tuna fish hit the far wall, then the floor. It spun before coming to a rest on the linoleum tile. Maddox answered the phone. "Hello."

"Mads?" It was Darcy.

"Hey," Maddox said.

"Yeah, hey." Darcy's voice had a tentative quality to it, as if every word, meaningful or not, was chosen with care. "I don't know if you'll think—"

"Listen, Darce. You've known me for forever, right? You know I'm not a tactful man. Sometimes shit comes outta my mouth; I dunno where it comes from, not really. But then I regret it, because I know it hurts people," Maddox said. "So, y'know."

"I do know," Darcy said, "mostly that you're shit at apologies."

"True."

Darcy's voice crackled. "I forgive you, again. And next time, too. But Mads, I don't wanna talk about any of that. I called, 'cause... I don't want you to think that I got my brains spilling out of my skull, but here's the thing: I think you should come over. Now."

"There's snow. The roads aren't clear," Maddox said.

Darcy laughed, but it sounded more frightened than amused. "Truth is, I need you to come over. There's a knock on my door. I open it, and you'd never guess who's standing there looking back at me. I mean, you'd *never* guess... Mads, I swear that I'm serious here... *but Stan's been sitting at my dining room table for the last twenty minutes.*"

The muscles in Maddox's chest tightened. "What's he doing?"

"Nothing," Darcy said. "Just sitting there, staring."

"Staring," Maddox repeated under his breath.

Darcy's voice lowered almost to a whisper. "Just watching me. You remember the calls we'd get, stray dogs in residential neighborhoods? That look in their eyes? When the animal knows he's where he doesn't belong? That's what it is."

"I'm coming over." Maddox ended the call.

Maddox's eyes refocused on the glass window on the microwave oven. His face was reflected there in a ghostly translucent image. He recognized the expression immediately: the father of a child who died in a meaningless fire.

He was out of the house before he slid the first button through its hole on his coat. Locking the door behind him, he pocketed the keys. The snowplow had been through once again. A four-foot-high wall of packed snow stood between his car and the street.

A junior high-aged boy wearing a snowsuit and knit cap called up to him from across the street. A long tendril of white vapor came out with his words. "You want to get shoveled out?"

"What'll it cost?" Maddox asked.

"Twenty-five," the kid answered. He stabbed his round-point shovel into the snowbank beside him and reached for a second handle protruding from the mound. He pulled a golf putter free and swung it down onto a patch of ice at his feet. The ice shattered.

Maddox glanced towards the intersection. "You get it done in five minutes?"

"Hell no," the boy answered as he replaced the golf club with the shovel and scooped up the shards of ice. "Not for twenty-five. Got other customers lined up. Fifty gets you front of line."

Maddox shook his head. "It'll melt."

He headed to the intersection, crossed the road, and continued on. The wind rushed in like high tide and struck the barricades of snow lining the street with enough force to draw up a fine mist. The air felt wet against his skin and tasted metallic against his lips. Each inhalation set off an uncomfortable jangle of pins and needles in his lungs. He squinted and kept moving, navigating down a thin clearing on the sidewalks, careful of the icy spots. Breaking his neck in a fall wouldn't help Darcy. But Maddox hurried just the same.

Two bundled figures stood at the bus stop. From a distance, he couldn't tell if they were men or women. As he stepped up beside them to wait, that didn't change. Their beige winter jackets, scarves, and caps hid all but their eyes. He supposed he could have stared and been able to tell, but looking into the eyes of strangers had never been his favorite pastime. Sometimes he saw more than he bargained for. Victims and victimizers: both were painful to recognize.

Facing forward, he stood there motionless and shivered until the white public transit bus pulled up. The door opened and a torrent of warmth billowed out, drafting a haze in the air. The two waiting passengers boarded. Once they were clear, Maddox followed. He paid the fare, nodded to the middle-aged Rastafarian behind the wheel, and took a window seat in the front row.

Hip hop blared out from a cell phone's speaker from one of the passengers in the rear of the bus. He caught only a few spare words here and there; he wished that he heard less. But inside the shouts and electronic beats, he thought he heard something else: a snippet of an acapella voice played on a loop. He sighed. "You'll Never Know" by Dick Haymes. *Of course.*

A layer of condensation on the window blurred his vision to the white world scrolling outside. He reached up to wipe it away, then stopped, and instead wrote *MIA* with his index finger. The letters held for only a moment before dripping away into a meaningless blotch. He wiped the rest of the window clear. The snow brought a rare calm to the streets. He knew that in another hour, after the car owners were done digging out their rides, the peace would give way to the normal city bustle. Nature couldn't hold back mankind for long.

The houses, shops, and traffic lights on Bellmont and the northern tip of Lincoln Park were dark. Maddox remembered the aftermath of Hurricane Sandy—a ghost of a city lit only so long as the sun was in the sky. Since then, a new 655-megawatt gas plant had been built on the shore of the Passaic River. *Didn't matter*, Maddox knew, *lines down and transformers blown. Can have all the juice in the world, but if it's not hitting the lamps, we're all in the dark.*

Maddox rested his temple flat against the window and closed his eyes. So *tired.* Not lacking rest, tired. A lifetime of tense moments and stressful situations weighed on his body and mind. He'd never run from danger, but that confidence took its toll: bouts of insomnia; osteoarthritis; hearing loss; restless leg syndrome. He hoped he'd accomplished enough good over the decades to balance the books because he felt the cost every day.

The bus pulled up to his stop with a lurch and a squeal. The driver glanced at Maddox with bloodshot eyes as he passed. He stepped down onto the snowy curb. A mist of fine snow greeted him on the sidewalk, kicked up by crosswinds. He slid his hands into his coat pockets and walked the three blocks to Darcy's house.

He knocked on the door but didn't wait, instead trying the handle. It turned. He took a tentative step inside and called out, "Darce?"

"In here." Darcy's voice came from the kitchen.

With the power out, the kitchen was lit by two candles, one on the counter and the other on the table. The flickering orange glow kept everything it illuminated in constant motion; shadows reached and contracted with a slow, steady rhythm. Darcy stood by the refrigerator with his arms crossed. His flushed cheeks and wet eyes told the story of a man who had freefallen through a wide range of emotions in a very short time. He nodded towards the table. Stan sat at the far end, his face half-lit by candlelight.

"Thank you," Darcy said, "for com—"

"Shuddup," Maddox said. He waved a hand. "You never need to thank me for anything. Never."

Darcy nodded. "Didn't know what to do. Still don't."

Maddox stepped up to the table and placed both hands on the nearest chair's backrest. He looked into Stan's glazed eyes. Without any motion, or even a dilation of a pupil, Maddox felt a snap as the stare was returned. "Good morning, Mads."

"You want me to call you *Kloum*?" he asked. Darcy shuffled behind him. "Because you need to know goddamned well that I won't call you *Stan*."

Stan's expression didn't change, but Maddox heard a smile on his lips when he spoke. "That's fair."

"Why're you here?"

"I'm not," Kloum said.

Maddox asked, "If not here, then where are you?"

"I'm in you." Kloum pointed Stan's finger to his temple and tapped. "In here. And in Darcy, too. I think you understand that much by now."

Darcy paced from the refrigerator to the doorway, then back.

"Did you kill Stan?" Maddox asked.

Kloum leaned into the light. The wrinkle lines and uneven skin tone receded from Stan's face, restoring his features to the condition of a man in his thirties.

Darcy closed his eyes and turned away. "Oh, Jesus."

"Do you remember him?" Kloum asked.

"Yes," Maddox said.

Kloum smiled. As his lips curled upward, the folds and spots returned to Stan's face, bringing him back to his seventies. Kloum reclined, once again retreating into half-light. "Then it should be obvious. I don't kill. Ever."

"What about Mia?" he asked.

"Mia?" Darcy asked. "Who're you talking about, Mads?"

That hurt. As hopeless as he knew it to be, he wanted to explain; wanted to share his memories of their friend; wanted for Darcy to remember. Instead, Maddox ignored him, bit down on his bottom lip, and waited for an answer.

"You pique my interest," Kloum said. His voice fluctuated from precise youth to slurry old age. "She should be gone from you, but she isn't."

Maddox asked, "What did you do to her? To any of them?"

Kloum tilted his head back and opened his mouth. A wisp of white smoke escaped and snaked its way to the ceiling. "I dreamed them away."

"Then dream her back," Maddox said, voice crackling like static.

Kloum leaned back into the light. His features rearranged in the orange glow. Cheekbones rose. Lips filled out. Pigment darkened. Just as Mia's face took form, it disappeared. Stan returned. "What would you give me in exchange for her?"

Maddox felt a chill shoot through his veins like a bolt of electricity. He wasn't sure if it was excitement or fear—but whichever, it was pure. In the candlelight he found it impossible to discern the color of Kloum's eyes, but they seemed darker than Stan's baby blues. Decades of reading intentions in suspects' pupils didn't help now. Was Kloum only toying with him? No way to know. "What'd you want?"

He followed Kloum's stare to Darcy, then to a set of steak knives on the kitchen counter. "Would you trade?"

A second bolt of electricity surged through Maddox's system, but this time without ambiguity. Fear. Not that the monster across the table would ask him to sacrifice one friend for another, but because he found himself considering it. Maybe only for a moment, but it was a long moment. "No."

Kloum's eyes returned to meet Maddox's stare. "Then I'll just take him anyway. Tonight. I'll give you the rest of the day to say goodbye. You'll need it. Tomorrow will be... difficult for you."

"What'd you mean?" Maddox said.

"He won't remember that I was here."

An intense burst of light announced the return of power to Darcy's home. Maddox shielded his eyes with a hand as bulbs flashed bright white. The afterglow receded and Stan was gone.

"Whoa, buddy." Darcy voice came from behind him. "Hope that didn't blow any fuses. When the juice finally came back after Sandy, had to replace that whole box. You remember?"

"One of the very few things I do," Maddox said softly. His heartbeat quickened and he went lightheaded. Darcy was the last of his friends he had left. He glanced up at the digital clock on the stove. How much time did he have left with Darcy? His stomach turned.

Darcy came around and sat opposite him across the table. The confusion and fright was gone, replaced by his usual dour yet content expression. "Glad you came over. Been a long time since we didn't talk like that. It ain't worth staying angry anymore. We're too old."

He studied Darcy's face and tried to memorize every detail he could, from the variations of gray in his hair to the prominent pores on his cheeks; the thickness of his eyelashes; the slight split on his bottom lip; the inch of skin between his eyebrows; the deep wrinkle lines that crossed his forehead like wave ripples. He wanted to remember everything he could. *Needed to.*

"You okay?" Darcy asked. "Jesus, I don't mean... You look a little shaken."

No, I'm not okay, Darce. I'm already missing you.

Maddox nodded. "*Okay* is a word, doesn't mean much to me anymore. But yeah, sure, I'm okay. I'm just dying. You're the one that's been sick."

Darcy propped an elbow on the table and rested his head in his hand. "Just a cold. Thought it might be pneumonia or something, but no, just a persistent goddamned cold. Still tired from it. You ever think you got a bug shaken but then it pops back up and lets you know it's still got you?"

No, I'm not sure I can shake this bug.

146

"Like hemorrhoids?" Maddox said. The words came out staggered and awkward, as if he wasn't completely sure what they meant. The joke–and its expected ritual response–lifted a little of the weight off his chest. *A little.*

Darcy laughed. "No one likes hemorrhoids. You wanna play cards?"

"I do. More than you can imagine."

Darcy pointed to the far end of the counter. "In the jar."

"You keep playing cards in the cookie jar?" Maddox said as he stood up and crossed the room. Lifting the lid, he dug through coupon books, matchbooks, and dozens of knickknacks before uncovering a box of cards. "This thing's a damn junk drawer. You need all this shit?"

Darcy shrugged. "I clean it out, I'll put cookies in there."

"Go figure," Maddox said. He returned to the table, slid the cards out of the box, and separated the jokers. He shuffled the deck. "Wouldn't that be a hell of a way to use a cookie jar."

"Blair used to buy low-fat cookies for me from the health food store. Remember when those things were sprouting up everywhere? She used to go to the one in Lodi and buy these tasteless sugar-free chocolate chip cookies. I say tasteless to be charitable."

Maddox thought of Mia's homemade cookies and lost his focus. The shuffling cards escaped his fingers and sprayed out on the table. He swore under his breath as gathered them back up. "She was a good woman; she meant well."

"Yeah," Darcy said. His eyes lost a little of their glow. He opened his mouth to continue speaking, but then paused and curled his lips. When he did speak, the words came out in a slow, deliberate pace. "She had the biggest heart. She was a beauty, you know that, and I never was handsome. You were, but not me. She stayed with me even though she could have done better. That's why I forgave her for having an affair with you."

Maddox froze. "Darce, I–"

Darcy shook his head. "You have a good heart, too. Took a few days longer, but I forgave you, too. Never bothered telling either of you that I knew; didn't see the point. Used to think that I was just too afraid to lose both my wife and my best friend, but that isn't it. Truth is, I'm not even sure who I am without the two of you. I don't think I want to know."

The tears Maddox had suppressed moments earlier came. "I'm so sorry, man. It wasn't an affair; it was only once. Drinks–"

"You don't have to."

"But I should," Maddox said, pulling the last few cards into his hand and squaring them up in his palm. "I'd just lost Catherine and you'd just bought that godawful Chrysler–"

"She hated that car," Darcy said.

"Two of you fought. We didn't plan it. You were on nights, Stan and I were days. She went to Hop's after you went to bed, just for coffee cake and tea, or whatever. Stan had to rush home for some reason. Sad, angry, lonely; those feelings do things to people."

Darcy gestured to the deck. "Just deal–I already did."

They played the same game they had since the late '70s: five-card stud, two up and three down, loser dealing the next round. Nothing wild except for the bottle of Turkey in the liquor cabinet, as Stan used to say. Tuesdays had been card night for so long that Maddox had never seen an episode of *Happy Days* until it hit syndication. Even after retirement, the games stayed put, even though they could have played any time. At first there were eight players, but age and disease whittled them over the years. Now he and Darcy were the last ones left. Maddox glanced back up at the clock. Card night would be hands of solitaire from here on out.

Darcy won the first three hands.

It's only a game of chance if you don't cheat, Maddox remembered Mia saying when asked why she was the first one to leave each week. *And I don't wanna play any game where the winner is the one who doesn't get caught.*

But she came every week, always with baked goods. " 'You know, Mads," Darcy said as he peeked at his face-down cards. "You're the one with the disease; I just got a cold. So why don't you tell me why you're looking at me like *I'm* the one dying."

Maddox had a pair of sevens. He wanted to be honest with Darcy and explain. But that seemed impossible. "Just... got dealt a bad hand."

"That's true," Darcy said. After a moment, he added, "But you had a good run, right? For a while there, when the gang was all still here, we had it good, right? Had to get old, everyone does, and things've gone to shit, no doubt.

But you know what I remember? A lot of good times. Smiles. Laughs. Tears, the good kind. If we don't have much left, that's okay. I feel like we've been luckier than two sons-of-bitches like us deserve."

When the cards turned, Darcy held nothing. Pair of sevens won.

Maddox cocked a thumb towards the liquor cabinet. "You have a bottle up there?"

"Sure. Doubt you're going anywhere in this mess." The snow had started back up. The window next to the refrigerator was a blur of white motion.

Maddox retrieved the bottle and two shot glasses.

Darcy raised a hand. "You know I haven't—"

"Yeah." Maddox poured two fingers of bourbon into the glasses and slid one across the table. "But I'd say it's about time to slide backwards on eight or nine of those twelve steps. Consider it one of my final wishes."

They drank. And played a dozen more hands.

Tipsy, Maddox asked, "You remember Mia Cresswater?"

"Some girl? No, don't remember," Darcy said. "Why?"

Maddox turned over his cards. He had nothing. "Ran into her a while back. Black meter maid, used to work the coin-ops on Ferry Street down by the red bricks."

"Damn," Darcy said. "And they say *you're* losing your memory."

Maddox slid the cards back to Darcy. "*She* remembered *you.*"

"Yeah?" he said as he shuffled the cards. "If I saw her, maybe it would jog my memory, but I dunno. Been so long, she probably looks too different. I only recognize you because I've seen you every damn day since we retired."

Maddox said, "Not *every* damn day."

Darcy nodded. "Wish I had, man. Maybe I'll go down to Hayes Park one of these days. If she's still down in that area, maybe I'll see her soon."

"Maybe you will."

Darcy rapped the empty bottle with his knuckle. "Grab another?"

"Sure," Maddox said. He grabbed the empty, stood up, and turned. It loosed a short, elegant echo when he set it down on the counter, a sound that reminded him of a ringing bell being silenced. He reached for the liquor cabinet door.

"Mads?" Darcy called. "On second..."

Maddox glanced over his shoulder. Darcy was gone, along with the furniture and most of the paint on the far wall. Dust balls and cobwebs littered the empty floor. Maddox stood in an abandoned house.

The last man standing, he thought. But not for long. His knees buckled at the same moment that tears flowed down his face. He dropped to the floor and wept.

A panic attack came. He didn't fight it. He was grateful to lose consciousness.

December 16th

A steady stream of wind whistled through a tiny hole in the living room window. Maddox slid his hand into the path of the miniature jet stream and watched with fascination as the hairs on his knuckles twirled like streamers. The hole had all the tell-tale signs of a BB gun's pellet. He'd seen dozens of cases of bored kids shooting through the windows of abandoned buildings. He guessed that Darcy's house qualified.

The snowfall hadn't relented yesterday, adding another five inches of powder to the streets. Trudging home through a foot and a half of snow after losing Darcy hadn't been possible yesterday. Mentally and physically, he wasn't up to it.

Are you now? he asked himself.

His reflection in the jaundiced windowpane answered the question for him. Heavy pockets hung under his bloodshot eyes. His complexion vacillated between unhealthy pale and bruise-blushed. Purple veins bulged from his temples. *Old* seemed the least of his problems.

Rubbing his shoulder, Maddox headed for the front door. His muscles ached from sleeping on the hardwood floor. As he pulled open the door, a blistering glare invaded the darkened house. The sun had found a gap in the cloud cover and sent an intense barrage of light screaming down into the city. Reflected off the snowy landscape, the light beams intensified into a blinding prism. Maddox squinted, shielded his eyes with one hand, and stepped out onto the porch.

A crow perched on the stairs' handrail squawked in protest. It cocked its head from side to side as it turned to face Maddox. At the top of its head, a row of disheveled feathers stood on end, giving the bird an absurdly ferocious look. Maddox took a forceful step forward. Unintimidated, the crow jutted its head out and released a louder caw.

"*GO–*"

The crow stood up straight and extended its wings to full span. It released a string of staccato chirps, rising and falling in volume like maniacal laughter.

Maddox retreated a step and stood in the doorway. The bird relaxed, retracting its wings and settling down on the rail.

Doesn't want to let me leave. What does it want?

Another caw broke the silence, but this one came from across the street. On a sloping snowbank, two more crows trotted around a pigeon with a broken wing. The smaller bird shrieked and turned in circles, clearly trying to keep its eyes on both of its attackers. One crow lunged in and pecked at the pigeon, tearing feathers free. The pigeon fluttered backward, into the second crow. A coordinated strike followed, each crow sinking its beak into the pigeon's neck from the opposing side. Black feathers converged on white. Droplets of red stained the snow. The pigeon went limp. The crows turned on each other, nipping at the air and chirping angrily.

The crow on Darcy's porch rail bristled. Maddox's gaze met the bird's dark eyes. He saw no trace of emotion there, only mechanical instinct. *You're no harbinger,* he thought. *You're nothing that helpful. You're chaos.*

Turning, the crow launched into the air with a violent flutter and flew across the road. It snatched the dead pigeon off the snow and headed for the rooftops. The other crows quit their combat and took flight after him. Once the birds disappeared from sight, silence returned to the city block. The only evidence of the pigeon's murder was a few spots of blood and some discarded feathers.

The snow would melt. The wind would scatter the feathers.

Maddox closed Darcy's front door. It closed without making a sound. He wished it had creaked like a demonic laugh or slammed shut with a thunderous clap—some kind of ambient eulogy. Darcy deserved at least that.

A thin layer of snow covered the sidewalks. Maddox slid his hands into his coat pockets and walked with a slow, pensive gait. In his thirties he'd fallen and fractured his ankle. Six weeks off his feet taught him to be wary that fresh snowfall might hide patches of ice. The sound of his footfalls reminded him of the crunch of breakfast cereal. Breathing in, a metallic flavor zinged across his taste buds. Winter in the city.

He walked like an old man: shuffling and defeated with his head down and face dour. He imagined himself as a young man watching from across the street and shaking his twenty-five-year-old head. *I'll get old, yes, but I won't get old like that.* But he had. Somewhere along the line his internal piano had lost its tune. Now each key produced only the same flat note. Worse, he still *felt* like the man who could carry a tune, but the music was long gone.

Déjà vu struck him hard enough to stop his feet mid-stride. At the bus stop, two figures stood wearing beige winter coats. What were the odds of crossing paths with the same couple? He approached them slowly, watching carefully for any sudden movements. As he got closer, their faces came into focus. Startled, Maddox froze in place. Although normal-sized for adults, their features were that of androgynous children–tightly compressed eyes, nose, and mouth, bulbous and freckled cheeks, all surrounded by an expanse of baby fat.

Maddox wanted to run.

Wait, he told himself. *Masks. They're wearing plastic baby-doll masks.*

At any other time in his life, strangers wearing masks would have kicked up a hornet's nest's worth of anxiety. Today, Maddox breathed out and stepped up beside them. "You two on your way to a protest or something?"

The baby dolls didn't react.

They waited in silence. A chill came and went.

The bus rolled up. Tires rolled over slush. The door opened. Maddox hesitated when the baby dolls made no motion towards boarding. Going in first made him uncomfortable. The cop in him distrusted having his back to strangers.

"You ridin'?" the driver asked.

"Yeah," Maddox said, and stepped up onto the first stair.

A hand clasped onto his arm from behind. He spun around. One of the baby dolls leaned forward. He could see her eyes through the eyeholes in her mask. An older woman. She whispered, "Don't go home."

Maddox swept her hand off his arm and hurried up the stairs. The door closed behind him. As he paid the fare, he said to the driver, "Strange people, right?"

The driver glanced at the closed door, then back to Maddox, and rolled his eyes. Maddox took a seat. Settling against the headrest, he turned his attention to the window to catch a glance of the baby dolls. On the glass, the letters AIM were written in an uneven hand. He placed his index finger against one line. The width of the letter matched his fingertip. He recognized his handwriting but felt puzzled: How had it returned? Why was it backwards? How had any of *that* happened? He moved to wipe the window clear. Nothing happened.

There was no condensation on the window.

The writing was on the outside.

The baby dolls stood at the bus stop, masked faces upturned while staring directly at Maddox. As the bus lurched and pulled away, the baby doll who'd spoken to him raised one hand in a tepid half-wave.

Don't go home.

Maddox went home.

*　　*　　*

Exiting the bus, Maddox trudged over a ridge of snow built up on the curb. The sidewalk was clear except for the occasional dusting of rock salt and chloride pellets that crunched under his heels. Infected by the city's filth, the mounds of snow bookending the streets were stained dark brown and littered with trash and gravel. Nothing on the streets stayed pure for long.

As Maddox turned past a tall, curving snow dune, Steven's house came into view. His car was completely submerged under the snow—the result, no doubt, of a city plow driver's disregard for anything other than clearing the streets. His gaze shifted to the house. It took a moment for his brain to catch up to his eyes and fully process what he saw. Every window and the front door were wide open. *Had he left the door unlocked? Open, even?*

A man's silhouette in the doorway darted inside.

"HEY–"

Maddox's hand dropped to his hip, police training and instincts kicking in. Retirement had other plans, however. His fingers slid across denim. No holster. No gun. Eyes wide, he surveyed his surroundings for a weapon. He thought of the kid-sized aluminum baseball bat he kept in the backseat of his car, but discarded the thought as soon he considered it. It would take too long to dig through the snow. He needed something else—fast.

A metal pole with a rubber grip protruded from a crescent-shaped knoll of snow on the far side of the driveway. Maddox hurried over and lifted it out. It was the miniature golf putter that the neighbor kid had used to break up the ice on the sidewalk. The handle's coarse texture seemed to burrow under his calloused hands. Freezing. As he walked towards the house, he held it in both hands and choked up. He kept his eyes trained on the dark doorway. *Did he catch a fleeting glimpse of motion there? Had the silhouette returned? Or was it nothing at all?* Out in the cold, with his eyes squinting and watering, it was impossible to tell for sure.

Maddox stepped onto the first porch stair. His foot slid under him. Ice. He released the golf club with one hand and steadied himself with the handrail. He wondered what defense he could muster in such a stance if someone rushed out of the doorway. He rushed up the second and third stair so he didn't have to find out.

The house interior was pitch black.

Stepping up to the doorway with the club raised, he called into the house, "STEVEN?"

No answer. *Of course not*, he thought. Steven hadn't been home in days. And if he were, he certainly wouldn't open the windows in this weather. The man who installed a key lock on his bedroom door wouldn't ever leave the front door open. No, the silhouette he saw was someone else. A looter?

Kloum?

Maddox stepped inside. As if recovering from a flash bulb, his eyes took a moment to adjust. When they did, his breathing stopped. The foyer was gone, replaced by a wide hallway with peeling wallpaper and paper-thin carpeting. The stench of marijuana and mildew hung in the air. Numbered doors alternated as the hall stretched on. At the end of the hall, two lanky black men sat with their backs against the wall. Maddox turned his head and found another hallway. More men, of a variety of ethnicities, milled around, heads down.

The Prince Street Projects. *Couldn't be. Was.*

Maddox released his breath in a long, stuttering exhale.

Not real. Any of it. Just get out of there.

And go where?

He stepped forward. His foot landed on the shredded remains of a zebra-print dress. It squished under his shoe. A pool of blood spread out from the fabric. One of the Johns pointed and laughed. "Shit, man, that's some real dark blood right there. If you want a chance at her, better hurry–don't think she's got long."

Another said, "'Less you don't mind y'pussy room temperature."

They laughed.

Maddox lifted his foot off the dress. The blood receded back as if sucked back into a sponge. He continued down the hall, leaving red footprints behind. The two seated johns raised their faces as he approached. Their eyes had no pupils. Maddox flinched. They giggled madly and held up their open palms. One asked, "You got a few bucks, man? We're just a little short."

"Don't worry," his partner added, "we won't cut the line. Don't like it tight, anyways. Always better all stretched out and sloppy."

Maddox pushed open the last door in the hall. Before entering, he tossed the johns a backward glance and mumbled, "All of you animals deserve to die."

He stepped inside Gerald and Melissa Shelton's studio apartment. Three dim lights cast an uneven glow over the room: a child's half-moon nightlight plugged into a baseboard outlet; a microwave oven with its door open in the small kitchen nook; the blinking LED display of the bedside alarm clock. 12:00 eternal. An old disco song screeched out from the alarm clock's speakers, the radio station not precisely tuned, static crackling along with the heavy bass, driving drums, and crashing cymbals.

On the bed, Gerald Shelton gripped a fist of his wife's hair and yanked her head back with each thrust. Blood glistened on her pale skin. Her broken nose rested flat against her cheek, its tip pointing up towards her right eye. Her open mouth gaped open, revealing a set of rotting teeth dangling from diseased gums. One eye was open wide; the other sealed shut by swollen purple bruising. Her hands were tied behind her back, the knot so tight that her skin overlapped the cord and the flesh blushed as deep a red as any garden flower. On her right shoulder, a flap of peeled-back skin dangled over a huge oval wound. As her husband rode her, the fold of membrane swung from side to side, flashing the tattoo that had nearly been severed from her: a smiling grim reaper standing over a tombstone.

Gerald Shelton, his emaciated body contorting with every push and pull, grunted as he rammed himself in and out of his wife's bleeding body. He'd painted his own handprint across his chest in Melissa's blood. Lost in excitement, Gerald bit down on the single scissor blade he held between his teeth, cutting his top lip. He spat it out. The blade landed on the pillow beyond Melissa's head. His blood dribbled down onto her ass.

Gerald wasn't fucking *his wife*; he was fucking a hole he'd made *in his wife*. Just as he had done decades earlier, he turned to Maddox and said, "Bitch passed herself around town. Don't want to share what they'd had. Made my own place."

The golf club wavered in Maddox's hand as if an electrical current ran through it. Rage flared up inside him, overwhelming his fear. *This is the one memory you can have. I'd all but forgotten this, hadn't thought about it in years, but you've brought me back here.*

Melissa let out a sob that sounded as if it'd started in her chest. A lock of her dark brown hair whipped against her face and stuck. Gerald yanked her back, drawing her head against his chest. Her neck bulged from the pressure. Veins surged to the surface.

"Fifty if you want some," Gerald said as he peeked out from behind her. His eyes had a wild quality to them, unfocused and yet super-aware, the eyes of a newborn praying mantis still groggy from birth but already searching for its first victim.

Fifty bucks. That's what she was worth to him. Going rate to break into a dead man's house, grease a crime-scene informant, or to clear the snow out of a driveway. Maddox's eyes caught a glint on Melissa's finger: a gold band and a solitaire diamond. Even if the ring was electroplated and the stone was cubic zirconia, it had a greater street value than this woman's *life*.

Life seldom gave men second chances. In 1973, he'd killed Gerald Shelton in cold blood. It hadn't been self-defense. He'd never even tried to convince himself of that. To say he'd agonized over that choice in the years afterward would have been an overstatement. Gerald Shelton deserved to die. Again.

But it would be different this time.

If Kloum wanted a show, he'd get it.

"Yeah, I want some," Maddox said and lowered the putter. He freed up one hand and withdrew his money clip from his back pocket. He tossed the entire roll onto the bed.

Gerald pulled out of his wife's wound. Snatching up the money, he fanned out the bills and smiled. "Shit, bro, for all this you get to pull the goddamned plug on her."

During his autopsy, the medical examiner found the tip of a blade lodged in the costal cartilage of Gerald's ribcage. He'd had a knife broken off inside him and, because of his occupation as a drug dealer, hadn't been able to visit the hospital. The wound healed naturally, sealing the steel nib inside, but the pain must have been insufferable. The ME speculated that the man self-medicated to ease the suffering, escalating from a mild cannabis habit to a cocktail of street heroin, amphetamine, and barbiturates. That would turn any common street criminal into a monster—at least, that was how the theory went—but Maddox knew better. Gerald was no *victim* of his environment... he *victimized* everything in his environment.

Maddox returned his free hand to the golf club and fastened down his grip until his knuckles cracked. He glanced back at Melissa's face and felt a sympathetic pang of vertigo. She appeared weary beyond the point of feeling pain. She'd gone to that place where life itself became an anchor, with pain as the tether, and the only hope of escape was death. Hope had vanished.

I can't give you hope, Maddox thought, *but I sure as hell won't surrender it to this asshole.*

Maddox rushed forward and swung the club. The toe of the putter caught Gerald above his right eye. The hit sounded like the collapse of an ancient tree. He rocketed back, disengaged from his wife, and toppled off the edge of the bed. Melissa collapsed flat to the mattress.

Rebounding off the floor, Gerald clasped a hand onto his head over the point of impact as he scrambled onto his knees. A line of blood trickled out from between his fingers. He gritted his teeth and let out a vicious growl.

"FUUUUUCCCCCKKKK—"

Maddox raised his weapon.

"—YOUUUUUUUUU—"

He brought the club down, faster and with more force than the first time, and struck the peak of the younger man's head. Gerald fell away, unable to get a hand under himself quickly enough to brace his descent. His chin hit the floor with a crack. His jaw visibly dislodged; the contours of curved bone strained against elastic skin. His face reddened and swelled. He screamed.

Maddox didn't hesitate. The third strike hit the back of his neck, shattering the topmost spinal atlas and propelling Gerald's head backward at an angle that would have been impossible had the vertebrae not collapsed. He gagged as he curled up. A quick coughing fit followed, until a spray of blood and bone pellets escaped his destroyed mouth. His hands shook as he raised them in a feeble attempt at self-preservation.

Maddox sprang forward again, this time lunging out with the putter and forcing it into Gerald's teeth. The top incisors tumbled loose as the gum shelf crumbled inward. He pushed and twisted the handle until the club hooked under the unseated jaw. Maddox stepped back, yanked, and dragged Gerald, kicking and squirming, across the floor. Grunting, Maddox lifted the putter and brought Gerald up like a fish on a hook. Blood gurgled out of his nose and mouth. He reached out and took hold of the club's shaft, but his hand slid down its length when Maddox rocked it back and forth.

Melissa pulled herself to the edge of the bed. Her eyes peeked out from the top lip of the footboard. Her tiny, constricted pupils projected unbridled terror.

Maddox tore the club out of Gerald's mouth. Most of his jaw came with it and tumbled across the floor. Gerald tried to scream, but with only torn flaps for lips, he could only gargle out a loud, faltering mumble. His breathing became wet panting as he pushed away from Maddox on all fours. A steady rain of blood fell from his face onto the floor.

Maddox set down the putter and went to the bed. Melissa reached out for him. When his ear was close to her lips, she whispered, "...he *ruined* me..."

She handed Maddox the scissor blade. "...please... ruin *him*."

Maddox kissed her forehead.

He stared down at the cast-iron blade in his hand. He'd never thought of Gerald's death as self-defense, but it wasn't *this* either. He'd simply beaten the man to death, not tortured him.

"...please..."

The bedsheets were drenched in her blood.

Gerald crawled towards the door.

"*...ruin him...*"

Maddox closed his eyes. *Stan in his casket. Mia curled up beside him on her couch with tears in her eyes. Darcy folding his last hand of five-card stud. Fuck Kinda Question putting a gun to his head. Hadassah Boutros. D'ester. Troy Turring. Janey. So many had been lost. How could he show mercy to a piece of shit like Gerald Shelton when so many good people received no reprieve? This one deserved to disappear, if only to balance the scales.*

He opened his eyes and launched himself toward Gerald. Reaching down, he grabbed hold of the fleeing man's ankles and pulled him back. Gerald clawed for purchase, but found none. His naked skin slid without resistance over the blood-streaked floor. He screamed out three quick and garbled syllables. Had his mouth been intact, Maddox was certain the wet barks would have translated to 'No, no, no.'

Ruined me.

Maddox lowered the scissor blade and slid it between Gerald's buttocks. He hesitated there, steeling himself for what came next. His hand shook. *I can't do this. It's too much.*

Don't want to share what they'd had. Made my own place.

He tightened his grip on the scissors and locked his lips together as tight as he could. Tears filled his eyes. How many victims over the years? How many innocent people piled into ambulances and coroner's vans? How many battered wives? How many children?

Persephone Alford.

Maddox rammed the blade into Gerald. It sliced into the soft tissue between sets of rigid muscles. Gerald lurched himself forward and screamed. Maddox pulled back on the blade, tearing through the rubbery final inches of Gerald's large intestine and grinding into the rectum's wall. Bracing himself, Maddox changed his grip on the scissor, placed both hands flat on its handle, and pushed. The tip of the blade broke through the tight muscle weave of his pelvis and tapped against the floorboard.

Gerald emptied the contents of his stomach in a burst of liquid vomit. Attempting to crawl forward, he slipped and fell face down into the mess. He wept, gasping and sputtering with every labored breath.

That's enough. He's paid up.

In his peripheral vision, Melissa sat up. Her nipples were gone. Small knots of red flesh remained. Maddox knew wounds. They hadn't been cut off. No, Gerald—or possibly one of his paying customers—had gnawed them off.

Melissa's head tilted down. Her unfocused eyes gazed down at her body. She brought her hands up and cupped her bleeding breasts. As realization struck her, she screamed.

Ruined me.

Maddox found the putter, lifted it up, and swung it down on the scissor blade's handle. The blade dug in, pinning Gerald to the floor. He convulsed–shoulders, back, and pelvis bucking–as his muscles seized. He vomited again, but this time ejected only blackish blood. Internal bleed.

Maddox looked to Melissa. Holding her breasts, she shivered and sobbed, chest shuddering with each breath. Then a cold, determined expression settled onto her face and she nodded.

Maddox returned the gesture.

Gerald clawed at the floor until Maddox dropped his feet onto the prone man's hands, straddling him. He lined up his shot, wavering the putter an inch from Gerald's nose. The wounded man drew in a breath and held it. Maddox wound up, feet slightly bent, and swung through. Gerald's head snapped to the right on impact. His neck released a dry pop like a firecracker igniting, followed by a series of crackles. As he settled, two large blood bubbles inflated at the tips of both nostrils. The nasal bone protruded from a tear in the skin, rising up like a tiny shark's fin.

Maddox pulled back and swung again. Gerald's right eye disappeared into its socket, the lid left dangling over a rapidly filling recess. The third swing crushed his Adam's apple. Gerald wheezed, neck bulging and blooming bright orange. Maddox stepped off his hand. He wasn't going anywhere. He turned the putter over in his hand until the toe faced straight down at the occipital protuberance, the tiny button on the back of Gerald's skull.

He raised the club over his head and kept his eyes trained on his target. He paused for a moment and thought, *Is this what you wanted to see, Kloum? Then watch closely, bastard.*

Melissa was still screaming.

Maddox brought the putter down. Gerald's skull cracked open and caved in. Maddox pushed down hard, planting the weapon deep in the exposed brain tissue. Releasing the club, he stepped away. The putter remained upright like a flagpole. Gerald shook. His fingers and feet flopped like rubber. A pool of urine spread underneath his body.

Without turning to face her, Maddox said to Melissa, "He's ruined."

Her scream withered away. Then a male voice shrieked, *"DAD–"*

Dad?

Maddox snapped his head towards his son's voice. Steven knelt on the far side of the bed, naked except for the bedsheets drawn to his waist. Tears streamed down his face. Gerald Shelton's dingy apartment was gone, replaced by Steven's blue marigold bedroom. Contemporary abstract art hung on the walls. An expensive jar candle burned atop a restored antique bedside table.

"WHY... GOD... FUCK–"

Maddox felt lightheaded and confused. A painful chill spread through his body, sending his extremities into fits of pins and needles. *How?* Right on top of that thought came, *Kloum.* And then, *What've I done?*

The man Steven had brought to Hop's lay on the floor at Maddox's feet. He shifted his attention from the dead body back to his son. Steven screamed and clutched at his bedsheets. "DIDn't DO ANYTHING... WHY DID..."

"...Steven," Maddox said in a voice he didn't recognize as his own. He took a tentative step towards his son, but then retreated two back when Steven flinched and slid to the edge of the bed. Maddox raised his hands to signify he wouldn't attempt to approach. Thick blood dripped down from his fingers, over his knuckles, and down into his sleeves. *Jesus.*

Steven's eyes were wild with fear and shock. Maddox wondered how much different his own must have looked in that moment. He inhaled deeply, turned, and left the room. He closed the door behind him. The door creaked like a demonic laugh and slammed shut with a thunderous clap.

He stumbled down the hall and into the kitchen. He retrieved the phone and sat down at the table. Hands still shaking, he dialed and put the receiver to his ear.

"911. What's the nature of your emergency?" a dispatcher asked.

Maddox opened his mouth to speak. Instinct told him to say, *I've got a 745* and rattle off the address, but he had a different role to play. "There's been a murder."

"Has the suspect left the building?"

"No," Maddox said. "He hasn't."

The dispatcher asked, "Are you in a safe place?"

Was he? "Yes."

"Stay where you are and don't make contact with the suspect. I'm dispatching police and an ambulance to your location. Is there anything I need to tell—"

"The front door's open," Maddox said. The rest of his words barely escaped before he began to sob hysterically. "And they'll find the suspect sitting at the kitchen table on the phone with 911."

December 17th

The strength of the scent of body odor came and went, sometimes forced out by the harsh chemical odor of industrial cleaning solution, but lingering always. Holding cells never really came clean. The criminals and drunks brought their smells in with them: wet armpit balm, carcass breath, and rotten meat flatulence. The cleaning crews had a difficult enough task without dealing with the occasional dirty protest–urine, feces, blood, or all of the above. The Green Street jail remembered every one of its occupants. With every breath, so did Maddox.

Seated on a wooden cot, he stared at his cell and absorbed the details. Dimpled concrete floor. Gray bars. A yellow cinderblock wall. Stainless steel toilet and sink. A single florescent light fixture overhead.

The light buzzed like an insect. A mumbling voice drifted down the cell-block hall. Maddox couldn't hear the words but from the cadence decided it was a drunken recitation of the Lord's Prayer. He doubted that a rod or a staff–regardless of ownership–could help the poor bastard out in this place.

How many criminals had he sent here? No idea–too many to count. Low-rent offenders did their time here awaiting trial, time served. But those pulled off the streets for major felonies were shipped over to Doremus Ave. Somewhere along the line the word *prison* fell out of vogue and *correctional facility* became the term. That building was a green and white monstrosity with a tower of black-tinted windows and enormous HVAC systems growing out of its roof like cancerous nodules. Maddox guessed neither *prison* nor *correctional facility* was what he should call it now. A simpler word would soon suffice: *home*.

A plainclothes detective stepped up to the bars. Maddox recognized the type immediately: dry clean only; weekend Little League umpire; microbrew beer only. He combed his hair to cover the receding hair on either side of his prominent widow's peak. Maddox would have bet good money the man owned a house in Montclair listed on the Register of Historic Places. An inner-circle cop, chasing a politically connected paycheck more often than criminals.

Behind him, a uniformed cop held a clipboard in his hands and a felt-tip pen between his teeth. The opposite of the detective, he dressed in warm-water-washed workplace blue and black. Department-store frames on his prescription glasses. A real cop.

"Kind of asshole?" the detective asked.

Maddox stood up. "*'Scuse* me?"

"I'm just wondering..." The detective pointed a thin finger at Maddox's chest. "...what kind of an asshole breaks into a house and kill a man, but doesn't have the balls to tell us his name. See, I'd think the hard part would be denting in a guy's skull with a golf club, not manning up afterward."

"I gave you my name," Maddox said. He didn't mean the detective, of course, but the arresting officers. He couldn't imagine that information not making it into the report. It didn't escape his notice that *this asshole* hadn't introduced *himself*. "Maddox Benjamin Boxwood."

The detective smirked. "A repetitive asshole, is that right? That's the kind you are? I'll tell you, we ran that name. You know what came back out of the computer?"

Maddox shrugged.

The detective turned his hand and touched his pointing finger to his thumb, a big fat goose egg. "I forget now, what was the phrasing, Office Crane?"

Crane removed the pen from his mouth. "No results found."

"*No results found*," the detective said. "As in, the scumbag you've arrested is lying to you. Probably don't understand we can prosecute you as a John Doe all the same. You think you'll be the first nameless piece of shit to work a mop up and down a cellblock for a stretch?"

That made no sense to Maddox. There was no way a retired law enforcement officer *wasn't* in the system. They shouldn't have had to refresh the screen before the State Bureau of Identification spit out his work history, paystubs, and disciplinary action file. Hell, there were still a few veterans in the office who went to his retirement party. He said nothing.

"Okay, *Maddox*," the detective said, making his name sound like the punchline of a very unfunny joke, "we can do this the other way. Turn your ass around and put your belly up to the wall. Then lock your hands behind your neck. And stay that way."

Maddox knew the routine. He'd been frisked on the scene and again during processing, but he'd seen suspects snatch improvised weapons out of thin air, seemingly. He pressed himself against the wall and complied. The cell door opened and the men entered. One pair of shoes squeaked against the floor. Probably Officer Crane, the soles of his catalog boots going bald from too many hours on the job. Hands patted him down.

"Turn around," the detective said. "Hands in front."

Office Crane handcuffed him. They led Maddox out of the cell and down the hall to a tiny interrogation room. He sat at the desk across from two chairs. They left and locked the door.

Maddox nodded. The waiting game. They'd leave him in the room, staring at his own reflection in the two-way glass, for an hour or so. *Let the perp perc*, the saying went. Force any man to stare at himself for long enough and he'd only be able to see his flaws. Tell him that he could escape from the room—and his life's shortcomings—just as soon as he confessed and he'd cop to skeet shooting on the grassy knoll, sharing his frequent flier miles with Mohamed Atta, and dropping a glove on Nicole Brown-Simpson's front lawn. Maddox closed his eyes and waited.

Without his sight, the soundproof interrogation room faded away from his senses entirely. He lifted his feet off the floor. It was as if he were floating in space. Without any other stimuli, Maddox became acutely aware of how it felt to inhabit his body: flesh like a heavy coat; feverish skin; heavy bones. Human. *Too* human.

Time passed. Maddox didn't let himself think. Instead, he willed himself into a deep, resonant silence. He was neither awake nor asleep, but ignorant of any sense of self-awareness.

After a while, the door opened with a click. Cool air rushed in.

Maddox opened his eyes.

The detective entered the room, followed by a younger woman in a business suit. She could have passed for a lawyer, but no, Maddox knew better. Another detective. In its purest form, good cop/bad cop lost its effectiveness in the mid-'80s, but variations survived, mostly focused on race, gender, and age. Mix an attractive woman with an older male suspect, add a bad-tempered interrogator, stir and bake. It was a surefire recipe for a confession.

They're trying too damn hard.

"Detective Hoult, let me introduce you to John Doe," the male detective said, pulling out a chair for Hoult. She crossed her legs as she sat. "I know, name sounds familiar, right?"

Hoult shook her head. "No, Bill, I'd remember if we'd met."

You sure about that?

"Dunno, I think he's just got one of those faces. I look at him and think, 'Jesus, do I know this guy?'" Detective Bill said. "But then I go, 'What the fuck am I saying?' I don't meet many guys capable of breaking into a stranger's house and ramming a golf club through his lover's skull."

Hoult's eyes widened. "You did that?"

Maddox sighed. "You two can cut the bullshit."

"Bullshit?" Detective Bill said.

"Yeah," Maddox said. "You prod at me and she bats her eyes and tells me she just wants to hear my side of it. You get louder, she gets softer. You roll up your sleeves, she undoes a button on her blouse when I'm not looking. About right?"

Hoult snorted.

"You watch a lot of cop shows on TV?" Detective Bill asked. He kept the swagger in his voice, but a quick glance over at Hoult betrayed a hiccup in his confidence level. "Sounds like you do. You gotta know that none of that shit is real. It doesn't work like that."

Maddox leaned forward. "Who do you have lined up to call you in the middle of the interview? Y'know, to give you the excuse to step out for a few minutes when things have gotten pretty heated in here? And then Detective Hoult can try to goose an *'I did it'* outta me?"

"You don't know what you're talking about," Detective Bill said.

He did.

"Let me make your day a little easier," Maddox said. "I came home today. Door was open. Picked up the golf club. Thought someone had broken in. It was dark and I hadn't slept much. Didn't realize my son was home. Or that he had... a guest."

"Wait, wait, wait," Hoult said. "If you want a lawyer—"

"Why would I want that?"

"You were read your rights?" she asked.

168

"Of course. And I understand them." Maddox abandoned Detective Bill and turned his attention solely on Hoult. "*I called 911.* I'm not trying to duck this thing. You need a statement for the report. I'll give it to you. I'll answer questions from the prosecutor later. I know the drill."

"You sound like a cop," she said.

Detective Bill blurted out, "More like an asshole."

"You're living proof that you can be both," Maddox said.

Hoult put up both hands. "You boys want me to leave so you can whip them out and measure?"

Detective Bill huffed. "You want me to listen to this bullshit?"

"As a start, yes," she said.

Maddox clapped. "You're both good at this. But maybe you missed the part where I made it clear that I know this game. I know it's difficult to change up the script, but really, drop the high school drama club act. I'm guilty. I killed that man."

Silence.

Maddox's cheeks raised and his eyes squinted. Tears were close. "He was my son's lover and I got confused. I have this... disease. Fucks with my memory, with my thoughts. And I thought he was someone else. From another time. And... I killed him."

Impatience set into Detective Bill's face. He leaned forward. His breath smelled like old tuna fish. He put a finger in Maddox's face. "You killed that man, that's right. But that's the only true thing you've said. The homeowner isn't your son. His name is Steven Lindsey and you're not his father. So cut the shit."

Lindsey. Catherine's maiden name.

"You told the 911 operator the same story," Hoult said. Her voice was smooth and calming, the polar opposite of Detective Bill's braggadocio. "We asked Mr. Lindsey about it. He never knew his father. His mother told him that he ran off right after she got pregnant. Just disappeared. So... who are you, John?"

"Maddox Ben–" Maddox said, drawing out the syllables.

Detective Bill finished his name. "–jamin Boxwood. Yeah, we got all that already. The man with no fingerprints on file. No school transcript. No voting records. No address. A face the computer can't match. If you're Maddox Benjamin Boxwood, why can't I find anything on you? Why didn't you have ID on you?"

"It was stolen," Maddox said. In his head he added, *Both the state-issued cards and my identity itself, apparently.* He was tempted to tell them the full story—Persephone Alford, Gerard and Melissa Alford, Kloum—but an insanity defense was still a defense, and he didn't intend to present one.

"Jared Fleet. That's the name of the man you killed," Detective Bill said. The wagging finger dropped down and tapped the table. "Did you know him at all, or was this a random thing?"

Maddox stared in Detective Bill's eyes. Forgone conclusions were all he saw. He sighed. "Know what? I didn't know him. He was a stranger. I walked into the first house I found with an open door. Surprised them. Things got outta control. And then I killed him. Isn't that what you want? All you need to prosecute me?"

"It probably is," Detective Bill said.

"Then let's stop talking right here. You fill in the details on the report. Whatever you want. I'll sign it. Even read it into the court record for you." Hot tears raced down Maddox's face. "But hurry. I don't have much time. I don't want to die before you get to send me up."

Detective Bill nodded and stood up. "Sounds good to me."

Hoult put a finger up. "You're confessing?"

"Yes," Maddox said.

"To events you remember differently?"

"Yes," he said.

In that same soft tone, she said, "Tell us who you are."

Maddox grimaced. "I guess I'm nothing at all."

170

December 18th

Eyes closed and half-asleep, Maddox heard the click of a key entering a steel lock, followed by the rattle of the mechanism turning. *Chunk-ch-ch-ch-clink.* He opened his eyes. The cell door opened. Even with the lights turned down low, Maddox could make out the face of Officer Crane. He held a day stick in his hands. Maddox remembered the feel of the wooden baton in his hand. In some ways, handling a truncheon was more reassuring than even a sidearm. He'd never had the experience of having one brandished against him. Until now.

"Stomach to the wall," Crane said.

Maddox groaned and sat up. "What time–"

Crane took another step forward, releasing the day stick from one hand and swinging it down to his hip. "Not gonna tell you again. To the wall."

"Yeah," Maddox said, swinging his legs off the side of the cot and bellying up to the cinderblocks. He'd misjudged the cop. Working class, yes, but with a fire in his gut to escape that life. He'd do what he had to. "My favorite wall, anyway; I was missing it."

It was cold.

Crane moved in. "Hands behind your back."

Maddox complied. Handcuffs locked around his wrists. *Tight.*

Crane spun Maddox around and held the day stick against his chest. "Word came down from the front desk that you didn't fill out the hotel register properly, John Doe. That's a problem. You don't think we can have you stay here in the presidential suite if you don't wanna cooperate, do you? Gonna have to move you to more communal lodgings."

Stepping back, Crane prodded him towards the door.

Maddox's heart raced. Another textbook play. Take a disobedient suspect, put him in a holding cell with a group of violent thugs, and let him sweat out a night. The next interrogation would go smoother. "Hey, listen to me, I confessed. You don't have to do this."

Crane pushed him out into the cellblock hall. "Do what?"

A loud male voice called out, "What's you doing there?"

Another: "Where he going?"

"Doggie on a shit-walk?"

Maddox shuffled down the hall. In the holding cells, he caught glimpses of men on cots; men leaning against walls; men pacing and mumbling; a man sitting on a toilet. All of their faces were locked in the same terrible expression: fear masquerading as hate. "Detective Bill tell you to do this?"

Crane pushed again. "Bill Reisz? Gotta be kidding me. Man's a pussycat. In a couple of different ways."

Hoult. He'd misjudged the good cop/bad cop routine after all.

At the end of the hall, Crane herded him to the right and down a hallway without cells. Triggering an electronic door to unlock, they exited the holding area. The section beyond was affectionately nicknamed *long-term parking*, a run of secluded cells meant to keep "at risk" suspects out of the main lockup. Rival gangs were kept at arm's length from one another here. Psychotics awaiting evaluations. Child predators who wouldn't survive a day in general confinement. The worst of the worst.

"Don't got to do this," Maddox said.

"No," Crane said. "Absolutely do not."

The expressions on the men here were different than in the regular holding cells. These perps weren't just angry, they were furious and fearless. *Hardened.* They didn't pace, they swaggered. A white skinhead held a bloody shirt to his chest, *1488* tattooed onto his forehead. A thin Latino, five-pointed crown on his neck, leaned against the bars. Prison sets scarified into forearms. Teardrops under eyes, five dots, cobwebs on elbows: mementos of long prison stays.

Crane stopped him at the last cell. Unlocking it, he swung it open and gestured for Maddox to step inside. Maddox stared into the cop's eyes. He saw too many years of double shifts and frozen pay rates. There was no reaching him. "Please."

The tip of the day stick pointed into the cell.

"If I don't go, you gonna hit me with that?" Maddox asked. He knew what the answer would have been had their roles been reversed. He'd never threatened to do anything without being willing to see the act through. He hoped that Crane was a better man than he.

"Do what I have to," Crane said.

Maddox stepped inside.

There were six perps in the cell. Maddox sized them up in a sweeping glance. Two young black kids, no more than nineteen apiece, looking straight off a street scuffle. A steroid-and-barbell Hispanic wearing a torn T-shirt. An older black man with gray hair and glasses sitting on a cot reading a paperback. A white boy with a full sleeve tattoo of a tangle of women engaged in a host of sexual acts with each other. The sixth sat on the far cot and faced the wall.

"The fuck we need him in here?" one of the black kids yelled.

The white boy added, "Specially not no old man."

Crane closed the cell door behind him. *Chunk-ch-ch-ch-clink.*

"Have a good night, *Mr. Doe*," Crane said as he walked away.

The prisoners stepped up to him, an impenetrable wall of muscle and callous. The white kid moved in closest, cocked his head to one side, and sniffed the air. "What you been here, an hour, a day, what is it? 'Cause your breath still smells good. See, we here for longer, and all our breath stank like shit, 'cause the food."

Maddox said nothing.

The kid's lips puckered into a circle. He took a deep breath and released the air up into Maddox's nostrils. Maddox turned his head. The kid was right. It smelled like fish rotting on a beach.

The *at-risk* prisoners laughed.

"Leave him," a familiar voice said.

The perps froze in place. Their eyes glazed over. After a moment, they shuffled in place as looks of confusion spread across their faces.

"Let him through," the voice said. They retreated to the sides of the cell, leaving a clear path to the man sitting on the far cot. He turned himself around. Stan. *Kloum.*

Maddox approached slowly, eyes flickering between the ·perps and the creature in the shape of his dead friend. "You don't have to worry about them," it said. "They don't see a scared old retired cop. They see one of their own."

"That's a lot of power you have," Maddox said.

Kloum patted the cot beside him. "Not power. Burden. Imagine juggling the memories of thousands. Replacing old recollections. Making sure some never form at all. Used to be less people. It was easier then. Now... I fail sometimes."

"Why?" Maddox asked, sitting beside the demon.

"*Why* is the most pointless invention of all humanity," Kloum said. "This insistence that everything happen for a reason. I am not a *why*. I am a *how*. That's all I am, actually."

Maddox asked, "Then *how?*"

Kloum smiled a smile Stan never would. "A better question. Necessity, that's the best answer. Nature abhors a vacuum and all that. I exist, as much as I do, to fill a void. To beat back the chaos that you resist so vehemently by asking *why*. You need a reason, I become it."

"How in the hell does erasing people do *that?*" Maddox asked, letting his anger season his words. He didn't feel fear. There was nothing more that Kloum could take from him.

Kloum said, "A child. Autistic, but very functional, very bright. She'll grow up to develop a series of hybrid methods of next-generation gene therapy. She'll cure virtually every disease and disorder plaguing mankind, including her own. Her influence won't simply be medical. By saving the world from pestilence, she'll become the greatest ambassador of peace this world has ever known. She will unite all of mankind. And unlike others before her, she'll reject the advances of those who will attempt to build a religion around her."

"Why are you telling me this?" Maddox asked.

Why. He grimaced.

"Jared Fleet," Kloum said. "Your son's lover. A good man. Drinks socially, but not an alcoholic. On New Year's Eve, this year, he'll have one too many glasses of wine and get behind the wheel of Steven's car. Your son will be in the passenger seat, asleep before they get halfway home from the party. Jared will swerve across the center line, then jerk the wheel hard to the right to compensate. Loss of control. Just as Steven wakes up, they'll strike an oncoming minivan. Head-on collision. No survivors."

Maddox's brow furrowed.

"The driver of the minivan is the father of that autistic child. The hood of Steven's car will force the steering column of the minivan through his chest. The daughter will survive the initial crash, but only for minutes. She bleeds out from a head wound." Kloum leaned forward and folded his hands together. "If the car accident happens, millions die unnecessarily. If Jared Fleet is murdered by his lover's father, they don't. It's not *why*. It's *how*."

Maddox said nothing.

"You chose to kill Gerald Shelton," Kloum said. "In part because you didn't trust the system to punish him enough. But more because you knew that he would eventually kill his wife. Isn't that right?"

Maddox nodded.

"Places like this," Kloum said, spreading out his hands. "Spaces to lock criminals away, out of sight. Most of the people who will lead your species astray don't deserve to die. So, I remove them from the minds of society. Make them impotent. But sometimes that's not enough. *I* can't kill anything. But I *can* bring another to the point where they'll do just that."

"You could have chosen anyone," Maddox said. Unsaid: *Why me?*

"I didn't choose you," Kloum said. "I wasn't even aware of you. You came looking for me. You made me choose you. I can't touch the vast majority of people. But the rest of your life had no impact on the future. You were already dying. No ripples. You were a perfect candidate."

Maddox balled up his fists. "You destroyed my life."

Kloum turned his head and stared into Maddox's eyes. "Of no consequence."

"Fuck you."

Kloum's eyes narrowed. "Have you considered what became of Melissa Shelton after you murdered her husband? You may think she straightened out her life and managed to leave her traumatic past behind. That didn't happen. The doctors repaired the damage on the outside, but not on the inside. She met another man, another Gerald, and died on the bathroom floor with a bandana tied around her forearm. A new dealer came with a bad batch. Do you know what her last words were? Nothing profound, not something worthy of an epitaph. Just *Hey, you Bobby?*"

Maddox's fists loosened. *What was the point?*

"Chaos," Kloum said. "The only truth."

Maddox drew in a deep breath. "It's all pointless."

Kloum nodded. "Entirely. There's no redemption to be had. No salvation;

175

no enlightenment. Those are all creations built on *why*. For all of your kind, the end comes as pain and indignity and futility. Grace is self-delusion."

Exhaling hurt.

"What now?" Maddox asked.

"A choice," Kloum said. "I cannot offer you any kind of reprieve from this world–and I owe you nothing–but I can act out of sympathy. If you wish, I'll remove you from the memory of this world. Your other choice is a short stay with the gentlemen in this jail cell. Both choices have their benefits, I suppose."

The wallet or the dog's teeth.

Maddox told Kloum what he wanted.

December 19th

A Polaroid photograph. Maddox sat in the cell, surrounded by men oblivious to his existence, and remembered the camera he'd bought in 1971. Triggering the button, a square, white-framed sheet emerged from the machine. The picture started as a block of light purple. Then shapes appeared, hazy at first, but growing sharper until the chemical process expired and the photograph took form. Over time, the colors faded. After decades, the image disappeared entirely.

I don't remember what became of that camera, Maddox thought.

Who was your third-grade math teacher? he asked himself. *What was the name of the joint on West Kinney Street where you and Stan used to pick up hot pastrami on Italian hoagies? Where did I go for fireworks on the bicentennial Fourth? What was the name of the bully who tormented Steven in junior high?*

No answers. Nothing. Gone.

He wondered how memorable he would have been to the criminals that shared his cell. Had he not asked Kloum to erase him from their minds, would they have remembered him at all as the months passed? Would he have become only another faceless beat-down, not worth the effort to recall? Would they remember him if they put him in the jail infirmary? If they killed him?

How many years had he not thought about Gerald and Melissa Shelton? If Kloum hadn't pushed him, would he have ever thought about them again?

Sometimes Maddox would buy a pack of Polaroid film without checking the expiration date. Those photographs were vague splashes of color and random shapes, if they developed at all. Many times the paper just darkened into a gray square.

Even the best photographs faded; details got lost.

Maddox stared down at the bedsheet on the cot. It wouldn't take much effort to twist it into a rope. Follow that with a simple slip knot. Snake the free end through the top bars. Another knot. All he'd need to do is kneel down and wait.

No one would mourn. No one would even *know.*

Time to fade.

"That look on your face, I used to see it in the mirror a lot."

Maddox turned towards the voice. The young Dominican he'd met outside Hadassah Boutros's home stood on the other side of the bars. He smiled, bright white teeth gleaming. "Hello, Mr. Maddox."

"It didn't work," Maddox said. "My luck."

"Oh, no, it worked." The Dominican chuckled and pointed towards the criminals lounging on the other cots. "These men here, they pay you no mind, yes?"

Maddox said, "But you can see me. So it didn't work. Not very well, anyway."

"See? Everyone sees you. Remembering? Not as much." The Dominican's grin didn't waver. "Bad ol' Kloum, he marks you up. People look at you and their brains read the instructions he left behind. Do not remember. And it works that way for almost all. Not for those he's already marked, though."

Maddox glanced at his cellmates. "They can't see you either?"

"Don't know I'm here."

"When did it get to you?" Maddox asked.

"Long time back. I was only a boy. A boy on a bicycle."

"But I was able to see you outside—"

"Yes," the Dominican said, "and that is very interesting. We think it's because of the disease in your head. The chemistry is changing there. His influence is not as strong."

"We?" Maddox asked.

"We." The Dominican nodded. "*The Displaced*. Forgotten. We keep an eye on Kloum. It was only natural we'd find you when you found him. His interest in you interests us."

The Dominican raised a hand. He held a keyring.

Maddox stood up. "Where'd you get that?"

"Off the guard at the desk upstairs," he said. "You've a lot to learn. When they can't remember you, they can't remember *what* you do, either. Their brains refuse to notice; they fill in the gaps with what makes sense to them. If I don't return these on time to his belt, he'll assume he put them down somewhere and go look. Feel foolish. And then they'll show up. Confused for a minute, maybe, but they're all quick to accept."

"You've come to bust me out? Why?" Maddox asked.

"Kloum spent a lot of time with you. More than usual." The Dominican shuffled through the keys. "The Displaced want to know why. We know about the disease—"

Maddox stepped closer to the bars. "You spied on me?"

"Not me personally. I'm a recruiter."

"Thought you were a priest," Maddox said.

"Is there a difference between the two?" The Dominican settled on a key and tried it. *Chunk-ch-ch-ch-clink.* He nodded with obvious satisfaction. "On the first try. At first you couldn't see us. Your keys out of your pocket, returned before you missed them. Into your son's house. Listened to the answering machine messages you didn't bother with. Read your mail. Later on, you started to notice us. Just people a little out of place."

The cell door opened. The perps failed to notice.

The Dominican stepped into the cell. "I'm not here to force you to do anything. You can stay here and finish thinking up a way to kill yourself. You'll leave behind a rotting stench that the guards and prisoners won't consciously smell. But they'll know on a deeper level. A sense of discomfort. Nothing they can explain. Is the world starting to make a little more sense to you, Mr. Boxwood?"

"More sense," Maddox mumbled, "and less."

The Dominican offered his hand. "My name is Saulo. If you decided to leave this cell and come with me, I can make that *and less* disappear. You won't like everything I can show you. But it can be an honest world finally, if you'd like."

"I'm tired. I don't think I care anymore," Maddox said.

Saulo's hand remained outstretched. "We have a way to kill Kloum."

"You do?" Maddox asked.

"Again, not me personally. Our leader."

Maddox took Saulo's hand. Instead of shaking, the Dominican gripped it and drew him close. Saulo wrapped his free arm around Maddox brought their bodies together. After a moment, the embrace ended and Saulo released him. He gestured to the cell door.

Maddox stepped out.

Saulo's smile withered. "A demonstration."

One of the black gangbangers stood by the cots, finger drumming on his hip. Maddox recognized the nervous energy as an early symptom of withdrawal. Head down, the kid mumbled in a voice too low and indistinct to be heard as anything more than a hum. A prayer? Ruminations? Lyrics? On the cot below him, the white perp watched him with suspicion.

Saulo took a step towards the black kid, placed both of his hands on his back, and pushed. Then he turned and rushed out of the cell, shutting the door behind him. *Chunk-ch-ch-ch-clink.*

The cell exploded into violence. The black gangbanger fell into the white boy, who immediately grabbed ahold of him by the ears. They tumbled off the cot onto the floor. The second black kid joined in, leaping onto the back of the white perp. The other inmates were quick to react, rushing into the fight.

"We go now," Saulo said, leading Maddox down the cell block. As they passed by, the sounds of the scuffle reached each cell. The perps scrambled to the bars, straining their heads to see down the hall. Shouting and barking following. Then pushing and shoving for the best position. More fights broke out.

Saulo pushed through the doors and they exited long-term parking. As the door closed behind Maddox, he said, "You've spoken with Kloum. He's told you his lies. Those brawls I started, maybe someone will die. Who knows how that might affect the future, right? A chain reaction. Uncontrollable. But had Kloum not come into my life when I was a kid, a little boy from a home broken even worse than my English, then there'd be no shove, no fight, no death. You see? He is not the enemy of chaos he claims to be. He's just the same."

The suspects in the holding cells rested on their cots, paced in circles, and spoke to each other in hushed tones. Not a single eye glanced into the hall as Saulo and Maddox passed. Not just invisible, Maddox noted, but soundless and scentless. He felt both superhuman and absolutely inconsequential at the same time.

They turned at the end of the hall and passed through another doorway, into a maze of booking officers' cubicles and aisles of filing cabinets. Detectives chatted on landline phones. Uniformed cops processed handcuffed suspects at their desks. Administration personnel scurried from one station to the next, delivering file folders and clipboards. The room smelled like coffee. Twenty years ago the lingering odor of burnt tobacco would have buried the scent of joe.

Detective Bill Reisz leaned against a partition wall speaking to a young woman in a tight business suit. Her eyes were focused on his moving lips. His were on her chest. "Court on Monday with that Dollar Store thing. Should be out early. I know they have you working the weekends, but maybe you could request—"

"Be just a minute," Maddox said as he broke away from Saulo.

The Dominican stopped. "Don't have time for this."

Maddox stepped between Reisz and the young woman. A stab of confusion darted across the detective's face, then he leaned back, adjusting his vantage point, and resumed staring at the woman's breasts. "—off by noon? There's a Brazilian restaurant in Elizabeth. They have lunch specials. Big, full plates—"

"The pussycat detective," Maddox said. "A word of advice. I know, what should you take a word from a guy like me for? A man with no fingerprints on file and no school transcripts. No voting records or last known address. A face that no computer can find a match for. But still, there's something of value here for you, so listen. Next time you play the bad cop, do everyone a favor. Eat a breath mint first. I might deserve to spend the rest of my life behind bars, but I don't deserve to smell your fucking breath."

Maddox reached into his pocket and fished out the detective's wallet. Reisz didn't seem to notice. Removing the identification cards, he slid the bi-fold back into Reisz's pants. As he rejoined Saulo, Maddox dropped the cards into the plastic bottle recycling bin near the door.

"That feel good?" Saulo asked.

Maddox nodded as they left the processing block. "Yeah."

"Hope it's outta your system now, though," Saulo said as he led Maddox past the front reception desks and towards the front doors. "Because you can't do that sort of thing too often."

"Why not?"

Saulo held the door open for him. Maddox stepped through.

"Too easy to get addicted to mischief. You get bolder and bolder. Take stupid risks. Don't ever start to believe that you're more than a man. If you cut me, I bleed–that hasn't changed," Saulo said, stepping out onto the Municipal Building's steps. "Too many of us have convinced ourselves we're immortal. Eventually, they've all been proven wrong."

Snow still bordered Green Street, reducing the width of the curbs by half, and narrowing the street. Signs restricted parking on the northbound side, but a single white van waited there nevertheless. The few uniformed cops milling around the stairs paid it no mind. Saulo pointed. "That's our ride."

Maddox stepped onto the red brick crosswalk. A taxi careened across his path, no slowing. Saulo put a hand on his shoulder and tugged him back. "Looking for a proof that you can still die? They can't see you, but they can run your ass over."

Maddox laughed. His world had changed; the treats were out of sync with his normal reasoning. He could steal a cop's wallet without fear of detection, but crossing a 25 mile-per-hour roadway might prove fatal.

The next car was still a distance off, so they hurried across Green Street. As they reached the other side, the van's side door rolled back.

Two men and a woman jumped down. All three wore baby-doll masks. "What's–"

Saulo put a hand on his back. "Calm, man, just wait–"

The woman held a syringe between her fingers like a cigarette.

"–the fuck–"

The men moved in fast. Saulo's hand reached up and seized Maddox's neck. Fingers latched onto his arms and squeezed. Maddox struggled, thrashing from side to side, but their grip didn't falter. They pulled him to his knees. He screamed. The cops on the stairs remained oblivious.

The woman stepped up. She raised the needle.

"Just a precaution," Saulo said.

The woman leaned down. "A little bee sting, that's all."

Maddox jerked back. The men in the baby-doll masks tightened their grips and brought him back forward. He stared into the mask holes of the woman. Pretty eyes. "Please–"

She leaned farther down until the plastic lips brushed his earlobe. Slightly muffled by the mask, her voice sounded at once very far away and entirely too close, as if projected from a great distance directly into his thoughts. "Hush now. You don't want to remember where we're going. 'Cause then *he* might know, and we're all safer without *that*."

The hypodermic needle lanced his neck. He felt a quick, cold stab and then a numbing sensation spiraling out from the puncture. His thoughts fragmented. His vision blurred and darkened.

Not a heart attack. Not a stroke.

Of course it wasn't.

The men released Maddox's arms. He slumped forward, only prevented from freefall by Saulo's firm grip. The woman withdrew the syringe and backed away. The outline of her body distorted like an image on a dying television set.

"Don't dream," Saulo whispered as the last of the color and light drained away from Maddox's sight. "They're cheap imitations of memories. They'll betray you."

Consciousness escaped; Maddox dreamed.

December 20th

"Methohexital." Her voice drifted through Maddox's thoughts. The tone was calming and gentle. "You're feeling washed out right now, like you're drifting at sea, but that'll fade. Unfortunately, what comes next is a headache. A nasty one. Can you feel that?"

With great effort, Maddox peeled back his swollen lips and whispered, "Yes."

"On a scale of one through ten?" she asked.

"Five," he answered.

"Barbiturates don't always play nice with other drugs," she said. "If we'd had another option, we'd have used it. But we didn't just need you unconscious, we needed to induce short-term amnesia. Once Kloum loses your scent, it takes him a while to find you again."

Maddox feebly cleared his throat. "Had no right."

"That's true, we didn't, but the risks are too high."

Maddox forced his eyes open, cracking through a rheum seal. Blinding light exploded against his pupils. He slammed his eyes back shut. With a moan, he said, "Seven."

"I'll dim the lights," she said. Soft-soled shoes padded away. The intense glow beyond his pink eyelids faded. The footsteps returned. "That better?"

"Yes," he said.

"There may be aftereffects. Nothing permanent. You'll let me know if you feel any nausea, shortness of breath, or tightness in your chest?" She put an icy hand on his forehead. "No fever, that's good."

Maddox tried again to open his eyes. Even the subdued light caused him to wince, but he managed a squint. She was tall and dark-haired with a tiny, pursed set of lips and dominant, unturned eyes. Not quite pretty, but pleasant enough. "You a doctor?"

She guffawed. "I wish we had a proper doctor. Back when I was remembered, I was a fry cook and part-time maid taking classes to be a nurse. They borrow some books and supplies from St. Joseph's. Somehow I keep us patched up. Like a middle school nurse."

"What's your name?" Maddox asked. His voice gained some strength.

She smirked, "My name used to be Mae."

"What's it now?" he asked.

She said, "Mae Bee. It's a joke about the odds of survival."

"It's good. Funny," he said.

"If you say so."

"Back to five," Maddox said.

"Good."

Mae Bee plucked a prescription bottle off the countertop behind her and held it up. "These are normally for epilepsy patients. Derrick DeMagginio. That's the name on the bottle. He's a little heavier than you, but I think we're in the ballpark."

A defensive rumble filled Maddox's voice. "What's *that* for?"

"Increases cognizance," she said, cracking open the bottle's top. "We couldn't have Kloum's thoughts in your head on the way here, but before we let you in any further, we need to know exactly what he's put in there. Think of this as psychological reconnaissance."

"There's no drug for that," Maddox said. He strained to sit but a canvas strap across his chest held him tight against the cot. His wrists, forearms, and ankles were similarly restrained. Otherwise, however, he was naked. He opened his eyes wide, ignoring the pain. His surroundings bore only a superficial resemblance to a hospital room: cinderblock walls covered in a thick coat of white paint; yellow water-stained ceiling tiles; an old stainless steel industrial sink in the corner. "Take these off. Let me up."

Mae Bee shook two pills out of the prescription bottle into the palm of her hand. "Problem with that is, Kloum can't do violence. He can't do *anything* physical, so far as we can tell. He exists only in our perceptions of him. But he can confuse otherwise good men. Place false memories. Change what they see. How they feel. He's done it before. We were too trusting that time. We lost six of us. Shot dead in the middle of the night. That won't happen again."

"I didn't come here by choice," Maddox said, growling his way through his consonants. "You people *abducted* me. What kind of goddamned assassin plans to get drugged and kidnapped as part of a master plan?"

Mae Bee closed her fist around the pills. "You're still not level-set. You can't think in the same way as you did before Kloum came into your life. He's changed everything. Those experiences that you've build your entire sense of logic upon? You can't trust any of them. Neither can we. There's nothing about our pasts we can rely on. He could feed you any memory and you wouldn't know the difference."

"You're insane," Maddox said.

Mae Bee moved her free hand over Maddox's mouth and squeezed his jowls. The pressure increased until his jaw moved and mouth opened. She pressed the pills between his lips. "That's a possibility as well."

Maddox caught the capsules with his tongue and trapped them against the roof of his mouth. The pills' coating began to break down and coat his tongue in a layer of greasy liquid. He struggled against the restraints, twisting from side to side, but the canvas straps held.

"You were right when you said there's no drug that will tell us what memories Kloum has put in your head." Mae Bee went to a metal door and pushed it open. Two men wearing baby-doll masks entered. One carried a pile of towels in his arms. An ice pick dangled from the other's hand. "That's why we don't rely on drugs alone."

Towel Man dropped his load on a rolling metal cart and pushed it bedside. Mae Bee handed him a plastic half-gallon jug marked ANTISEPTIC ALCOHOL SOLUTION.

"Kloum has a weakness, Mr. Boxwood. His ability to affect memory depends on the mental state of his victim. Your disease, for instance. You were able to see us even before he marked you. He has trouble influencing schizophrenics and the like." She reached onto the cart, withdrew a hand towel, and doused it in the sink. "But everyone has a natural resistance to him. *Fear. Panic. Pain.* We're never more aware of our world then when we're hurting. It cuts right through his false memories. We think that's why he's drawn to the most traumatic moments in history. He cannot control those in anguish. That's dangerous to him."

The coating was gone. The taste of chalk and minerals filled Maddox's mouth.

"So we've got to hurt you. Not just a little bit, unfortunately. We're experienced at this. Won't leave any lasting damage. This is surgery without anesthetic by design. Pain is the cure."

Maddox attempted to kick but managed only a feeble shuffle.

Ice Pick Man used a towel to wash down the blade with alcohol. He worked with the care and precision of a gourmet chef preparing his knives. Dark brown Asian eyes peered out from the mask's eyeholes, full of concentration and patience. His accent confirmed his race. "Try not to squirm. It'll only make it worse."

Steam rose from the sink. Mae Bee lifted the hand towel out of the stream of water and spread it out in her hands. A torrent of water escaped the fabric and ran down her arms, leaving her pale skin pink in its wake. "Ready?"

Maddox screamed, "NO–"

The remainder of the pills fell into his throat. He choked.

Mae Bee dropped the hot towel onto his face, covering it. Maddox's face swelled, the flesh rising as if reacting to bee stings. Water rushed into his nostrils and streamed down into his lungs. He shuddered violently, head rocking back and mouth gasping. The limited amount of air he could draw through the towel's tight weave gave no relief. His windpipe convulsed and threatened to collapse.

Through the cloth he could see only dark silhouettes against a gray background. Ice Pick Man leaned in close, until the outline of his head nearly eclipsed out the overhead lights entirely. "There won't be much blood so long as you don't move."

Maddox's heart raced, beating even faster than during his attacks. His neck muscles bulged. His muscles clenched. He started to shake.

"Let's get this over with," Mae Bee said.

Ice Pick Man lunged forward. An icy jolt of pain burst in Maddox's lower abdomen. He felt the blade's path under his skin and between the tight weave of muscle beneath. He bolted to his right to escape the blade, but the restraints blocked his movement. A pair of hands–Towel Man's, Maddox assumed–latched on to his thighs and held him in place. Ice Pick Man twisted the blade slowly, threading the stainless steel deeper into his body.

"Told you not to move," Ice Pick Man said with a grunt.

Towel Man added, "That's a lot more blood than usual."

"Listen to my voice," Mae Bee whispered into his ear. "I need you to think back through your life. Search for the most awful moments. Use the pain you're feeling; it'll guide you. Focus on those moments of grief."

Maddox couldn't think at all. The agony overwhelmed his senses and reduced him to animal instinct. He understood her words but couldn't attach meaning to them. They were only raw sounds that he knew meant *something*, but the pain obscured anything more.

"Your worst moments. Relive them. Know them."

The blade turned in his abdomen.

Ice Pick Man pulled back. "This will hurt worse."

The blade retreated from Maddox's flesh, scraping and dicing along its escape route. His skin puckered close once the ice pick was out. The muscles surrounding the wound fluttered. Ice Pick Man was correct. Removing the blade brought infinitely more pain.

"What does it remind you of? Find it. Search until it's clear," Mae Bee whispered. "It's there, hidden under the scar tissue, waiting for you to unearth it."

Towel Man released him and swabbed him down. The towel's coarse texture grated against his bruised and punctured skin. Then cold alcohol splashed across his body. A spark of pain erupted from the tiny hole in his abdomen, followed by a flash of heat. The towel returned and wiped away the moisture.

The silhouette of Mae Bee moved out of his sight and returned with the unmistakable shape of a bucket. She held it up over Maddox's head and overturned it. A fresh wave of steaming water cascaded down on the towel over his face. His chest tightened. His sinus cavities flooded. His ears popped.

The ice pick slid under Maddox's right nipple. Instead of digging deeper, the blade navigated overtop the muscle membrane and tugged at the skin from underneath. The tip struck a bundle of nerves. Searing pain spread out over his chest. An intense wave of nausea struck him. His stomach lurched.

Ten, he thought with sudden clarity, *the pain's a ten.*

"Find it. Seize on it."

The ice pick's tip broke through the skin of his armpit.

"A *lot* more blood," Towel Man said. "You didn't hit a major artery, did you?"

"Never can tell, but I don't think so." Ice Pick Man pulled the blade out of Maddox in one fluid motion. Agony. The little exit wound in his armpit stuttered like a pair of lips. Towel Man wiped him down, sanitized the area, and dried him off.

The ice pick, cold from a fresh douse of alcohol, snaked down from his ribs to his belly button and kept moving south. It stopped at his inner thigh. Mae Bee lifted the towel's corner and brought her lips to Maddox's ear. "This one's gonna be the worst of all, I'm afraid. It's called the genitofemal nerve. It's right on top of the psoas major. That's the muscle that makes your testicles rise and fall. It's gonna feel like someone is reaching inside you and tearing you inside out."

Please no.

The blade punched into Maddox's body and set in motion a series of violent explosions of pure sensation. He went fully rigid. Every muscle in his body contracted to its limit. Pain of the highest order surged through him like an electrical charge. Mae Bee was wrong: it didn't feel like being torn inside out. It felt like exploding in slow motion.

It didn't fade, even as the moments passed.

"Remember the truth," Mae Bee whispered.

Ice Pick Man wiggled the blade.

At seven, Maddox fell from a street sign he'd climbed and broke his arm. That pain returned to him. *He recovered from hernia surgery at nineteen; a stab wound early in his years on the force; the death of his mother in a Jersey City hospital bed; nose broken in a drunken stumble up his apartment building's front steps; a root canal; Dad dead on the living room rug, one hand frozen in a clawing gesture; the moment he heard that Dan Wilkson, a patrolmen friend, had been shot responding to a domestic dispute; Catherine—*

"You need to listen to me. She's not coming back this time. The respirator will keep her breathing and the IV in her arm will keep her nourished, but she'll never regain consciousness. She's at her end," Dr. Van Stiehl said, standing beside Maddox. The doctor faced him; Maddox stared down at his wife on her hospital bed.

"Does she know I'm here?" he asked. "Can she hear me?"

"No," Dr. Van Stiehl said.

Maddox wiped away the freshest tears. "How can you know?"

"The EEG chart is flat."

Dr. Van Stiehl pointed to a clipboard hanging from the foot of the bed. The chart resembled sheet music. There were no notes, only empty staff lines. Maddox glanced away. "But you can't know, right? Really know?"

"We know," Dr. Van Stiehl said.

Maddox steadied himself with a hand on the bed rail. Catherine's face was pale except for the dark purple blotches under her eyes and the two small birthmarks that punctuated her right eyebrow. Her hair, thinned out by her disease, clung to her sweaty skin. She'd been so beautiful. "What can I do?"

"You can say goodbye and let her have her dignity."

His grip on the rail failed. Dr. Van Stiehl guided him over to the chair beside the bed. He knew what the doctor meant. Order the machines to be turned off. End his wife's life.

He couldn't. There was no way. Impossible.

"You need time with her alone. To make your peace," Dr. Van Stiehl said and left the intensive care room, closing the door behind him.

The respirator moaned and sucked.

He knew he was supposed to speak to her. To tell her he loved her and would miss her. He wished he could have done more for her. Been a better husband. Saved her somehow. Brought home flowers more often, or her favorite coffee Danish. Apologized for the vacations that never happened and the evenings at home cut short by calls from the precinct. He could think all of these things but say none of them. Said aloud, they were words of surrender. He took her hand and sat with her in silence.

The heart monitor bleeped. Paused. Bleeped.

He ruminated on their courtship in restaurants, movie theaters, and hotel rooms. On their marriage at her parents' Presbyterian church. On their honeymoon trip to the Grand Canyon. On the night she told him she was pregnant. Holding her after that first miscarriage. The birth of Steven six years later. The smile on her face as she held her newborn son for the first time. Her pride as she watched Steven graduate high school, then college. Their first day retired together, lounging on the couch watching game shows and reruns of old sitcoms. The day she collapsed in the bathroom. The diagnosis—

He wouldn't sign an order to remove the machines. The thought of a nurse drawing an hourly paycheck unplugging the ventilator and pulling the IV out of her arm repelled him. She deserved better than to be put out of her misery like a stray dog by a veterinary assistant.

After a long time sitting, Maddox stood up and left the hospital. Before he did, however, he did two things: he turned off the ventilator himself and swore to himself he'd never think *of it again.*

He nearly succeeded.

"You found it, didn't you?" Mae Bee whispered.

Ice Pick Man pulled the blade out of his thigh. Towel Man sanitized the area. Mae Bee pulled the hot towel off his face and tossed it into the sink.

Maddox sprayed the air with water and vapor.

Mae Bee loosened the restraints. "You're free. Anything Kloum put inside you has been flushed out. There may be aftereffects. Moments of confusion where you have two sets of memories of the same event. But you'll know which is real."

Maddox leaned over the side of the cot and hacked up the remaining liquid from his lungs. He ran a hand to each of the wounds Ice Pick Man had inflicted. Only small bumps and irritated skin remained. As promised, there would be no lasting damage.

Maddox stared up at Mae Bee and panted until his throat relaxed and lungs filled normally. She wiped his face with a clean washcloth and smiled. "Clarity is not a gift; everyone must fight for it. You've earned this."

"Goodbye," Maddox said in a whimper. "I love you."

"Excuse me?" Mae Bee asked.

He shook his head. "Wasn't talking to you."

December 21st

Morning came through the small octagonal window, first as a yellow ambient glow, then building to prismatic bands of sunlight. Dust glittered in its breadth. Maddox stared up from the bed with the awe and wonder of a two-year-old child. After the last few days, the idea of a simple, beautiful ray of light was as close to a religious experience as he could imagine. He lifted a hand into the brightness and turned it slowly, examining every crease, wrinkle, and blemish. All his imperfections, each a memento of a moment in his life, were brought into a spotlight. No lies; only honesty.

He felt eyes watching him from the doorway but refused to allow himself to become distracted. It was good moment. He'd enjoy it. The figure in his peripheral vision waited without any sign of impatience. Once the sun rose higher over the horizon and the light leveled out, Saulo came to the bed and sat. "It's like being reborn, yes?"

Maddox shrugged. "I really don't know what it's like."

"You feel good?" Saulo asked.

"No," Maddox said in a soft tone. "Wouldn't say that. But I can *feel*, more than I have in a very long time. Not all of it is good, but it's better than not feeling at all."

Saulo nodded. "That sounds right."

Maddox's stomach growled. "Is there breakfast?"

"Not really," Saulo said. "Everyone usually takes care of themselves. We don't prepare to accommodate guests. But I'll ask around. I'm sure someone will share something."

"I'm surprised," Maddox said. "I'd have thought you would all look after one another, like a commune, y'know, share the resources."

Saulo stared down at his folded hands. "We're not hippies. People come and go. Have to understand—unless we find them early, they spend time out there alone. Really alone. Invisible among the crowds. No one to talk with. No nothing. Good people get damaged pretty quick like that."

Maddox could relate. He'd begun to feel like that even before Kloum.

"That said," Saulo said, "we've been busy recently. You've made him busy, which kept us active. You proved to be a recruiting goldmine."

Maddox's brow dropped. "What's that mean?"

Saulo stood up. "C'mon. Got some people waiting to see you."

Maddox didn't move.

"Promise you, no more syringes or any of that."

Maddox said, "And that's it? Now I trust you?"

It was Saulo's turn to shrug. "You really should. If we meant to kill you, we had the opportunity. I wish it worked some other way and we didn't need Mae and the guys to do their thing, but we do. It protects everyone."

"Your pep talks are shit."

Saulo offered his hand. "Yes, but I can find you breakfast."

The Dominican opened the door and led Maddox out into a wide cinderblock hallway. Half of the overhead florescent lights were out, producing a pattern of light and dark patches down the linoleum tile floor. They passed a faded and curled poster advertising a high school drama class production of *Bye Bye Birdie*. The performance date read Friday, February 18th, 1983. "This was a school?"

Saulo pointed to a series of bullet holes in a classroom door. "Not a real one. Cold War. I don't know the whole story, but the military built this place as a training ground. In case the Soviets invaded or something."

"Never heard of anything like that," Maddox said.

"Which is why it's perfect for us." The hallway forked ahead. Saulo gestured to the right. "Kloum isn't omniscient. He only knows what he pulls out of people's heads. Very few know about this place. That protects us here."

Maddox peeked through an open door. A female mannequin stood at a chalkboard with a pointing stick in her hand. Plastic children stared back from five rows of desks. None wore clothes.

"They must not have ever done much with the building after the Berlin Wall fell, because they left everything in place. Cans of rations in the cafeteria cupboard. Washed and pressed fatigues in the laundry. Even the armory is still stocked. Government, you know. It's like they just forgot about it all. We call it the Rumor Mill."

They took another right turn and the lighting improved. The school hallway transformed into rows of office cubicles. More naked mannequins at desks staring at typewriters and rotary phones. There were bullet holes in the partitions. "There's a few more settings in the other wings: a grocery store, a disco, a bowling alley. They're all fake. Empty cereal boxes on the shelves, painted white dots on the floor instead of a working disco ball, plastic bowling balls glued to the lanes. Almost seems like more work than just making the real thing."

Saulo held a metal door open for Maddox. Ducking under the man's arm, Maddox stepped into a small, undecorated room. A single bed waited under an octagonal window. It was identical to the room in which he'd awakened.

Hadassah Boutros sat on the edge of the mattress.

"I'll go fetch you a bagel," Saulo said as he left.

Hadassah stood up and ran a hand down her skirt to smooth out the wrinkles. She spoke in a dry rasp but an upbeat tone. "I was wondering if y'all'd find yourself a way in here."

"They didn't give me much choice," Maddox said.

"I just suppose they probably didn't," she said as she stepped up to him. He flinched as she wrapped her arms around him in a firm embrace. She squeezed and then pulled away. "They're not all that much on manners, but they're trying to right a tremendous wrong. Sometimes there's no polite way to do that."

"Your face's gone pale. Paler than usual even," she said. The corners of her lips turned up in a playful smirk. "What's the matter, you seen a ghost? A spook, maybe?"

"I just... never thought I'd see you again."

"Poor boy," Hadassah said. "Been getting pushed and pulled in all kinds of directions, haven't you all now? Kloum and us, the Displaced, playing a game of tug-of-war with your head. You've had it rougher than most of us. That's 'cause Kloum has a special interest in you. Me? He didn't take two notices until you came sniffing around looking at me. And I *knew about him*. I just wasn't no kind of threat to him, I guess."

Maddox stared down at his shoes. "I'm sorry. I didn't know—"

"Sew those regrets back up," she told him. "Don't you trip over any kind of regrets over *that*. It didn't hurt none. And now, well, I'm back with my children. I only helped their mommas give birth to just a few of them, but they all feel like my babies all the same. The people who've forgotten me? Naw, they all forgot about me a long time before you came around asking questions. I should thank you."

"No, you shouldn't," he said solemnly.

She tossed her head to the side and fixed him with a one-eyed stare. "You think I was living on the high? Running a food stamp card through the machine once a week to buy bags of white rice and ramen noodle packets? Even the moment that I saw Kloum standing there on the street, waiting for me to come back from the park, I knew things would only get better. It's not that way for most people he touches, but for me, I got no regrets about any of it."

"How did you know it was Kloum on the street?" Maddox asked.

Hadassah smiled. "He was too perfect. My husband, dead nineteen years, still looking like he did when he passed. Waved at me from the sidewalk with his little finger down, just like he always did. It's exactly what I'd wanted to see. That's his biggest weakness for sure. He'll use our memories and our wishes against us. But he's not creative... My daddy told me never to scratch a silver fork against a silver knife. Maybe nothing happens and you really have what you think you've got. More likely you end up holding stainless steel in both hands wishing you still thought they was precious."

Maddox knew the feeling. "You let him do it."

"No, baby," she said, "I *asked* him to."

Hadassah stepped up to her dresser, opened the drawer, and removed a shoe box. She pulled out a long blue ribbon and a black permanent marker. She stretched it flat across the dresser and wrote MADDOX. "Hold out your wrist."

"I don't need that," he said.

"You're one of my children now," Hadassah said, lifting his hand and encircling his wrist with the ribbon. She tied it off in a single fluid motion. "No one has given you anything since you got forgotten, right? Don't you take this off. Don't insult me by throwing away your first gift since your new birthday."

Running a finger over the silky ribbon, he nodded. "My doctor says I won't live to see another year, so this is probably my *last* birthday gift as well."

"Listen now," she said. "No one knows nothing about that."

Saulo reappeared in the doorway holding a bagel. He raised it up. "I'd say breakfast is served," he said, but then tapped it against the door frame. It sounded as solid as a hammer. "But I'm not sure you could gnaw through this thing."

Hadassah grinned. "Maybe we could use it as a weapon. Hold it up over some poor brother's neck. *Give us all your donuts and coffee or else we'll beat your bones down to dust.*"

Saulo chuckled. "I think maybe it would just be better if we went out for a bite."

"Out?" Maddox asked. He hadn't even considered it as an option.

Hadassah reached for her yellow knit coat. "None of us are prisoners here. You come and go as you wish. In most cases."

"There are precautions," Saulo said as he tossed the bagel into a wastebasket in the corner. It landed with a thud. "But you've just been through the cleansing. Shouldn't be no kind of problem."

Saulo spun on his heels and headed back into the maze of cubicles. Maddox and Hadassah followed. At the end of the office vignette, Maddox's foot landed on a small-caliber shell casing. He leaned down, swiped it off the floor, and slid it into his pants pocket. Saulo glanced back at him with a quizzical look on his face but did not slow his pace. In another moment and after a few more turns, they arrived at a set of reinforced steel doors.

A man wearing a baby-doll mask stood guard. The assault rifle in his arms was a larger caliber weapon than the shell in Maddox's pocket. Saulo barely afforded the sentry a glance. They exited without even a word from the guard.

A short alley opened up onto a residential street. Maddox turned back to the alley. He'd driven through the neighborhood countless times but had never noticed the entryway to the facility. Two-story brick houses lined Gotthardt Street, separated only by wrought iron fences and narrow driveways. It seemed impossible to Maddox that he could have overlooked the mammoth building nestled behind the homes. Hadassah snickered. "I see what's on your face. Had it on mine, too. Hidden in plain sight, or is it something else? That's what you're thinking."

"It's not that complex," Saulo said. "People are too busy with their own lives to look beneath the surface and see what's really there. Too busy and too comfortable. Don't wanna know. The government and Kloum both rely on that."

Maddox mumbled, "Doesn't seem possible."

"That word lost its meaning a long stretch back," Hadassah said.

Saulo waved a dismissive hand in the air. "What's it matter? We are where we are; things are how they are. For right now? There's a little Columbian café a few blocks over. Good coffee, okay pastries. This morning, I don't think we need to be more existential than a foam cup filled with java."

They walked in silence. The sun broke through the clouds. Snow drifts glistened with an almost metallic intensity in the bright light. An old Cadillac, rusted at all its edges and coughing through its final miles, rolled down Gotthardt and turned onto New York Ave, slowing at the intersection. An elderly black man stepped off the curb into the car's path. Brakes squealed and men yelled. For the driver and the pedestrian, it was a normal day filled with the usual frustrations, Maddox realized. How long had it been since he'd felt that way?

Maddox shivered and wished he had a coat. Hadassah looked warm.

Saulo trotted down New York Ave to a tiny corner café nestled under three floors of apartments. The Dominican opened the door and hustled them inside. The proprietor, a lanky white man in his late forties, pointed to the last man in line to be served and barked, "Close that door. All the way. Goddamn wind'll keep blowing it open if y'don't."

Hadassah slid inside just as the customer yanked the door closed. She pursed her lips and blew. His bangs danced. He fixed his hair and muttered, "Close your own fuckin' door. Paying customer here, not some doorman."

Maddox leaned over to her ear and whispered, "There's no wind."

Hadassah laughed. "You don't have to hush. They won't hear you even if you scream. Took some getting used to for me, but you'll take to it. Same as the wind, in a way. They need an explanation for why the door opened, so they say the wind did it. Don't matter that the air's still out; they gotta believe it. Otherwise, they run risk of actually knowing something."

Saulo cast her a harsh look. "That's a little unfair."

"Maybe it is," Hadassah said. "But true, too."

Saulo pointed to the only open table in the small café. "They don't have a big menu, but everything's better than you'd expect. What can I get you?"

Taking her seat, Hadassah ordered, "Muffin. Whatever they have."

Maddox sat down beside her. "Whatever... I guess."

"You're worried about this?" Saulo said as he reached over the counter and retrieved three muffins. He jutted out his chin in the direction of the line of customers. "They're not seeing muffins float across the room or anything. They just don't see them at all. They ignore it because it would lead them to questions they don't want to have to answer. So these muffins never existed in the first place."

Maddox sighed. "It's still theft."

Hadassah laughed again. "You serious?"

"Yeah," he said.

Saulo set the muffins and three large Styrofoam cups of coffee on the table. As he sat down in the remaining chair, he said, "Imagine you go on vacation. While you're away, a guy comes into your backyard and digs up a bag full of pirate treasure. Then he closes the hole and replaces the grass perfectly. No sign that anything was ever touched. You never knew the treasure was there. Or that he was ever on your property. Did he steal from you?"

"Yes," Maddox said.

Saulo winked. "But you see the point, right?"

"I guess," Maddox said. He turned his attention to the window beside him. A woman in a baby-doll mask stood across New York Ave, motionless and staring back at him.

Saulo leaned over the table and, following Maddox's gaze, squinted. "Precautions, I told you. We call them Custodians, because they clean up our messes. Not everyone goes through the process of being forgotten as well as Haddie and I. Some... lose things. Perspective. Morals. Sanity. The Custodians serve a good purpose. They protect the hive. But they're also... volatile."

"Nuts," Hadassah said with a nod. "Crazy people."

Saulo straightened up in his chair and bit into his muffin. Crumbs cascaded down his chin. "They keep us safe; we value that. And also, who would be the one to tell them they're not wanted."

"They're volatile," Maddox echoed back.

"Exactly," Saulo said.

An hour later, they returned to the Rumor Mill. At the front door, Saulo knocked in a quick melody with his knuckles and fingertips: knock-tap-knockknockknc tap-tap-knock.

The guard Custodian on the other side opened the door.

Passing inside, Maddox asked, "That'd keep Kloum out? A secret knock?"

"No," Hadassah said.

"There are others," Saulo said. "Confused. Kloum gets into heads, turns minds all around. Maybe someday a man shows up here with a gun or a bomb. We think we're invisible, but not to Kloum. We have to take precautions."

"Confused," Maddox mumbled, "like I was."

"Yes," Hadassah said. "Exactly like you."

December 22nd

"Say you were standing on the edge of a cliff. A Wile E. Coyote situation where the road just stops and it's straight down from there. You dig so far?" the old hippy said. He took a moment to make eye contact with each of his listeners.

Maddox stared back at him with mild curiosity. He'd met enough men and women at the Rumor Mill to understand that none were completely sane. Being forgotten changed people. He wondered how long it would take before he'd be affected.

The old hippy continued, "The fall doesn't have to scare you, because it's just a chance to fly, even for just a moment, and you've never flown before. You know you'll die, but hell, that's gonna happen eventually, right? But flying, that's not something that many people get the chance to do."

The listeners mumbled. A few sounded skeptical, but most seemed to consider the old hippy's words as meaningful. A young woman with a shaved head and large brown eyes tilted her head and said, "That's beautiful."

"It's not flying," Maddox said. "It's falling. To your death."

The old hippy grunted. "To you, maybe."

"No," Maddox said. "To everyone. I've seen what happens when people jump off buildings. Off bridges. You want to know? Your bones break on impact. And every shard of your skeleton becomes a missile inside you, cutting through all your internal organs as swift as razorblades. You bleed inside and out. Not like in the movies, either. Jumpers don't always die the instant they hit. I've seen them last ten minutes, looking up, neck broken at an impossible angle. Nothing but pain and regret. None of them thought they were flying."

"But," the old hippy insisted, "they *flew*. They did."

Maddox turned away and left the group standing in the school classroom training vignette. Saulo had told him that the onset of insanity came faster for those who tried to live outside the sanctuary of the Rumor Mill, but he wondered if that was entirely true. Maybe they just traded one form of madness for another.

As he entered the hallway, he passed a poster of a kitten clinging to a tree branch. A bullet hole marked the center of the picture–a dime-sized hole, tiny tears spider-webbing out, black seared edges–too fresh to be a relic from the Cold War. He'd bet the hole matched the .223 caliber Remington shell casing he still carried in his pocket.

They're probably training to protect themselves against Kloum. The thought brought a guilty smile to his face. He couldn't fool himself into thinking that anyone could believe that Kloum could be shot. *No, that's not it, exactly. They're protecting themselves against Kloum getting someone inside. Someone who'll attack from within.*

The hallway was filthy. He hadn't noticed before, but as his hand grazed the wall he felt a layer of grime build up on his fingertips. *A colony of forgotten people, cloistered up inside a grimy fortress,* he thought. *A community of rats scurrying around, scavenging for food. Can I live this way? Would I even want to?*

Mae Bee appeared at the end of the hall. As Maddox approached, she crossed her arms under her breasts and rolled her eyes when his gaze hesitated on her chest. "She's asking for you."

"Who?" he asked.

Mae Bee dropped her hands to her sides. "Just follow me."

He did, through a maze of corridors and down a flight of metal stairs. As they went, the scenery changed from the dated decorations of the vignette scenes to whitewashed cinder walls. Tile floors gave way to smooth concrete. Harsh overhead florescent lights vanquished all shadow and texture from sight.

Mae Bee stopped in front of a red metal door and held up a hand. A glimmer of doubt passed through her eyes a moment before she said, "Are you the sort of man who wants answers? You search for them, I get that, but do you really want your mysteries solved?"

He nodded. "I am."

She nodded, but the trepidatious expression remained. "I think we all believe that we are. I've seen a lot of disappointment in many, many faces. Tells a different story. If we walk into this room, you might not like the answer you get."

"I don't even know what question I've asked," he said.

She snickered. "As if there are all that many questions."

Mae Bee held the door open and gestured for him to enter. Maddox looked the nurse in the eyes. How much trust could he place in a medical woman who used torture as medicine? Where had she led him? Instead of answers, he saw an alarming physical abnormality imperceptible at a distance: her irises were slightly different sizes. Once he'd noticed, her entire being took on an unbalanced appearance. Unnerved, Maddox broke off his stare and passed through the doorway.

Hiss. Pop. Hiss. Pop. To his right, an antique child's phonograph rested on a short chest of drawers. The needle rode the final loop of the groove, tittering each time it came to the end before jumping back to the beginning. *Hiss. Pop. Hiss. Pop.*

Mae Bee shut the door behind him.

He stood in a child's bedroom filled with furniture better than half a century old. An ornate four-post bed dominated the center of the room. The silhouette of a thin figure faced him from behind a panel of faded pink drape. A frail female voice asked, "Play it again, once more? For me?"

Maddox reached for the stylus and lifted it out. A sound like a zipper being pulled burst out of the built-in speaker. He dropped the needle at the beginning of the forty-five. Dick Haymes harmonized with the Song Spinners. "You'll Never Know."

"Thank you," she said, then hummed along with the music for a moment. Her head swayed back and forth. After a moment, she parted the drape. "Now you come and step up. My eyes don't work too good, to match the rest of me."

Maddox approached the bed. The woman was propped up by a stack of large frilly pillows. She wore a child's floral dress on her emaciated form. As she pulled the drape along its rod, her arm shook. *Not much more than a skeleton and skin*, he thought. The gravity of his own advanced age evaporated as his eyes roamed over her. "Hello, ma'am."

"Ma'am?" she said with a cackle. "That's not me."

"I'm sorry," Maddox said. "What should I call you?"

"Just my name is fine," she said. Her eyes, set far back and ringed by dark circles, glimmered. Her expression was innocent and kind. "You just call me Purse. They all do."

"Purse," Maddox said. He felt tears welling up unexpectedly, accompanied by a rush of heat that spread across his face. With trembling lips, he asked, "Persephone Alford?"

She covered her mouth with one unsteady hand and giggled.

Maddox felt weak. How many cops had spent their retirement years searching for answers to her mystery? Had any of them believed they could have found her alive? How close had they come to standing here in front of her? "I had a friend. Stan. He spent years searching for you."

She lowered her hand and revealed a wide smile. The upturned corners of her lips pressed into folds as dry and rigid as seafaring rope. "I keep asking them to put a chair in here, but they never do. So, I guess you'll have to come and sit by my side here, even if it doesn't seem proper." She patted the bed beside her. "C'mon now."

He sat on the edge of the mattress. It sank as his weight came down. Bedsprings creaked. For a moment, they sat in silence. Then Persephone dropped a hand on his. Cold.

"Your face," she said. "I thought it'd be hard and mean. But it's not. You pretend to be cold, I think, but inside you're warm. Maybe that's what's different. Why you were the one to find me."

Maddox shook his head. "I never meant to come looking."

"Or maybe *that's* the reason," she said. She gestured around the room with her free hand. "When we came here, they built my bedroom. I told them, '*The mirror goes there, the chair with the teddy bear over there.*' All from memory of how it all was. But none of it's right. How could it be? That bear? It's the same kind as Mr. Puffles, but it's not him. He's long gone. The furniture too. It all looks right, but it's all wrong."

"This is your bedroom from the house on Clinton Ave?"

Persephone's smile straightened. Her pupils dilated. Her hand patted his and then moved to her lap. A long moment passed. Maddox waited in silence.

The record ended.

Hiss. Pop. Hiss. Pop.

Her voice crackled like the record. "Like to hear a story?"

"Yes, please."

"Could you bring Mr. Puffles to me?"

He did. She pressed the bear to her chest.

"It's not a happy story, I've got to warn you. It's not even an important one. Not every story has to be, I suppose... It's about a little girl and her mom and her dad. Immigrants, though the girl was born here. They came here to escape, to forget about the horrible things they'd seen in the old world. But they could never truly forget, so they lived with a little shadow of fear. At all times."

Hiss. Pop. Hiss. Pop.

"She never went to school, never played out in the streets or in the park with other children. Didn't even know there *were* other children in the world until the day a boy appeared in her window. She was scared of him at first, but then they became friends. As close of friends as you can become with a pane of glass separating you. She couldn't hear him and he couldn't hear her, so they pantomimed and played guessing games. In winter, he blew on the glass and fogged it up. Then he wrote his name. It was backwards on the window."

"Troy Turring," Maddox whispered.

Hiss. Pop. Hiss. Pop.

"He was as honest with her as he could be. But she didn't tell him the truth. She held things back. But what would you expect? A little girl to tell her only friend things that might scare him off? No, a little girl doesn't explain the welts on her arms or the marks on her neck. She certainly doesn't try to tell him about Daddy's visits into her bedroom."

Hiss. Pop. Hiss. Pop.

"And, above all, she doesn't mention the man with the terrible face, like a baby who didn't get born, who asks her if she wants to be free... Sometimes her friend would bring books and hold them up to the glass, page by page. Big cardboard pages and brightly colored drawings. Stories about animals and kids and talking trees, all sorts of funny things. But once, after a particularly bad night, he brought a book that told the story of Peter Pan."

Hiss. Pop. Hiss. Pop.

"That night, the little girl wrote a letter to her friend. Construction paper and a yellow crayon. It told him she loved him. And goodbye. She taped it to the window. Then she told the man with the horrible face that she wanted to go to Neverland. And he took her."

Hiss. Pop. Hiss. Pop.

"Where did he take you?" Maddox asked.

Persephone's pupils lost focus. "Just... away."

Hiss. Pop. Hiss. Pop.

Her fingers tightened around Mr. Puffles. A large, pearl-like tear formed in each eye. "She wanted to get away from her father's hands and her mother's... ignorance. But she always thought that running away meant running *towards* somewhere."

Hisspop. Hisspop.

Persephone's fingernails dug into the stuffed bear's wool fur. Its head twisted from the pressure until it faced Persephone's chest. "But the man with the horrible face took somewhere away from her, too. *All* of the somewheres. There was no Neverland."

Hisspop hisspop.

Stuffing erupted from between her fingers as Persephone tore into Mr. Puffles. Her hands disappeared into the toy and pulled until the fabric tore apart at the seams. The bear's body, deflated, lost its shape and transformed into a limp bundle of brown cloth and white fiber.

Hisspophisspop.

Persephone's eyes snapped back to focus. She stared down at the mess in her hands. Slowly she withdrew her fingers from inside the remains of Mr. Puffles and let him fall to her lap, then off the bed entirely and onto the floor. In a sad, quiet voice, she said, "Oh."

Maddox stared at the carcass on the floor. Plastic eyes seemed to return his gaze. He held his attention on the destroyed stuffed animal even as he heard Persephone move towards him on the bed. Her breath tickled his earlobe as she breathed. And when she whispered to him, the scent of black licorice filled his nostrils.

"We do horrible things sometimes," she said. "When no one can see us. When no one seems to care. My father did unspeakable things to me and my mother let him, but they never broke me. Kloum needs to pay. No matter how horrible the price for all of us."

Hiss.

Pop.

December 23rd

"Wake up," Saulo said, prodding Maddox's arm with two fingers.

Maddox opened his eyes. "Wasn't asleep."

The Dominican's attention shot to the doorway. A rustling sound echoed down the hall. Saulo crouched down and crept up to the entryway. He ducked his head out quickly.

"What's got you spooked?" Maddox asked as he sat up on his cot.

Without looking back, Saulo said, "Get dressed. Thing's wrong."

Throwing off his comforter, Maddox reached for the pants folded on the bedside table. "What do you mean? What's wrong?"

The .223 Remington shell dropped from the pocket as he unfolded the pants. It struck the floor with a metallic ping and bounced across the floor. It came to rest at Saulo's feet. "Most of the Custodians are gone. So's Purse. And some others."

Maddox hurried into his pants. "What you mean, gone?"

"Just gone, man. Must have taken her with them," Saulo's lips quivered as he spoke. "I've been here for years, never nothing like this. Something's up... something bad."

"Kloum?" Maddox asked.

Saulo shook his head. "Maybe. Dunno."

Running footsteps replaced the rustling sounds coming from the hall. Saulo retreated from the doorway. A second set of footsteps joined the first. Three quick cracks of gunshot sounded. A young woman's body skidded to a halt in the hallway. A thick trail of blood spread behind her. Her bare feet twitched, then didn't.

A jolt of adrenaline surged up inside Maddox and propelled him to shamble past Saulo. As he swung the door shut, he caught a glimpse of a man wearing a black suit and a baby-doll mask swaggering down the hall, an AR-15 in his hands. There was no lock on the door.

"Chair!" he yelled.

Saulo spun in a circle, head whipping from side to side, until he found the high-backed fiddleback in the corner. He snatched it up by its top rail and flung it at Maddox.

Maddox caught the chair, changed his grip, and slammed it to the floor. It broke into pieces. Maddox dropped down onto his haunches and reached for the longest rod.

The door burst open. Shards of wood trim rained down on Maddox.

Slapping his fingers around the rod, he swung it back like a baton. It struck the Custodian in the ankles as he stepped into the doorway. He howled in pain and pulled the trigger of the AR-15. Bullets sprayed into the room. Saulo dropped to the floor, both hands covering his head. The Custodian toppled forward, still firing off shots. Maddox skirted across the floor and out of the Custodian's path. As the large man hit the floor, Maddox raised the chair leg over his head and brought it down on the intruder's hand. The rifle fired once last time before it left the Custodian's wounded grip.

Maddox scrambled for the rifle but, in a clumsy panic, only managed to push it farther from reach. The Custodian rolled over, cradling his wounded hand to his chest, and started to rise. Maddox spun towards him and swung again with the rod.

The Custodian caught it in his good hand.

Maddox's fingers tightened on the weapon and tried to free it by wrenching it back and forth. The Custodian held tight to the other end. As the man rose to his feet, he pulled Maddox across the floor. If Maddox relinquished the rod, he had no defense against the larger, younger man. He glanced at the AR-15. *Can I get to it before he hits me with this thing?*

The Custodian yanked back. The distance to the rifle increased.

No, I cannot. Can't let go.

Another yank on the rod, this one to the right, slid Maddox in a wide arc. He hit the wall, hard. The breath rushed out of him as he felt–and heard–the impact. Still, he clung to the chair leg with shaking hands.

The Custodian stared at him through the eyeholes in the baby-doll mask. The impact with the floor had pushed the disguise off-center. The Custodian's chin peeked out from its bottom. The voice that came from behind the mask wasn't a vicious snarl, a ham-fisted chortle, or a villainous growl. The man sounded *normal*, like a substitute teacher or tax consultant, not a murderer. "It doesn't have to be difficult. Let go and I'll help you."

Maddox felt his grip loosen. "I don't wanna die."

"You're already dead," the Custodian said. "We all are."

The Custodian pulled back on the rod again. This time it came free from Maddox's hand. The Custodian stumbled back into the doorway. Maddox pushed off the floor. Equilibrium faltering, he slapped a hand against the wall to steady himself. He eyed the AR-15 again.

Odds haven't gotten any better.

But there wasn't any better option. Maddox went for the rifle, skidding to his knees as the Custodian stepped forward, chair leg raised. His hand closed on the buttstock. An intense shockwave of pain jolted through him as the Custodian brought the rod down on his lower back. His eyesight blurred.

Maddox pulled the rifle towards him.

The chair leg came down on the gun's hand guard, stopping its movement and pinning it to the floor. The pain in his back still raging, Maddox released the rifle and twisted around. He stared up at a smiling baby-doll face. The Custodian's eyes were lost to shadow.

The corner of the intruder's mouth, just visible at the edge of the cockeyed mask, raised. A smile beneath a smile.

The Custodian released the rod and took Maddox by the throat in one swift motion. Heat exploded at contact, rising to fill his face. Tears flooded Maddox's eyes. The Custodian squeezed.

Maddox's hands raked at the Custodian's chest, but with every second his dexterity failed more and more, until both arms fell limp to his sides. His blurry vision darkened.

A sound cut through the haze, a hearty collision of hardwood and bone. The fingers around his throat retreated. Maddox coughed. Saliva burst up from his lips and landed back on his face. The wavering outline of the Custodian stumbled off him and into the wall, bouncing off, his basic shape becoming clearer in Maddox's vision as the large man brought his good hand up to the back of his head. Saulo stepped back and pointed with the second-largest piece of the broken chair.

Maddox pulled the rifle back into his hands.

The Custodian straightened up and faced Saulo.

Maddox pressed the butt of the rifle between his chest and shoulder and took aim. He wiped his eyes. The Custodian rushed at Saulo and swiped the chair leg out of his way.

Maddox released a deep breath and pulled the trigger.

A crater opened in the wall behind the Custodian.

Missed. Dammit.

But he hadn't.

The Custodian dropped to his knees, both hands—wounded and good—snapping to his neck. Blood sprayed from between his fingers. He slumped forward, chin pressed against breastbone, and then collapsed to the floor. The baby-doll mask came loose and slid across the tiles when his head hit.

"Take it," Maddox said, pointing.

Saulo leaned down but stopped with his fingertips an inch from the mask. He swallowed hard, then shot Maddox a desperate look. "It's got blood on it."

"Everything here does," Maddox said. "We should go."

Saulo lifted the mask off the floor with two fingers, careful to avoid touching any of the red droplets that marked its face. "Don't understand this. How did Kloum get to the Custodians?"

Maddox shrugged as he peeked out the doorway. Besides the dead body on the floor, the coast was clear. "You'd make a shit detective. Don't assume. We don't know anything yet."

Saulo stayed close as Maddox headed down the hall.

At the end of the hall, they turned right and entered the mock high school classroom. The chairs and desk were scattered across the tile floor, most overturned, some broken. A dark splash of red ran the length of the chalkboard. A dead man lay crumpled beneath the American flag. His head was in pieces.

Maddox kept moving, through the door and into the next vignette, the office. Fresh bullet holes dotted the cubicles. A single shoe rested on the floor next to the water cooler. A corpse with one bare foot was draped over the nearest desk.

"They trained for this," Maddox said. "Right here."

Saulo mumbled something under his breath.

"Kloum didn't get to the Custodians," Maddox said as they passed through another doorway and re-entered the main hall. "Crazy bastards planned to do this, practiced it, waited."

"Waited for what?" Saulo asked.

Persephone, Maddox thought, but instead said, "Permission."

"This isn't right," Saulo said.

"What gave you the first clue?"

"No," Saulo said, pointing to the door at the end of the corridor, "this hallway. It never went so far. Walked it a thousand times; it was never this long. And that door—"

Maddox finished his sentence. "Was never there."

But it *was* always there, Maddox understood. Apparently, Kloum wasn't the only one able to manipulate memories. His thoughts drifted to Mae Bee and her operating table. What damage had she done to him there? To all of the Displaced? As they approached, an illustration etched into the door came into focus. A grinning Grim Reaper standing over a tombstone. The name on the grave marker was KLOUM. Over the skeleton's head, written in yellow crayon, were the words:

COME AND FLY

Maddox opened the door and stepped through. He was greeted by eight rows of seven desks, each with a blank two-fold presentation poster sitting on it. Otherwise, the large room was empty.

"What is this?" Saulo asked as he stepped inside.

"Dunno." Maddox headed down the narrow center aisle between desks and tightened his grip on the rifle. He half expected a Custodian to leap out from behind one of the white cardboard displays. Passing the final row of desks, his foot brushed against the first of dozens of presentation posters littering the floor. Some were torn. Some had bullet holes. He kept walking until he came to another door.

He turned the knob and pushed it open.

Saulo's eyes widened.

They stepped into a large hexagonal room. Sixteen rows of folding chairs circled a long desk in the center of the space. In each sat one of the Displaced, posed in the same position—hands folded in their laps, shoulders flat to the backrest, heads tilted back, mouths and eyes wide open. They were naked. And dead.

"Christ," Maddox blurted out.

"No," a male voice responded. The old hippy sat behind the desk in the center of the room. Mae Bee stood behind him, a hand on his shoulder. A half-dozen Styrofoam cups and a clear pitcher, a quarter filled with red liquid, waited at his fingertips. "People know who Jesus was, even two thousand years on. Nobody gonna remember any of us. Kloum made sure of that."

Maddox moved his finger to the trigger and led Saulo through the maze of dead men and women. He felt the Dominican's hand tighten around the tail of his shirt. As they passed by, Maddox scanned the lifeless bodies. He flinched at each one of their waxy, screaming faces. He felt a pang in his chest when they moved past D'ester, the church organist. Maddox's foot brushed aside one of the many cups scattered on the floor.

"This your own little Jonestown?" Maddox asked as he approached the desk. He leveled the rifle at the old hippy's chest. "Red punch for the willing, bullets for the rest?"

Mae Bee shook her head. "All part of the natural order in desperate times. Have you heard of the pea aphid? A little green bug, nearly transparent, looks like a tiny fat grasshopper. They live in colonies and they're very loyal to the group. Ladybugs find them tasty. It's a problem for the aphids. But they have a defense mechanism built into their instincts. When a ladybug comes to their nests to harvest them, they wait for it to get close and then they explode. It scares away the predator. It's selfless. Beautiful."

Maddox gestured at the first row of dead bodies with a sideways flick of his chin. "Doesn't look to me like there's anyone left to protect."

"Kloum will fall," the old hippy said. "It's already in motion. But we can take no chances. Everyone he's touched is a threat to our success. Even you. Even us."

Mae Bee smiled. "Once Kloum loses, all of our lives will be remembered again. We will be restored. Our birthdays will mean something again to the people we've loved. That's worth this."

"See?" The old hippy gave a stern nod. "We flew."

Mae Bee took a step up to the table and lifted the pitcher. As she poured out four cups of red punch, she said, "It really was inevitable for all of us, anyway. Some last days, others years, but eventually the loneliness gets to be too much. At least this way we all go together."

The old hippy picked up a cup and offered it to Maddox.

Maddox's finger curled around the trigger. "No, thank you."

The old hippy shrugged and tilted the cup towards Saulo.

Saulo shook his head.

Mae Bee's smile flattened. "You do know you won't leave here?"

"We'll see," Maddox said.

The old hippy brought the cup to his lips and drank. Once it was emptied, he tossed it over his shoulder. Beads of red liquid clung to his beard. "I ain't gonna see nothing."

Mae Bee lifted another cup with her thumb and forefinger, pinky extended. She sipped, then opened her mouth and spilled it down. She squinted as she swallowed. "Too sweet."

The old hippy pushed away from the table, folded his hands, and let his head roll back. He convulsed for only a moment before his mouth opened and he went still. Mae Bee looked from right to left, but there were no more chairs. She lowered herself to the floor gracefully, crossed her legs, and exhaled. Then she slumped forward and died.

Maddox turned in a full circle. His eyes passed over each dead man and woman. He and Saulo would probably be the last to see any of them and retain a memory. He felt like there should have been some responsibility imbued in the situation, but if there was, he couldn't find it. "We should go."

He took a step towards the exit. Saulo didn't.

"Maybe... I shouldn't."

Maddox glanced back at him. "What you mean?"

"I dunno," the Dominican said. He gestured towards the dead bodies around them. "I was just a regular man. Not someone special. You told me why Kloum came to you. I've never known. One night I come home from work and my family, they don't see me. They *can't*. I lived out on the streets, snuck into hotel lobbies, anywhere warm. Then the Displaced found me. I was pretty far gone. Talking to myself, hearing voices, seeing things. But these people—as crazy as they could be—they cared for me. Brought me back. Saved me."

"You're okay now," Maddox said. "You can leave."

"*Can*, yes. But should I? Why? I know what's out there. A world that won't acknowledge me. Here, there was structure. Purpose. Outside these walls? Just loneliness and slow death. Maybe it's better that I stay here." Saulo plucked a cup off the table.

"You really thinking about this?" Maddox asked.

Saulo stared down into the empty cup. "Like I said, I dunno."

Three quick blasts echoed from somewhere inside the complex.

"I've got to go," Maddox said.

"Yeah, you do." Saulo leaned against the table.

Maddox walked out of the hexagonal room. No drywall here, only red brick and pale mortar. Rough concrete underfoot. Overhead, water pipes hung from rusted swivel rings. They had to lead to an outer wall, he knew. Another gunshot sounded, no louder than a firecracker but unmistakable. He hurried down the hall, turned at a sharp left corner, and found himself approaching a pair of crash doors secured by a bright yellow blockade bar. Maddox rammed the bar out of its brackets with the butt of the rifle, then pushed open the door on the right.

He expected a barrage of gunfire. Instead, the door clanked against the metal rail of the fire escape beside it. The sun had broken through a small gap in the dense clouds over Gotthardt Street, its rays spiraling down in a rush of kaleidoscopic colors, blinding Maddox. He raised the rifle to his brow as a shield and squinted.

The clouds expanded. The gap closed. The sunbeam withered.

Three Custodians knelt on cracked asphalt, heads bowed, the palms of their hands flat against the blacktop. Hadassah Boutros stood behind them with her arms crossed. "Come on out, Mr. Boxwood. It's safe."

Maddox stepped out of the building. As he passed, he noted the total stillness of the kneeling Custodians, as if they'd been turned to stone. His attention turned to Hadassah. Her face was rigid. He gestured to the Custodians. "How?"

"They'd all been waiting for you. Didn't know you was so important, did you? The Displaced've been watching you for a minute. Kloum wanted something from you. And you did it, killed that man, took that stone outta his shoe. That worried them. They have a plan, and you weren't none of it, so they brought you here, keep you under wraps." Her voice was a rolling mumble of dispassionate syllables. "But now's the time. Hatching their plan. When I saw what they meant to do–kill all these people, my children... No. I wasn't gonna let that happen. *So, I brought* him *here.*"

Maddox whipped his head from side to side. Old buildings, windows, rooftops. No Kloum.

"He's gone from here," Hadassah said and pointed to the Custodians. "I was too late. He wiped them, completely, just by putting a hand on their heads. No memories at all, down real deep. They don't even remember how to stand up."

Maddox headed for the road.

"Where you going? There's nothing out there for you, you know."

He didn't turn.

"He still needs you–"

He spoke softly, without concern whether Hadassah could hear him or not. "Home. I'm going home."

December 24th

The wind gusted and Maddox's ears filled with a heavy fluttering sound, like a bedsheet on a clothesline in a hurricane. He tossed the AR-15 to the sidewalk and covered his ears. He closed his eyes and grimaced. A migraine headache was building. He'd spent the night in the backseat of an abandoned car he'd found on the edge of Independence Park. Deep enough into the night, an eerie quiet fell over Newark; he hadn't slept much, or well, or deeply.

He'd walked since dawn, traveling north along the tracks of the railroad through neighborhoods he used to patrol. He caught sight of a black-and-white police cruiser working the train station as the sun began to rise. A shit shift. He wondered what the officer had done to pull that short straw. Morning brought colder air and more wind. He just wasn't dressed for the weather. He removed his hands from his ears and folded his arms across his chest to preserve a little of his body heat.

He found a trio of homeless men camped out on Rector Street. Sometimes, he knew, they'd group together and share their meager resources in hopes of making it through the colder winter nights. These three were doing better than most. He spied an extra tweed coat resting in their shopping cart. He imagined how much warmer he'd be inside it. Stealing it wouldn't have been difficult in the least–they'd never even see him. He left it where it was.

The streets widened as he moved north. Rectangles of grass preceded the houses. Wrought iron caged trees interrupted the sidewalk at regular intervals. The *better* part of town.

Steven's house.

Maddox stopped at the edge of the property and stared.

He'd never noticed before how similar his son's home was to the one in which he'd been raised: white aluminum siding with wide black shutters, terracotta flower pots dangling from chains on the front porch, a dark-stained bench beside the front door. It wouldn't have been difficult to imagine Catherine sitting there, cradling newborn Steven to her chest, swaying back and forth.

Wind, not his dead wife's off-key lullaby, sang in his ears.

Maddox swiped the spare key out from the closest flower pot's water saucer, unlocked the door, and stepped inside. A rush of warm air met him and carried a sweet cinnamon scent to his nose. Closing the door, he glanced at the coat rack. His old gray two-layer topcoat hung there, untouched. *Unseen*, he thought.

The house was silent.

"Steven," he called out, well aware that his son wouldn't hear him. It didn't matter. He needed to hear his voice call out his son's name. He needed to feel that some connection still existed.

The small but impeccably dressed Christmas tree in the living room drew his attention. They'd never been religious–and Steven's lifestyle didn't map well to a mid-life spiritual rebirth–but the holiday itself was a family institution. After Catherine's death, Maddox had merely gone through the paces, but Steven's dedication never faltered. Each year a single new ornament was added to the tree, always an expensive blown glass piece, and always dated by hand on its underside. Maddox took a red and orange ball into his hand and turned it over. 1986. The elongated yellow and silver one was from '90. He squinted as his eyes crossed over a larger clear sphere that he didn't recognize. *This year's*, he thought, until he rotated it in his hand. 1994. He couldn't remember it at all.

Returning 1994 to its limb, Maddox's hand grazed another tradition. Hand-made cards traded between Catherine, Steven, and him. For so many years six cards hung from the tree, always opened on Christmas Eve. Then cancer stole away four of those cards, leaving only cards marked, *To Steven Love Dad* and *To Dad Love Steven.*

There was only one envelope on this year's tree.

Hand shaking, Maddox slid it free from the green ornament hook holding it to the tree branch. On the front, in Steven's careful hand, was the normal addressment, but on the reverse he'd written, *Look what I found packed away with the ornaments...*

Maddox took a deep breath and opened the card.

It wasn't a Christmas card.

The Boxwood family had another, similar tradition.

Handmade birthday cards.

Sliding his finger under the envelope's lip, Maddox opened it with a quick swipe, and pulled a folded sheet of construction paper out. The back of the card was hand-dated in black marker, 1982. Steven would have been seven. He turned the card over. Drawn in crayon, three stick figures paddled a canoe away from a waterfall. Captions floated above all three: *DAD, MOM,* and *ME.* The simple cartoon family was smiling. Steven loved adventure movies at that age and had no doubt based the drawing on something he'd seen on a Saturday afternoon UHF broadcast. It was bright and fun and silly.

Maddox opened the card.

In yellow crayon, Steven had written:

HAPPY BIRTH DAY, DAD.

Below the inscription, Steven drew another scene from the Boxwood family adventures. As the canoe dropped off the waterfall's cliff face, all three stick figures leaped out and reached for a long vine trailing down from the top right corner of the card. Rising out of *MOM's* mouth was an exclamation: "*HELP MEEEEEEEEEE*".

The final E intersected with the words above.

HAPPY BIRTH*E*DAY, DAD.

Maddox's hand shook. He dropped the card and envelope.

The soft clink of glass against hardwood turned his head towards the kitchen. As he approached, a strong whiff of red wine tickled his nose. He was no connoisseur. Maddox often told friends that he couldn't tell a sauvignon blanc from grapefruit juice, but he could identify this one instantly: Sangiovese, his grandfather's favorite, shared at Christmas for generations. Maddox bought a bottle for his own family each holiday, even allowing young Steven a small glass after dinner. To Maddox, this was the taste of Christmas—spiced sour cherry with a lingering zing of tobacco.

Steven sat at the kitchen table with a glass and a bottle.

Sobbing.

Dressed in his black bathrobe, Steven was leaning forward, elbows on the edge of the table. Teardrops hung from his eyelashes like icicles. Had he slept? From the look of him, not in days. He certainly hadn't shaven.

Maddox pulled out a chair and sat.

Steven poured another glass of Sangiovese.

"Steven," he said.

There was, of course, no reaction.

Maddox bit his bottom lip. His own eyes were no longer dry. He turned his head. The sink was filled with dishes, flatware, and an empty take-out Chinese container. The countertop was littered with dying sympathy bouquets and unopened greeting card envelopes. Maddox doubted many were Christmas greetings.

A mess. Steven's house was never that way.

"Steven," he tried again, still unable to turn his head back and look at his son. "I know you can't hear me. I wish you could. I want to tell you I'm sorry. For Jared. If I hadn't gone looking into this *thing*, he'd still be alive. Maybe here with you right now, sharing wine. Christmas."

In Maddox's peripheral vision, Steven took a long sip.

His voice cracked. "Who knows, right? Even the three of us, sitting at this table? Passing the bottle. I could tell him stories... about you growing up. And you'd... get embarrassed. And we'd... all laugh."

The phone rang. Steven made no move to answer it.

Maddox wiped his eyes and cleared his throat. "I know that I haven't been the right kind of father, not for a long time. No excuses. When Cath— When your mother died... I lost a big part of me. I wasn't all that good a husband, either, I know that."

Another ring.

"But what we had, we had. It was our lives. Without her... I wasn't a husband anymore. I'd only even barely known how to be one to begin with. And without her, a father? I couldn't hang on to it. I didn't know where to start."

Ring.

"You were just figuring out who you were and I was losing myself. We couldn't have been farther apart," Maddox said. The tears on his face were getting hotter as they trailed down his cheeks. "You probably thought that I didn't like the man you were becoming. I never wanted you to be like me. You choosing a different life? That was the best thing I could have hoped for."

Ring.

"You know the saddest thing of all? Missing her made me want to forget her, because it was too much. I got rid of the house and moved in here. Thought that having a smaller bed might help. No room for two. Even thought it might help bring me back to you."

Ring.

"It didn't. You give me a problem to solve and I can do it. Why I became a cop, probably. I need to feel like I can fix things. But her, and then you? I couldn't repair any of it. Beyond me. I think maybe I went looking for Persephone... because I'd realized that I couldn't find you."

Ring.

Steven's glass was empty.

Maddox turned his head slowly. Steven's face came into focus. The expression of absolute devastation on his son's face reminded him of Fuck Kinda Question.

'I just want things back how they was.'

The phone didn't ring.

Maddox reached out for the bottle of Sangiovese and tilted it back to his lips. It still tasted like Christmas, but someone else's holiday, and a very long time ago. He set the bottle back down in the spot where he'd lifted it from. It clicked against the table, glass on wood.

"I'm sorry I failed," Maddox said, "at everything."

The house was silent.

Christmas Day

From his chair in his bedroom, Maddox listened to the soft purr of the gas furnace as it blew warm air up from the basement and out from the floor vent. On a more moderate day, the furnace would turn on and off at regular intervals throughout the day. But not today. Overnight the temperature outside dropped into the single digits. The sunrise made no difference. The heater chugged on.

Maddox's bedroom was exactly as he'd left it. Maddox wondered if it existed to Steven at all. Could he even see the door when he walked the hall? Or perhaps he saw only a guest bedroom, sparsely furnished and simply decorated. No way to know.

Steven was still in bed. Maddox had checked on him earlier and found him lying on the mattress and staring at the ceiling. He had the impression it was very normal for his son to spend most of the day that way. Clinical depression? He had no doubt.

Every now and then the sound of a passing car would rumble by the window behind Maddox's head. The crackle and roar of an old car moving down the street made the quiet that followed seem even more absolute. If not for the air vent, he'd have believed that he'd gone deaf. Eyes closed, he felt weightless, as if gravity had lost its power and he'd floated off the chair beneath him. He felt himself drift towards sleep. Was this what death felt like? If so, he wouldn't resist.

The kitchen phone rang, as it had regularly since Maddox came back home. Steven never bothered to answer. Maddox understood. After Catherine died, the calls flooded in. He stopped lifting the receiver on the second day. There was only so much '*I was so sorry to hear...*' that he could take.

Christmas. Angels. Wings. *Something.*

Fuck it, he thought. *If I'm not dying I should just sleep.*

The second time the phone rang, Maddox's eyes opened.

What if Steven isn't ignoring the calls?

Maddox pushed out of his chair and stood up.

What if he can't hear the ring?

The third ring sounded louder, more urgent.

Maddox stormed down the hall and into the kitchen.

Plucking the receiver off its wall cradle, he said, "Hello?"

A familiar voice answered, "About time you answered, Mads."

December 26th

At dawn, Maddox dug out his car, turned the key, and drove. The streets were empty except for the occasional garbage truck or transit bus. The sky was clear. Unblocked by clouds, the rising sun's rays put an orange glow on the city's wrought iron, brick, and concrete. Soon, he knew, the snow would melt and the gutters would become rivers. How much of the trash, debris, and dirt would be washed away into the sewers? *Not enough* would be his usual answer, but not today. *Maybe just enough* seemed about right.

A smile grew on his face when the faded HOP's STOP road sign came into view. A cartoon waiter wearing a white apron leaned against the words CASUAL FINE DINING. There wasn't any fine cuisine on the menu, but it never felt like a marketing lie, either. For the paper napkin crowd, Hop's *was* fine.

Maddox pulled into the parking lot. There was a car parked in his spot under the old oak tree at the edge of the property. The yellow spray-painted X and the traffic cones were gone. *No*, he realized, *they were never there.* Twelve days earlier he'd been unable to see the truth.

He parked the car. The walk to Hop's front door confirmed his earlier suspicions: the wind on his face didn't have the same bite as it had a day earlier. For winter, it would be a warm day. The bell rang as he opened the door and walked in. He paused for only a moment at the greeter station before realizing that he might well wait there forever. In another hour, the place would be swamped with businessmen, retirees, and beat cops, but for now it was nearly empty. The counter stools were empty except for a single young man in a battered suit and tie. Maddox knew the sort—overnight manager at some megastore, fully aware of his low place in the pecking order.

His fingers twitched. *I'm nervous*, he thought, *but good nervous.*

He turned and stared at his booth. And smiled.

"My god," Mia Cresswater said, rising from her seat. Tears built up in her eyes even as a wild grin took over her face. She shook her head a bit and squinted her eyes. She was beautiful.

The second diner turned in his seat to face Maddox. Darcy drummed his fingers on the table, a quick and happy drum beat. "I told you he'd find his way back to us."

Maddox stormed across the restaurant and met Mia at the table. Wrapping his arms around her, he felt her body heat radiating through her clothes. She was shaking. He held her tight against his chest for a long moment before breaking off the embrace and kissing her lips.

"Be jealous if I don't get the same treatment." Darcy snickered as he too rose. They didn't shake hands. They too embraced. Not as tightly. And no kiss followed.

In another moment, they all sat down in their normal seats. The silence that followed felt comfortable and natural. They stared at one another with a mixture of elation and relief.

It was Darcy who finally spoke up. "So, how've you been?"

They laughed.

"Peachy. Things have been peachy," Maddox said.

"Tell me about it," Mia said, reaching over and taking his hand. "And I really do mean that—you tell us everything. Because we don't quite have this thing figured out."

Darcy smirked. "At all. I was never the smart one, remember?"

He told them.

"I was right there beside you," Mia said. "In bed. Heartbreaking, you not seeing me. I called out your name, but you couldn't hear me. I felt like a ghost. I was too upset to follow you when you left. But we weren't apart for long. You came in here and sat right there." She pointed to the next booth. "I was screaming at the top of my lungs, but no, nothing."

Maddox laughed. "You parked in my parking spot," he said. "But I didn't see your car. And I remember two women sitting right here. Loud women."

"She *is* as loud as two normal women," Darcy said with a grin.

Mia playfully flipped him the bird.

Maddox continued his story—the crow and the pigeon, the cop outside the courthouse, the Custodian's warning not to go home. He paused a moment before continuing, but with a hard swallow, told them about Jared. Their expressions changed, but the horror in their faces was tempered with understanding.

They were friends; they wouldn't judge. Then he went on to the detectives, Kloum's proposition in the jail cell, and escaping with Saulo.

"Guess we didn't warrant their attention," Darcy said.

"Hmmm-mmmm," Mia agreed. "Chopped liver."

"The Displaced were only interested in me because of what Kloum made me do," Maddox said. "They have some plan. I dunno what it is. I only just got there; I wasn't trusted. But they seemed to think I was some sort of threat to them, so they kept me under close watch."

He told them about Mae Bee's treatment to remove Kloum's influence over him. Mia cringed throughout the description. Her hand tightened on his.

"All those bodies," Darcy said when Maddox told them about the suicides and murders at the Rumor Mill. "What, they're just gonna rot away without no one knowing they're even there? Not right."

Maddox nodded. "All graveyards are full of forgotten people."

He told them he went home but left Steven out of his recap. Even so, the look on their faces told him that they knew that part anyway. "And then, yesterday, I got smart and finally picked up the phone when you called."

Confusion settled into Darcy's eyes. "Whadda you mean?"

"Yesterday," Maddox said, "when you called the house."

Darcy shook his head. "We've been coming here every day hoping you'd show up, but we didn't know you'd be able to see us. Or hear us. Mads, I didn't call."

The moment of silence that followed was *not* comfortable.

A horrible thought tumbled into Maddox's head. As he shifted his stare between Darcy and Mia, he studied their faces for anything not quite right. *Were they really here? Was any of this real?*

A voice whistled behind him, as strong as a teakettle but carrying a tune. A strong chill surged through Maddox as he recognized the tune. "You'll Never Know."

The young man in the rumpled suit swiveled his stool around.

"Holy mother–" Maddox began.

Mia finished, "of fuck."

The young man was gone, replaced by Stan Mancuso.

No, Maddox knew, *not* Stan. "Kloum."

Kloum straightened his threadbare tie as he stood up and walked towards their booth. There hadn't been any poker tell in Darcy or Mia's faces, but there was one in the way Kloum walked. He had none of Stan's swagger. In fact, it didn't have any personality in its step at all–it walked the way an alien creature might think a human would walk. Too perfect. Too much control. The chill underneath Maddox's skin jolted to his fingers and toes. Pins and needles.

Arriving at their table, Kloum placed a television remote on Maddox's placemat. Tilting its head, Kloum's vacant eyes met his. Though clear, it was like looking into a mass of cataracts. *It isn't seeing me through those eyes*, Maddox sensed. *It's altogether different than us. A whole other thing.*

Kloum turned and walked to the door with his perfect stride. He pushed the door open and left without the bell ringing. Maddox's eyes dropped down to the remote control.

In twenty-two days, choose channel 7.

The television that hung next to the pie case was off. Probably just too early, he figured. Either that, or they'd simply forgotten to turn it on. Maddox put his finger on the *ON* button but hesitated.

He breathed out. "It wants me to see something."

"Don't," Mia said. "Everything we've been through? I say no, we don't need to do one more thing for that *thing*. Whatever it wants, it won't be good."

Maddox turned his attention to Darcy.

"She's right," Darcy said, then sighed. "But when has that ever stopped you?"

Maddox turned on the television and pressed the button marked 7.

An insurance commercial burst onto the screen and concluded with a joke Maddox didn't understand. The picture cut to the local news affiliate's anchor desk. A pretty news presenter in her fifties smiled and welcomed viewers back. "*News and weather coming up at the bottom of the hour, but first we go to Willis Daniels, reporting on a special event that showcases some very talented young inventors.*"

The broadcast cut to Willis Daniels, a gray-haired African-American reporter, standing in a gigantic conference hall. Under his name, a caption read NATIONAL YOUNG INVENTOR's SCIENCE FAIR. After an awkward beat, Willis said, "*I'm here at the Passaic County Exhibition Center. As you see, nearly three hundred school-aged tinkerers and their teachers have gathered here to show off their latest and greatest inventions and innovations."*

The camera pulled back to reveal dozens of rows of tables set up on the center's floor. Children, teenagers, and adults wandered from one display to the next. Colorful two-fold presentation posters announced each station and explained every gadget in bold bubble letters and hand-drawn illustrations.

Maddox's heart sank. The room in the Rumor Mill.

"I'm here with event coordinator Darlena Hinsler, who in addition to putting together—"

Mia asked, "What is it, Mads?"

"You're right. It's bad."

Hinsler, clearly nervous, recited lines she'd obviously prepared. *"These are extraordinary young people, all only beginning their roles shaping all of our futures—"*

Movement behind the reporter caught Maddox's eye. "No."

A pair of baby-doll-masked Custodians seized Hinsler from behind and pushed her violently to her knees. She screamed. Another pressed a handgun to Willis's temple and then calmly stated into the camera, *"We are watching the broadcast. If the feed is cut, we'll kill everyone here. Everyone. Not even a quick cut-away. Understand?"*

"Yes," Willis said, trembling.

"Not you," the Custodian said. *"You."*

The cameraman answered, *"I... understand... yes."*

The Custodian pulled the trigger. Willis's head burst open from ear to eye. The reporter collapsed as blood sprayed and frothed from the head wound.

The convention hall erupted into chaos—yells, screams, the rumble of feet, the crash of tables upset. Then a flurry of gunshots sounded and the attendees all froze and ducked down.

"We have all the doors guarded. Any attempt to come in or go out will be met with deadly force. No exceptions," the Custodian said, black eyeholes directly facing the camera. "Repeating: this camera keeps rolling, the broadcast stays on, and no one enters or leaves."

"God," Mia said before slapping a hand over her mouth.

Darcy shook his head. "What do they wa—"

Maddox shushed him by raising a finger.

"Kloum," the Custodian said. "Come, join us. Your special girl is here. The one you've manipulated so many to protect over the last few years. Come here now or she dies."

Maddox reached into his jacket pocket and snatched his car keys.

"I've gotta go," he said.

"Wait," Mia said, putting up a hand with all five fingers extended. "You can't go in there. You're an old, sick man. They'll kill you in a heartbeat. Besides, what's it matter? Only those of us Kloum has touched can even see this, right?"

"No," Maddox said. "Fear and pain. A convention floor full of children held at gunpoint. Safe to say that everyone watching channel 7 right now is seeing everything that's going on. And word will spread. More will tune in. That's what they want: to expose Kloum. And then once the world has seen it, and fear what it is, it won't be able to operate in the shadows anymore. They'll have neutered it."

Darcy asked, "That's a bad thing?"

Maddox cocked a thumb towards the television. "Is for those kids."

Mia's eyes flashed from Maddox to the screen and back. Her brow furrowed and worry lines deepened. Without a glance in his direction, she said, "Darce, you have any plans for today, besides being invisible and miserable?"

"Guess not," Darcy said.

To Maddox, she said, "Then you ain't going alone."

Maddox dropped the remote control. "Let's go."

Darcy grabbed his coat and mumbled, "Sometime you two have to explain to me how 'I've got no plans' means risking certain death. I know I'm just a public-school diploma and a pension check, but damn."

The bell above the door chimed as they left. Maddox opened the passenger's side door for Mia. Darcy took the back seat. As Maddox turned the ignition key, Darcy asked, "So letting the real police—the young guys with good knees and fresh training?—deal with this... That's out of the question exactly why?"

"Because they don't know what they're walking into," he said, turning the wheel hard and pressing down the gas pedal. "They'll only see the Custodians who are holding guns to hostages' heads. Hostiles could walk right up to them and they wouldn't have a clue. They don't stand a chance."

Darcy grunted. "And we do?"

Maddox put the accelerator to the floor.

"Maybe," he said. His voice didn't even sound hopeful to his own ears. "But think about it. What's the Custodians' play? They can't walk out of there alive. Once Kloum is exposed, so are they. They're all dying anyway, so they need to cement the memory of the event, make it something Kloum could never overcome. And that means making it unforgettable. They won't let those kids survive."

Mia braced herself with her hands on the dash. Maddox took a sharp turn onto the Route 280 ramp. Darcy shifted from the left side of the car to the right. He swore.

"They'll cut the broadcast," Mia said.

Maddox nodded. "Channel 7'll want the police to make that call. The chief won't make a decision without cover from the mayor. Give or take a few opinions from political advisors, I think we have ten, twelve minutes."

"How fast can we get to the center?" she asked.

"Ten, twelve minutes."

Darcy steadied himself, one hand on the roof, the other clinging to the door handle. "What if Kloum doesn't show? Wouldn't that buy us more time? To drive safer?"

Maddox passed a hybrid on the right. "It'll show."

"How can you know?" Mia asked.

"It sees all the possibilities and tries to manipulate the outcome," he said. More vehicles joined the roadway as the morning commute began. "It came to Hop's to make sure I'd be in the fight."

Darcy said, "You saying that *thing* called in *backup*?"

A pickup truck cut across the lane. *Can't see us. Doesn't know we're here.* Maddox cut the wheel hard. The car bolted onto the shoulder of the road. The Prospect Street Overpass's supports loomed ahead. Maddox glanced in his rear-view mirror. Traffic was thick, but he slid back into the lane between a battered Ford Focus and a Liberty International Airport shuttle bus.

"Feel sick," Darcy moaned.

Maddox piloted the car back into the fast lane. The speedometer needle raced back up into the red. "I need you two to find the news van. Keep the broadcast live until..."

"Until *what*?" Mia asked.

"Until whatever happens *happens*," Maddox said. "Kloum must have some plan, some way to resolve this. I'm guessing you'll know it when you see it."

Darcy leaned forward, putting his head between Maddox and Mia's shoulders. "How are we going to keep the feed live? We don't know how to work that equipment."

Maddox glanced at Mia. "You'll think of something."

He cut the wheel hard and took the next exit. The convention center parking lot was filled with flashing red and blue lights. Maddox stomped on the brakes. The car skidded to a halt an inch from the two uniformed cops blocking the entrance. They continued their conversation, clearly oblivious to their close call. Maddox killed the engine and pointed to a news van in the corner of the lot. "There."

"I see it." Mia cracked open the door, but paused before stepping out. She leaned back and kissed Maddox's cheek. "Listen, you, get in there and do what you have to do. Then get back to me, okay?"

Maddox smiled. "That's the plan."

Darcy opened the rear passenger-side door. He huffed as he pushed himself out of the car. "*Plan* doesn't seem like the right word to me."

As she joined him, Mia plucked a two-way radio off one of the patrolmen and tossed it to Maddox. He caught it. She stole the second cop's radio, smiled, and said into it, "Stay in touch."

"*Stay in touch,*" the radio in Maddox's hand repeated.

The policemen continued their conversation.

Darcy and Mia walked towards the van. She glanced back with large, worried eyes. Twice.

Maddox opened the driver's side door and got out. He dismissed a quick pang of guilt as he turned his eyes away from the sight of his retreating friends. He hadn't *quite* lied to them, he told himself. The broadcast *was* important, but much more honestly, he wanted to keep them at a safe distance. *Babysit a news tech or two, but stay out here. Things about to get ugly.*

He passed an enormous mound of snow and ice that had been plowed to the edge of the parking lot. It would take weeks to fully melt, he knew, even if the temperature continued to rise. He followed a trickle of runoff down the sloping asphalt. Dozens of police cruisers interrupted a straight path across the lot. They were parked at odd angles for quick turnaround and pursuit if the need arose. Farther up, a line of black armored vans formed a protective retaining wall that shielded the police congregated there. The men and women wore black ballistic vests over their blues. Maddox remembered the heavy pressure of plated flak jackets he wore during the riots. These looked lighter and more flexible. He wondered if they felt as safe.

The cops weren't talking and he understood it well. Idle chatter always died in anticipation of real danger. They'd spend the moments before orders came down thinking about their wives and husbands, girlfriends and boyfriends, children and parents. Each of them, he knew, had a sealed envelope in a station locker—a letter meant to be delivered if they didn't come home. Maddox felt his own heartbeat quicken in his chest. He'd thrown out his envelope when Catherine died.

Maddox clipped the two-way radio to his belt.

Ear to his phone, Detective Bill Reisz crouched behind one of the vans. *Really must be all-hands-on-deck*, Maddox thought, *if they called this shitstain in*. As he passed by the detective, Maddox unsnapped the leather strip on the cop's holster and snatched up his sidearm. It was heavier than he expected. Glancing down at the weapon in his hand, he cocked his head to one side. He'd seen cops carry 45s, but the Heckler and Koch was an expensive gun. Maybe detectives made more money these days. Quickening his step, he released the magazine into his palm. Fully loaded. Ten in the box, one in the chamber.

Maddox pivoted right and followed the line of vans. The front entrance of the exhibition center was a set of six glass doors leading to a main promenade. The Custodians would set up shop on the staircase balconies on the second and third floors, rifles pointed down. A Dealy Plaza turkey shoot. No dice—he'd have to find another way in. One that was less guarded.

Tires shrieked. He glanced back at the long black vehicle skidding to a halt just behind the vans. Tactical Raid and Deployment, the Special Weapons and Tactics boys from Woodbridge. That meant the governor was awake. Not much time. He slid the Heckler and Koch's magazine home and thumbed the safety to *off*.

On the southern side of the complex, he found a three-bay loading dock with a narrow receiving deck. Climbing the stairs, he felt his heart quicken.

Was he really up to this? *I'm an old man, fat around the middle, and half dead from a brain disease.*

Didn't matter. Showtime at the Apollo. Cue the horns.

One.

Maddox stepped up to the metal door.

Two.

His knuckles and fingertips struck steel. Knock-tap-knockknockknock-tap-tap-knock.

Three.

The door cracked open.

Four.

Maddox rammed the pistol into the gap and pulled the trigger. A loud yelp followed the gun's report. He threw open the door and rushed in. A Custodian stumbled back. The guard's gun fell from his fingers. A red stain blossomed in the middle of his shirt. Maddox aimed for the center of the flower and fired again. The Custodian jolted back against the wall behind him before crumbling to the floor.

The door shut behind Maddox.

Maddox swung the weapon around. The hall was clear.

The Custodian gasped four times in quick succession, as if unable to catch his breath. His body tensed, then relaxed and didn't move again. Maddox knelt beside him and put Detective Bill's sidearm on the floor. Nudging the body to be sure the man was dead, he lifted the baby-doll mask off. Underneath, the Custodian's face was barely recognizable as human. Multiple layers of brown and pink scar tissue wove together a grotesque tapestry of hardened flesh.

They hurt themselves, he told himself. *To protect themselves from being manipulated by Kloum. Fear and pain. Or both.*

Maddox pulled the elastic strap over his head and slid the baby-doll mask over his face. His peripheral vision vanished, replaced by the blurry edges of the eyeholes. *Not optimal.*

He took the Custodian's gun, a shiny chrome IMI Desert Eagle, even heavier than the Heckler and Koch. Full clip; eight rounds. If Detective Bill's gun was a nasty bastard, this was a full-blown *motherfucker.* It went into his waistband. Maddox's knees cracked as he stood up.

The service corridor was lit by clusters of LED lights behind square frosted glass shields. Every six feet an overhead fixture provided a fresh shower of warm white light. Darkness crept in between each lamp. Staring down the hall, Maddox was struck by the impression of being inside a segmented bioluminescent worm. He counted the bright spots and multiplied by six: seventy-two feet. That meant the hallway bypassed the promenade and came out somewhere underneath the grand staircase that led to the exhibit hall. It would get him by the Custodians on the balconies.

Leading with the gun in his hands, Maddox headed down the worm. His eyes were fixed forward but his ears listened for sounds coming from behind. He passed a bale of cardboard next to a bright yellow compactor. He glanced inside as he passed to feed an irrational tingle of fear that a Custodian might be crouching in the machine, ready to leap out. *It's not a goddamn funhouse*, he reminded himself.

The two-way radio squawked. He fumbled to retrieve it from his belt and at the same time keep the Heckler and Koch level and ready. Mia's voice came over the radio—*loud*. *"We're at the van."*

Maddox scrambled to scroll the volume dial down. Then he hit the microphone button and whispered, "Get in there and make sure we're still on the air."

The reply, now softer, came immediately. *"Doing it now."*

Good luck, he thought.

At the end of the worm, Maddox found a set of metal crash doors. He took a breath, held it, and exhaled as he swung the right door open and stepped through. Two lines of orange reflective tape formed a pathway between walls of stacked cardboard boxes. Printed on the sides were abbreviated descriptions of the contents: *LGHT FXTS, FLR RLLRS, PWR SPLYS*. It was a storage area. He followed the orange tape through a maze of metal shelves and towers of brown cartons. *CLNG AGNT, SRVNG TRYS, DGRSER*.

Can I buy a vowel?

The storage area came to an end at a single-windowed door. Maddox approached it with caution, aware that it not only allowed him to see out, but also provided a clear view *in*. He craned his neck on one side and peered through at a hard angle. Two Custodians stood just outside. The taller of the two swung a shotgun by its stock like a clock pendulum. The shorter Custodian had her arms crossed over her chest. Her right hand held a snub-nosed small-caliber handgun. Neither were cheap guns. Stolen, without a doubt.

The shorter Custodian's eyes flickered to the window.

Shit.

Maddox opened the door and stepped through.

She asked angrily, "Why aren't you at the–"

Maddox trained the Heckler and Koch at her midsection and cracked back the trigger. The sound of the bullet striking her abdomen hit Maddox's ears before the gun's loud pop. The short Custodian screamed and spun. She fired her weapon twice as she staggered back.

The taller Custodian shuffled back and raised his shotgun.

Maddox had no time to aim. Instead, he fired off three quick shots in the man's direction. All three hit their mark. The Custodian fell back. The shotgun erupted, spraying buckshot directly into the woman's baby-doll mask. The tungsten pellets spun her head fully around as they punched through her skull. The powder blue wall behind her turned red.

The taller Custodian's legs gave out and he tumbled to the floor with an animalistic roar. Maddox rushed over, put the barrel of Detective Bill's pistol against the fallen man's temple, and pulled the trigger. The Custodian's right eye exploded as the round rocketed through his head.

Too loud, gonna draw attention, Maddox thought as the bodies collapsed. A line of blood spilled from the Custodian's jagged eye socket and ran parallel to the orange tape. He knew it must have been his imagination, but the gun in his hand felt lighter. *Four bullets remained in the clip, one in the chamber.* Back in his service days, he'd bought an ammunition dump pouch to store backup rounds. He never had to use it. Now he wished it were there.

Got to conserve. Make each shot count.

He pushed through another door into an employee break station. A cubical at the far end was marked *SECURITY STATION 3*. An arm extended out from the open door. The fingers were slightly curled as if frozen mid-unfurl from a clenched fist. *Poor bastard, probably netted twelve dollars an hour without benefits. Didn't deserve this.*

Workplace policy posters covered the walls. Walking past, Maddox reflected on the training rooms in the Rumor Mill. Too accurate for comfort. The Custodians had practiced for today in all-too-real environments. Security at the Expo Center never had a chance.

He kept moving, hustling past a wall of lockers and a dry erase board filled with scheduling reminders. So important yesterday, so utterly pointless today. Finally, he came to a door marked PUBLIC AREA BEYOND THIS POINT–REMEMBER TO SMILE. Maddox's lips did not move as he cracked it open and peeked through.

His heartbeat quickened.

A Custodian stood only feet away, back to Maddox, with a shotgun leveled towards a cameraman's midsection. Shaking, the photo journalist kept the camera trained on the Expo Center's hall. The bodies of Willis Daniels and Darlena Hinsler rested at his feet, their pooling blood soaking into his white sneakers.

The student inventors, parents, and teachers knelt on the floor, hands behind their heads, faces down. Eight Custodians prowled the aisles between the exhibit tables. Farther up, on the main stage, three more Custodians kept watch over the crowd from a better vantage point. Three children–two boys in their early teens and a girl a few years older–had been brought onto stage. They waited there, tears streaming down their faces, in the same prone position as the rest of the students in the hall.

Maddox let the door close and retreated a few steps along the cinderblock wall. Twelve hostiles. Thirteen rounds between the two guns. *Not a lot of room for error. What's the plan here?*

"*Mads,*" Mia's voice whispered through the two-way radio.

"Yeah," he said in a soft voice, moving another few feet from the door.

"*We locked the news crew out of the van. They could still kill the broadcast from the station, but on our end, we're staying live.*"

Maddox said, "Good."

"*But... things are getting more complex.*"

"Of course they are," he said.

"*The SWAT team are getting ready to go in,*" she said.

Maddox's mouth went dry. Not much time, then.

"*And there's another problem. Stan... Kloum's coming with them.*"

No time at all.

A commotion erupted in the ballroom. Individual screams and yells merged into a roaring cacophony. Gunshots sounded and the crowd fell silent. Maddox ducked down and stepped back up to the door. Pushing his head through, he gasped. On stage, one of the Custodians moved behind the girl. In his hand he held a long curved Hawkbill machete. The Custodian to his right called out across the room, "Focus that camera here."

The cameraman shifted his torso and corrected his aim.

"We've waited long enough!" the Custodian shouted.

The girl screamed.

The Custodian slid the blade under her chin. The hook at its end reached almost to her ear. An uneasy murmur grew.

Maddox kicked his way through the door.

The Custodian next to the cameraman reacted first, turning towards him and swinging the shotgun around. Maddox thrust the Heckler and Koch in his direction. Both fired.

Maddox felt an array of pellets tunnel into his left thigh. He yelled out as the pain of broken skin and torn muscle hit. He stumbled back, then fell. His vision blurred as tears flooded his eyes. He fell to the tile floor hard and heard bones crack.

The hazy shape of the Custodian dropped as well, the shotgun hitting the floor a moment before his lifeless body. Still holding the camera, the cameraman bolted to the edge of the hall.

The Custodians scrambled, running towards the back of the hall, guns waving. Maddox wiped at his eyes with the back of his hand. Six of the baby-doll-masked soldiers approached. He brought the handgun up and tried to aim at the closest. His hand was unsteady and his eyesight was a blotchy mess of colors and shapes. Four rounds in the Heckler and Koch; no ammo to waste on a wild shot.

Three Custodians broke through the final row of hostages.

They stopped, extended their weapons, and took aim.

Maddox took a deep breath and fired.

The Expo Center went dark. Children screamed.

They cut the power. Here they come.

Maddox rolled onto his stomach. Fresh pain surged from his thigh. He kicked himself up onto his haunches. A warm wetness rolled down his leg from his wounds. He ground his teeth.

A barrage of gunfire echoed in from the lobby. He could distinguish the hard and fast clatter of automatic weapons from the more robust thunder of shotguns and sharp claps of pistols—a symphony of firing pins and combusting gunpowder. A hum overtook the brief silences between shots. Generators.

Maddox straightened his arm and tightened both hands around the Heckler and Koch's grip. The lines of florescent light bulbs overhead flickered. He drew a bead on the closest Custodian. As bright white light returned to the exhibit hall, Maddox pulled the trigger. The shot took the Custodian high in his chest and sent him to the floor. Maddox shifted his aim to the next and fired again. A dead center hit; lead cracked through breastbone.

The third Custodian swung around and fired. A floor tile took the damage. Maddox squeezed the trigger twice. The first shot passed through the man's throat. The second passed up through the underchin before exiting through the top of his head.

The students, parents, and teachers panicked. Some dove flat to the floor, but others rushed towards the exits. The five remaining Custodians on the convention floor opened fire on the runners. A father with his daughter's hand in his was struck by a shotgun blast. His body collapsed back onto his child in a shower of blood. A sixteen-year-old boy made it to an exit door before a bullet tore a path from his ear to his eye. Two teachers were cut down as they stumbled over cowering students.

Maddox tossed the Heckler and Koch away. Empty. He reached into his waistband and brought out the Desert Eagle. He forced his knees to straighten. Ignoring another wave of pain, he stood up and took aim at the Custodian who had shot the student at the exit. Eyes still watering, he hesitated, unsure of the shot. Eight rounds, eight Custodians. Each one had to count.

The crowd surged towards the back of the hall like a cresting wave. They plowed through tables and displays. Papier-mâché, plastic tubes, and balsa wood crashed to the floor. The Custodians continued to fire into the fleeing swarm. Geysers of blood exploded up where the shots landed. The screams intensified with each fallen body. The youngest children fell under the trampling feet of the older kids.

Maddox steadied his aim as best he could. A Custodian guarding the western emergency exit reloaded his shotgun. Maddox put his sights on the baby-doll mask and pulled the trigger. The right eye hole doubled in size. Orange shotgun shells scattered across the floor.

The wave of students skidded to a halt as they approached him. *They've no way of knowing I'm not one of them. I'm just another man wearing a mask and firing a gun.* He waved and shouted, "*GO-*"

The echo of gunshots, the screams, and the thunder of shoes against the floor buried his voice. He studied the face of the closest student, a pimple-faced blond boy around fifteen, and saw only terror and confusion. The boy was frozen in place, eyes scanning for a safe exit.

Here. Past me. Go.

A large-caliber bullet struck the boy in the back of his head and exited through his mouth. He jerked forward from the blow. His jaw dropped open and blood, broken teeth, and skull fragments vomited out.

Hands trembling worse, Maddox followed the shot back to a Custodian moving in from the left side of the stage. He fired. The shot went wide. Tightening his grip, he squinted until the water in his eyes was forced out and rolled down his face. He pointed the Desert Eagle at the center of the Custodian's chest and squeezed. Another miss. He had no idea where the shot landed.

Too dangerous. *I'm gonna kill these kids myself if I keep this up.*

"*DOWN-*"

Maddox didn't know if the students could hear his voice, but he couldn't. He wobbled as he took a step into the crowd. The students hurried out of his path. He stumbled with his next step but remained upright. He wrapped his left hand around his right to steady the Desert Eagle. No use. He pulled the trigger.

The shot went over the heads of the crowd.

His chest muscles clenched and a bolt of pain struck him. The first stirrings of a massive migraine began to fester in his head. *Not now*, he told himself. *Not a heart attack. Not a stroke.*

A blonde teacher cut a path through the hall holding a young boy tight to her chest. Her wild eyes locked on Maddox for a fleeting moment. Even through the blur of his tears, he clearly saw her disbelief and terror. Then her face turned into a blur of red motion. She fell and disappeared into the crowd. It took a moment for it to register that she'd been shot—*in the face, with a child in her arms.*

Enough.

Maddox screamed and this time he heard his voice over the cacophony. His hands clamped down on the Desert Eagle's grip. He fired off two quick shots. The Custodian at stage left dropped his shotgun and clutched his throat.

Five Custodians remained on the floor, one on the stage.

One in the clip, one in the chamber.

The math isn't getting any better.

The ruckus from the lobby grew louder.

In a blind dash, a teenage boy collided with Maddox. They both spilled to the floor. The Desert Eagle tumbled from his grip. Maddox instinctively grabbed ahold of the kid. The boy struck out and landed a sloppy punch to Maddox's chin. He released the boy. Kicking off the floor, the student bolted out the exit behind them. It wasn't a serious blow. As a younger man, Maddox doubted it would have felt like much at all. But now, it *hurt.*

Searching for the gun from his new vantage point on the hardwood floor, he followed the trail he'd left behind since he took the shotgun hit to his thigh. He'd lost much more blood than he'd have suspected. How much more before he passed out? No idea. No time to worry about it.

The first four members of the SWAT team burst through the hall's main doors. They wore full riot gear-body armor, helmets, flak jackets—and carried MP5 machine guns. Once inside, they parted into two groups and dropped to one knee. A quick barrage of automatic fire laid down cover for the rest of the team to rush in.

A tall and lanky Custodian made his way through the hall. The crowd scattered from him. The weapon in his hands wasn't a firearm; he held a red-bladed fire ax. He moved with a forceful gait, plowing through the debris of science projects and fallen bodies without hesitation.

Maddox scurried backwards, propelling himself with his forearms and elbows. The pounding in his chest quickened into a drumroll. Intense heat spread out from his breastbone to his extremities. His mouth went dry.

The Custodian choked up on the ax handle as he approached.

Maddox's head struck the back wall. *Nowhere left to go.* He instinctively brought his hands up in a futile defensive stance, knowing that his old arms would be cleaved like firewood.

The Custodian raised the ax over his head.

The two-way radio in his waistband squealed.

The ax descended.

Maddox closed his eyes.

The ax's blade tapped the palm of his hand and stopped. He felt his skin part and blood rush to the surface. But not much new pain. The wound was barely more than a scratch. Maddox opened his eyes. The Custodian was frozen in place, still locked in a mid-strike pose. An index finger was pressed against his temple. It belonged to a member of the SWAT team standing alongside the Custodian. The cop pulled his hand away, but the tall man remained in place.

The cop removed his helmet and tossed it away, revealing Stan's face.

A stab of fresh panic surged through Maddox. He knew that Kloum's presence would set the Custodians' end game into motion. They would ramp up the sheer horror of the siege and sear the most terrifying images they could into the minds of everyone watching on television. That meant killing everyone. Maddox stared out at the hundreds of children still trapped inside the hall.

Kloum reached down and slid the baby-doll mask off Maddox.

"No more hiding," it said. "No more masks."

As it straightened up, Stan's face disappeared. The features that surfaced resembled an oversized unborn fetus's elongated face. The outer skin was translucent and glistening, allowing a hazy view of the subtly pink muscles underneath. Its eyes were clear, empty half-globes. The thing had no hair whatsoever.

The SWAT team filed in. Students rushed towards them.

The two-way radio squawked, "*MMMMMaddox–*"

Kloum pointed to the girl on stage held captive by the machete-wielding Custodian. The face Maddox was looking at couldn't convey emotions, but the tenor of its voice did all the work necessary. "She's the reason. Get her out of this place."

"MMMMMMaddox... got... problem," Mia's voice said through the radio. *"—Sharing the signal... going out... all channels. We can't... it off from here... WE CAn't TURN IT OFF."*

It wasn't uncommon for television news stations to share footage during major news stories. Even raw signals. It was no longer a simple matter of killing the feed in a single news van. The Custodians' plan was working.

The remaining Custodians leveled their AR-15s at the crowd.

No.

Maddox's hand wrapped around the ax blade. He pulled himself to his feet, then wrenched the weapon out of the Custodian's hands. Using it as a crutch, he hobbled across the hallway floor, not stopping as he swooped the Desert Eagle off the tile.

Gunfire filled the exhibition hall. The Custodians opened up on the students. The SWAT team returned fire. Dozens of students, parents, and teachers fell. Two of the Custodians went down in the first minute. A heavy stench of gunpowder spread.

Maddox skid to a halt in front of the cameraman.

The cops began to rush into the center of the hall.

A nine-year-old girl collapsed at Maddox's feet. Her blood sprayed against his shoes.

Maddox aimed the pistol and fired the remaining two rounds directly into the camera's lens. The cameraman jerked away, dropping the equipment before running for the exit. A Custodian's bullet struck him in the back and spun him around. A second bullet completed the pirouette, and his life.

We all might die, but they don't get to win.

The Custodians turned their attention to the SWAT team filing into the hall. The automatic gunfire intensified into a constant thunderous rumble. Maddox dropped the empty Desert Eagle and took several fumbling steps towards the stage. He focused on the machete-wielding Custodian and his young hostage and tried to ignore his peripheral vision. There were too many small bodies lying in blood pools surrounding him as he reached the middle of the exhibition center's floor. If his eyes wandered, his heart would break and his legs would surely fail. So *no*, he'd lock in on the baby-doll-masked monster and the trembling girl under his blade. He thrust ahead with the ax, then shifted his weight against its long handle as he propelled himself forward. Pain sparked up from his wounded thigh with each step. He grimaced, ground his teeth, and pushed on.

Kloum stepped up to his side, glanced at him, and passed him.

The Machete Custodian's eyes widened as he saw Kloum approach the stage stairs. His hand tightened on the blade's handle. The girl winced as the steel pressed against her throat. In a gravelly Southern drawl, he yelled, "YA KEEP BACK–"

Maddox quickened his steps. The pain increased. Blood flowed freely down his leg. He reached the bottom stair as Kloum stepped up onto the stage.

"I WILL KILL HER–"

Kloum raised both arms like a preacher appealing to God, except that instead of pleading, the gesture was unmistakably aggressive. The Custodian took a quick step back. He dragged the girl with him. The machete drew blood.

The gunshots reached the pitch of their intensity and became a blown-speaker din. Ignoring the pain strumming in his chest, head, and thigh, Maddox climbed the stairs. His feet wobbled under him and his ankles threatened to buckle.

Kloum circled the Custodian.

The Custodian kept moving, jerking the girl in a circle, keeping his eyes on Kloum. *"KEEP BACK–I TELL YOU–I'LL CUT HER GODDAMNED HEAD OFF–"*

Maddox planted himself in place. His legs shook as he lifted the ax blade off the floor and swung it back over his shoulder. The weight of the weapon nearly overturned him, but he managed to catch himself and stay upright.

Kloum's translucent face brightened as a swirling white glow ignited in the center of its head. The Custodian took another step back and to his right. Maddox stared at the back of the man's head.

The girl screamed.

Kloum's mouth opened wide. Tendrils of white light reached out and wagged in the air like a half-dozen serpentine tongues.

Maddox swung the ax.

The blade cracked into the Custodian's skull and severed the baby-doll mask's straps. It fell to the girl's feet. The machete followed. Then the

Custodian himself dropped to the stage. The girl cowered away from the body. Her face was covered in red speckles.

Kloum's mouth closed and the light dissipated.

Maddox reached for the girl. She took his hand.

Kloum pointed to a door behind the stage. "Get her out."

The girl tugged at his hand. Maddox swayed back and forth as he moved, never far from falling, but managed to keep up with the girl. All the same, he felt like an anchor. The gunshots became sporadic. As they reached the door, he glanced back. The exhibition center was a ghoulish museum of death: children, parents, and teachers in piles and sprawled out alone, their bodies forming a hideous tapestry: mouths open, hands clutching, eyes bulging. *If there's a hell, it's jealous of this place.*

"C'mon," the girl pleaded.

Maddox nodded. His voice was thin and dry. "Let's go."

They passed through the doorway into a long brick hallway. The lights overhead flickered and pulsed. Long patches of the corridor were completely unlit. *Emergency generators not cutting it back here.*

The girl put her free hand to her neck and winced. Maddox could see that the wound was superficial, but a small trickle of blood ran down from between her fingers. "You'll be fine, it's okay."

She smiled weakly and squeezed his hand.

The door closed behind them. Maddox took the lead, struggling but working his way down the hall. The girl followed, careful to stay a safe step behind. The sound of Maddox's footsteps was dense and shambling, a sharp contrast to the girl's delicate taps. His breathing grew louder and raspier. Drawing in each breath became laborious. Each beat of his heart felt like a punch to his chest. He wiped his watering eyes. His face felt hot and raw.

Not a heart attack.

Not a stroke.

A low, rolling growl echoed down the corridor. Maddox stopped and motioned for the girl to cower behind him. He sniffed the air. Wet dog. A lean figure leaned against the door at the end of the hall. The EXIT sign over its head blinked on and off. A harsh red glow flickered over a Custodian's mask. At his waist, a pair of animal eyes reflected light like tiny mirrors.

Bloomfield Ave.

The Custodian pushed off the wall and held up Maddox's wallet.

"Maddox Benjamin Boxwood," the Custodian called out. He flicked his wrists and the wallet opened, revealing a driver's license in a plastic sleeve. Once, it would have been a badge. "Have something that belongs to you. You want it back?"

The raggedy dog crouched down low and barked. To Maddox's ears it sounded as loud as any of the gunshot blasts he'd heard in the expo hall. The light may have been low, but the dog's teeth were all too easy to see.

"You can have it back," the Custodian said, waving the wallet. "We can still have it all back. All of us. You only have to hand over the girl. That's it, no more. You can walk through the door and not look back."

The Custodian's finger opened the tri-folded wallet even farther. A photo of Steven at age ten. Little League bat resting on his shoulder. A green baseball cap. Messy bangs. "All of it."

The pounding in Maddox's chest deepened from a bass drum's deep roar to the reverberation of a kettle drum struck with a mallet. It hurt more, too. Maddox opened his mouth to speak before his brain could even process what to say. The answer was primal, unavoidable, as if written in his DNA. "No."

The Custodian sighed and released the wallet. "Then I'm sorry."

The moment Maddox's wallet hit the floor, the dog bolted from it crouch and sprinted down the hall. Maddox spun around, crumbled overtop the girl, and wrapped his arms around her. The dog launched itself off the ground. Maddox ducked his head down until his chin pressed hard against his clavicle and braced himself. The dog collided with him at full speed. Toppling over from the force of the impact, he fought to keep the girl safe in his embrace.

Sharp incisors and penetrating canines sank into his shoulder. Maddox screamed. The dog thrashed its teeth from right to left. The bite wounds tore open wide. A deep red-brown stain spread down his shirt. The dog backpedaled on its haunches, dragging the old man to the wall. The base of his skull slammed against brick. The dog released him long enough to strike a second time, this time latching its jaws on Maddox's forearm. His hand shook.

—*Notaheartattack Notastroke*—

The dog bit down harder. Tooth struck bone. His hand went limp.

The girl shook in his arms.

The dog yanked back and tore strips of flesh from Maddox's arm. Licking its maw, it coiled back onto its hind legs before springing back onto them. This time its mouth closed around the hub of Maddox's jaw. Its teeth burst through his cheek. Jerking back, Maddox's face became exposed and the dog's bite cut deeper, until it had his jawbone between its teeth.

Maddox let go of the girl as the dog dragged him across the floor by his face. He struck the dog's side with his fist without effect. He could taste the animal's saliva mixing with fresh blood.

NOTAHEARTATTACKNOTASTROKENOTAHEARTATTACK–

Shock setting in, the girl hid her face and curled into a fetal ball. *No, run. Run now.*

The dog twisted its head until it dislodged Maddox's jaw, then released him and again retreated a step. Winding up, it released a tittering snarl. Maddox snatched the two-way radio up with his good hand. The dog leaped back to him. Maddox swung the radio.

It squawked as it connected with the animal's snout.

The dog fell, recovered, and twisted back to face him. Its growl deepened. *Hurt, didn't it?*

The dog rushed towards him again. Maddox thrust the radio upward, catching the animal under its chin. It whined and retreated again. It shook its head as if drying itself off. Maddox didn't wait for another attack. Instead, he launched himself at the animal and bludgeoned it with the radio. It dropped to the floor with a whimper. Maddox struck again. And again. When it no longer moved, he released the radio and fought to stand up.

The Custodian at the door shook.

Maddox placed the palm of his good hand under his chin and pressed his jaw back into shape. It hurt. Like everything else. When he spoke, his voice came out slurred. "Getch oud of da way."

The girl rushed to Maddox's side.

The Custodian moved out of their path.

As they passed, the masked man said, "It didn't have to be this way, you know. That girl is all Kloum cares about. We could have used her to make it expose itself. We all could have been remembered."

Maddox ignored him and stepped towards the door.

The Custodian reached down, picked up the wallet, and held it out. It fell open. Maddox glanced at the photo in the corner of his driver's license. He reached out, but instead of taking it, he closed the Custodian's hand around it. "That doesn't matter anymore."

Maddox slumped against the door's push bar. The daylight beyond was blinding. He staggered out. The girl followed. A flurry of voices met them. "HOLD. HOLD. HOLD FIRE–"

The police were blurry black silhouettes.

"Go," Maddox whispered to the girl.

She paused for only a moment. Then she ran.

Maddox took one more step, then stumbled, and fell to the asphalt. He could no longer feel individual heartbeats. His chest was a flurry of constant, painful motion. His throat swelled. He gasped for breath.

NOTAHE RTATT CKNO AST OKENO AHE–

Except this time, as the daylight around him dimmed, he was not so sure.

December 27th

Cold.

He drew the old frayed coat around himself as he lay down on the concrete. He stared out through a curtain of chain-link fence at the road beyond. What street was it? He didn't know. What was the city's name? His own?

Maybe he'd remember in the morning. Maybe.

He groaned as he rolled onto his side. His whole body hurt, but the exhaustion was more powerful, at least for the moment, so he'd sleep. The last sight he caught before his eyes closed was of the whitewashed brick wall behind him and the words sprawled out in graffiti across its face. NEWARK DREAMS.

He had no idea what it meant.

Maybe it didn't mean anything at all.

December 28th

The bleeding started again, darker this time. Looked worse.

When had he gotten hurt? He didn't know.

He'd found a rusted shopping cart outside a shuttered Hispanic market and had been using it as a suitcase and a walker. Both front wheels spun as they rolled across the hospital parking lot. What hospital was this? There were words on the building but he couldn't read them. Didn't matter. Ambulances parked outside of hospitals; that was all he needed to know.

He'd collected enough items off the street to fill his shopping cart. A flat bicycle tire. Bottles. An empty tissue box. A water-damaged paperback. A tennis ball worn down to its brown core. All trash left behind and forgotten.

The automatic doors opened, inviting him inside. The two women at the front desk didn't raise their heads to acknowledge him. He rolled his cart past them and down the hall. Doctors and nurses wandered from patient room to room. Food service personnel wheeled trays. Equipment technicians worked on a computer system behind a nurse's station. None noticed him.

At the end of the hall he found a quiet room with its door open. He turned the cart roughly and entered. Inside, there were two beds. One was occupied by a woman even older than himself. Unconscious, the woman clutched a teddy bear to her chest. *An ugly thing*, he thought, all sewn up as if it had been torn to pieces and repaired by a child. The old woman looked very pale. *Not much life left there.*

The second bed was empty, at least for a moment. Releasing the shopping cart, he climbed onto it and settled down. He stared up at the white ceiling. *This feels familiar.* But that's all he could muster. When had he been here? No answer.

He closed his eyes.

Time meant nothing. He might have slept for a minute or a week.

"Maddox," a voice called, waking him.

Cracking his eyes open, he watched as an old man in a police uniform came to his bedside. Again, the face felt familiar, but his mind couldn't dredge up anything more. "Whats y'say?"

"I'm a friend," the friend said. "Maybe. We used to know each other well, at least for a little while."

Maddox raised his hands and stared at them. One was locked in the shape of a claw, and the other shook. Both were covered in blotches. "Cans y'help me?"

"No," the friend said. "There never was any helping you. You were dead before I met you. That's what a man without a purpose is. Nothing. For a time, I gave you meaning."

He didn't understand. He moaned.

"I came to say goodbye. And to thank you," the friend said. "You've done so much for me. I thought that I could at least express my appreciation."

What is he saying? Nothing made sense.

"Who are you?" he asked.

"That's not important," the friend said.

Without knowing why, he asked, "You's God?"

The friend smiled. "I hope not."

"Okay," Maddox mumbled.

"There's another reason I came. And I know you probably won't understand, but I want to be honest with you. Chaos is the most formal form of honesty. There are no lies in the maelstrom. So, I want to tell you this: I've lied to you."

"'bouts what?"

"The girl you saved for me, the one that cost you your whole life?" The friend reached for a blanket on a rack from the wall. "I told you she will someday save millions of lives with her invention. That's why I couldn't let her die in a car accident caused by your son's lover, or by those confused men in masks. That wasn't true. She will be a great inventor, yes. But after the attack in the exhibition center, her interests will become more morbid. What she invents won't save lives, it'll harvest them. Her hands will bring death on a scale not seen in your history. And it will be magnificent to watch."

He shook his head. "Don't understand."

The friend smoothed out the blanket over Maddox, turning down its hem under his chin. "It doesn't matter. Just rest now; you've earned it. There's nothing more for you to fear."

He closed his eyes and muttered, "Goodnight."

"Goodnight," the friend said.

Then nothing.

December 29th

"You've *gotta* see this shit," Bryan said, flashing his phone.

Jimmy smiled in the cocky way only a fifteen-year-old could. He and Bryan had been best friends since kindergarten. Beginning in middle school, they'd shared hundreds of videos, always trying to outdo the other. It started with obscure European and Asian horror movies, then progressed to footage of real-life executions and traffic accidents. "This better not be that ISIS vid. Already saw it and didn't even think it—"

"Nah, man, no," Bryan said, tapping the screen. "That terrorist attack in New Jersey a few days ago? Remember how the networks cut the broadcast right as the police rushed the joint? Well, turns out this one blogger got ahold of the footage. All of it. It's... I dunno, you gotta see it."

The video started. Jimmy asked, "They ever figure out who these guys were?"

"No group took credit," Bryan said. "But that ain't what I want you to see. Keep watching. Right at the end."

The video concluded with a gun thrust into the camera and an abrupt black screen. "What the hell was that?"

"Here," Bryan said. "I'll go frame by frame."

A blurry figure filled the screen for a split second.

Two clicks later, for a single frame, a monstrous face appeared.

"Whoa. What *is* that?" Jimmy asked.

"Dunno," Bryan said as a strange expression took over his face. "And it's strange, 'cause ever since I watched this... I've been seeing... things."

Jimmy's brow dropped in disbelief. "Seeing things in the video?"

"No," Bryan said. A flash of fear glinted in his eye. "Everywhere. People who shouldn't be there. People that no one else seems to be able to see."

Jimmy laughed. "Ghosts?"

"I... No, I guess not," Bryan said in embarrassment.

Jimmy waved him off. "Don't worry 'bout it, man. You're tired. Too many overnights playing games. But I'll tell you what. This shit?" He pointed to the phone. "This is seriously freaky stuff. We should so repost it."

"Where?" Bryan asked.

"Everywhere."

December 30th

"You ready?" Mia asked as she lifted her nine-millimeter Beretta out of her hip holster.

Darcy nodded. "Think so."

She knocked on the door. After a moment, a man wearing a stained white wifebeater opened the door. He craned his head out into the apartment complex corridor and scanned left and right. Mia pushed past him. The renter stumbled into the hall as Darcy, too, pushed into his apartment.

The renter swore, dropped to his knees, and tied his shoe.

Darcy closed the door and locked it.

From the other side of the door, the renter shouted, "Shit."

"You take the kitchen, I've got the bedroom," Mia said.

"That," Darcy said as he turned right, "is how it's always been."

Mia raised her gun and entered the bedroom. Empty. But her ears caught a rustling from the closet. She whistled loudly. Darcy came running. She pointed to the wall. Darcy drew his sidearm and nodded.

Flinging open the door, Mia jammed the barrel of her gun up against a female Custodian's bare forehead. "You're real fucking ugly with all those scars. You want the chance to give see them heal, you're gonna tell us what we need to know."

The Custodian raised her hands as far as the closet would allow. Darcy reached in and removed a six-inch hunting knife from the woman's belt. She said, "Whatever you need."

"Where's Maddox Boxwood?" Mia asked.

"There's not many of us left," the Custodian said. "Scattered all over. Hiding wherever we think that Klum won't find us. Or...him, Maddox Boxwood... I don't know that much of anything anymore."

Mia pushed the gun. The Custodian's head tapped the back of the closet. "That's too bad. This asshole might not have a wardrobe worth wearing, but it'll be a shame to make him lug it all to the laundromat to get your brains out of his work shirts."

The Custodian gulped down air. "I... think he might be dead."

Darcy's expression darkened.

"We need to know for sure," Mia asked.

The Custodian's eyes filled with tears. "Only *it* knows."

Mia withdrew the nine and backed off. "Then I guess we'll just have to go and ask Kloum."

December 31st

When Safran was allowed to return to the barracks, he did so with the same mop he used to clean the selection platform. It was empty, except for the blood. The bodies were gone, already turning to ash in the crematoriums. The soldiers had killed them all, those who attacked Kloum and those who had not. Bullet holes peppered the walls. There would be a draft this winter. He knew the camp administrators wouldn't fix it. Nothing, he realized, could fix it. Nothing. *Kloum.*

Had they killed the demon as well? He doubted they *could*.

"Who?" the kapo had asked him, and he'd answered, "All."

They died because of his answer.

Then the same man had asked him his name, and, unlike the time when he'd been asked his age and occupation, he told the truth. "I don't remember."

Safran dropped down onto the bunk where the demon had sat.

A new train full of prisoners would come tomorrow. More men and woman and children would be processed. More blood would need to be cleaned off the platform. He wondered when the madness would end.

Just keep busy and don't think of it, he told himself, *and in time, if you can, forget all this.*

BLEAK
DECEMBER

Made in the USA
Middletown, DE
26 February 2018